# RIDING ON A
# DANGEROUS WIND

# RIDING ON A
# DANGEROUS WIND

Caroline Jay

The Book Guild Ltd
Sussex, England

First published in Great Britain in 2004 by
The Book Guild Ltd
25 High Street
Lewes, East Sussex
BN7 2LU

Typesetting in Baskerville by
Keyboard Services, Luton, Bedfordshire

Printed in Great Britain by
Antony Rowe Ltd, Chippenham, Wiltshire

A catalogue record for this book is available from
The British Library

ISBN 1 85776 855 8

*'Opportunity riding on a dangerous wind'*
*(translation of the Chinese symbol for*
*the word 'trauma')*

*For my family and all my friends*
*who saw me through*

# Foreword

It seems these days that there is hardly anyone who has not been affected in some way by breast cancer. For some it has been a mind-numbing diagnosis for themselves while for others it has been the pain of watching a loved one go through the turmoil and terror. There have been great leaps forward in dealing with the disease but, as patron of the Action Against Breast Cancer charity, I know how much work there is still to be done.

One of the most important things is to try to see the positive. In this story of a woman's life and how it is affected by the experience of having breast cancer there is a lot to learn. For the cancer patient reading *Riding on a Dangerous Wind* it is heartening to see that the diagnosis can represent the beginning of a new life; that for some the onset of breast cancer can act as a catalyst of renewal rather than decline. Written from personal experience, Caroline Jay has the insight and understanding to convey a difficult story with compassion and humanity. For the partner, relative or friend trying to support someone through the difficult days of diagnosis and treatment Caroline's book is a wonderful guide as to what is helpful and what is not. Caroline and I have been friends for many years and it is lovely to realise that through her writing she can extend that hand of friendship to those she has not even met.

Sandi Toksvig, 2004

# Chapter One

'There must be more to bloody life than this!' Nina was standing in her kitchen and shouting at an unresponsive washing-up bowl.

It was 1.30 on a Sunday afternoon, two weeks before her daughter Josie's tenth birthday. She was bent tensely over the sink, her hands yellow plastic gloved. The morning had been spent making breakfast, putting the washing in the washing machine, hanging it out to dry, cleaning the bathroom and toilet, tidying endless piles of clothes, making soup, preparing lunch and trying to help Josie with her homework. Nina never sat down and relaxed; somewhere in a distant childhood, it had been instilled in her that things were there to be 'got on with'; anything less felt like failure. She'd barely noticed her transition into a housewife and mother unable to see an alternative. Labouring daily under this self-imposed time pressure, born partly of a sense of duty and partly of a fear of failure, she had become a tightly coiled spring.

'I'm trapped in this bloody house,' she continued, still addressing the washing-up bowl, 'it's like a sodding prison. I hate washing up, I hate cleaning, I hate tidying, I hate ironing, It's boring, boring, boring. No one has a clue what I want from life. And it's not bloody this. I hate it, I hate it, I hate it all!'

What she could easily have added but didn't, choosing

instead to suppress the feeling out of guilt, was that most of all she hated her husband, Malcolm. She hated him for being oblivious of her needs. She hated him for being able to walk out of the house every morning and close the front door behind him. She hated him for being able to go away on business, safe in the knowledge that she would always be there to look after their daughter. His collusion in her situation made him her prison warder and she hated him most of all for that. Oh yes, and she hated him for who he was, a sort of Golden Retriever of a man, always anxious to avoid confrontation and ever eager to please.

For years now, Nina had felt she had to suppress all the anger she felt. She'd learned as a child what devastating effects anger could have. Whenever she got angry with Josie, she would feel immediately guilty and have to explain to her that it wasn't her fault. And what right did she have to be angry with Malcolm? He wasn't a bad father. True, he had never really learned to play with his daughter, he wasn't the getting down on the floor or putting on silly voices type of father, but he loved her very much. As she'd grown older, they'd grown closer, finding common ground in a love of computers and all things mathematical. He was a good husband, never making demands, always working hard and earning the sort of money that allowed them to live a comfortable middle-class life in a comfortable middle-class house in a comfortable middle-class area of London. He never complained. So what did she have to grumble about? Why wasn't she happy and contented? She slammed a plate down on the side and accidentally caught a glass which was already draining. It toppled over and, as if to spite her, rolled off the edge of the draining board and smashed into a million fragments on the stone-tiled kitchen floor. This was the last straw.

'Shit! Fuck! Bugger! Sod it, sod it, sod it all! It's just not fair! Why does it always have to happen to me? Shit, shit shit!'

Nina was now standing, unable to move, surrounded by shards of broken glass, tears streaming down her face, completely overwhelmed by the injustice she perceived to sum up her situation. Josie was wise enough in her youth not to put in an appearance; Malcolm was not. He came and stood in the doorway. 'Do you want some help?' Nina was now beside herself with rage and screamed at him, giving herself a sore throat in the process.

'No, I don't want your bloody help! I can do it. Just go away and leave me alone! I'll do it myself just like I do everything else around here.'

He needed no second invitation to disappear. He could have stayed and pointed out how unfair she was being, but chose instead to beat a hasty retreat; his usual response. Confrontation was anathema to him. A fact that was not lost on Nina, and which only served to fuel her fury. Why couldn't he answer her back? Why did he always let her get away with it? Why did he never, ever stand up for himself?

These thoughts were surging through her head as she began to retrieve pieces of glass with her bare hands and throw them in the dustpan. She didn't care what damage she did to herself; perhaps she deserved some punishment. She found herself courting some outward sign to show for all the inner turmoil she was feeling, a large gash on the hand or something worse. Then people would understand that something was wrong, then they'd feel sorry for her, then she'd have an excuse to stop. Try as she might, the most she could muster was a tiny dot of blood on the tip of one finger. She dragged the hoover roughly from its cupboard as if trying to lay some of the blame on another inanimate object. She crashed it roughly into several of the kitchen cupboards as she finished clearing up, and jammed it unceremoniously back where it had come from. Then she stood, unsure what to do with herself. Her heart was still pounding, anger still pulsing through her veins, her urge to scream as strong as ever and her throat rough from shouting. She had to get out.

Without stopping to get a coat or think what she was doing, she stepped out of the side door, slamming it behind her. The glass panes rattled in protest. The cold winter air hit her like a slap in the face. It felt right. She set off down the side path and up the road, defiantly stamping one foot out in front of the other, hands deep in her pockets, head down, desperately trying to get rid of the tightness in her chest and throat. Before she knew it she had reached the Thames which flowed grey and silent a few streets away from the house. She was panting heavily and stopped to catch her breath, vaguely aware that she must have crossed several busy roads without even noticing. Being Sunday, there were lots of people at the river's edge. Families feeding ducks, teenage boys with fishing rods and Walkmans, elderly couples making intricately slow progress along the towpath.

New feelings tumbled in to join forces with her anger. Why did she always feel so guilty for getting into this state? Wasn't anger a good thing, a helpful release of tension? Not in their house. Oh no. Malcolm's motto in life was 'it's not worth getting angry about'. So he never did. She could remember only one occasion in 15 years when she had seen him lose his temper and that was with someone he'd never met before over something which, to her, was truly not worth getting angry about, a hotel booking. He always looked so hurt and confused and nonplussed when she got angry. He was even uncomfortable when Josie got angry, which didn't happen very often as she seemed to have inherited her father's passive nature. No, anger was definitely a no-go area in Nina's life. She stood and watched the big grey clouds roll in towards her on the chill wind. She cried again, not tears of anger any longer but tears of sadness and loneliness and despair. How had her marriage degenerated into such a sterile state of tolerance and non-communication? How could she pretend to feel what she no longer felt? Was this all there was to her life? Was this her future? A relentless wave of snowballing feelings broke around her. She realized that the clouds, too, had closed in, and the people had gone. The towpath was deserted and she was bitterly cold. There seemed no alternative but to tread wearily back the way she had come, home to face the music.

She crept somewhat sheepishly in through the side door, madly resenting the way she felt.

'Are you alright?' Malcolm asked as he put his head round the doorway, not daring to come right into the room. To any other person at any other time this would have seemed like a perfectly innocuous, even caring remark. To Nina it was irritating in the extreme, proving as it did to her that this was all he wanted, for everything to be 'alright' and back on an even keel, for there to be no further unseemly explosions of temperament. She grunted an inaudible reply and brushed past him in the direction of the ironing.

The rest of the afternoon passed uneventfully. Josie and her father spent much of it in front of the computer, an activity which instantly excluded Nina, who loathed computers with a passion she only otherwise exercised in response to double glazing salesmen.

Her sense of pent-up frustration stayed with her all

through the evening. She cooked and they ate in front of television, obviating the need for communication. It was much later that same night, whilst nursing her sore throat and sitting in front of the open log fire which she had lit to warm her soul, that Nina found the lump in her breast. She sat on her own in the heat of the fire, feeling it again and again, hoping that the next time her hand touched the same spot, it would be gone. But no. She went to bed in a state of rising panic.

When she woke the next morning, for a fraction of a second, she couldn't remember what was so wrong. Then it hit her. Her hand went again to her right breast and yes, there was no doubt, it was still there. Once Malcolm had left for work and she had delivered Josie to school, she rang the surgery. She had to argue the point with a crusty receptionist and insist on speaking to her doctor. She realised she was almost panting with anxiety by the time she heard his cheery voice on the other end of the phone.

'I know I shouldn't panic but I found this lump last night and now I am! Panicking that is. Is there any chance you could see me today? I'd really appreciate it.'

'I'm sure it's nothing to worry about,' came the reassuring tones, 'but you obviously need to have your mind put at rest. If you can come right now, I can give you an emergency five-minute slot.'

'Oh thank you, that's great, I'll come at once.'

Nina put the phone down and collapsed into the kitchen chair behind her. She was shaking.

She was still shaking half an hour later as she sat up on the doctor's couch, her breasts bared to the world. He was very discreet, looking away as he felt all round the lump.

'I'm sorry my hands are cold. As I said, I'm sure you have nothing to worry about. You see, it doesn't feel like a cancerous lump; that feels different, more like a piece of chewing gum, solid and detached from the tissue around it. This is not like that. Please put your things back on.'

Nina dressed hastily and sat by his desk.

'I'll arrange for you to have a mammogram just to check. There's no real urgency but I'll make it sooner rather than later because I know you'll go on worrying. You should get a letter in the post with a date.'

'Thanks.'

'Goodbye, and please try not to worry.'

Fat chance of that, thought Nina, as she walked out into the raw winter air. The warmth of the house welcomed her like a cocoon when she stepped in through the front door. Charlie, her cat, appeared from nowhere and, as if informed by some feline apprehension, wound his tail and lean furry body round and round her legs, figure-of-eighting in and out as she tried to walk to the kitchen. She was putting the kettle on when the phone rang.

'Hi there! It's Mo. How's things with you?'

'Oh hello, Mo. Actually, not brilliant. I've just been to the doctor because I found a lump in my boob last night.'

'What did he say?'

'Oh you know, the usual sort of thing, not to worry, most lumps are benign, this one doesn't feel like cancer etc., etc.'

'Well, I'm sure he's right. Do you have to have a mammogram?'

'Yes. I have to wait for an appointment through the post. He said there was no urgency about it though.'

'There you are, then, he must think it's all OK.'

'Yes, but he doesn't know that for sure, does he? No one does.'

7

'No, but that's why you're having the mammogram, to make sure.'

'Yes, yes, I know.'

'You don't sound convinced. Are you worried?'

'Actually, "worried" doesn't even begin to cover it. My worst nightmare may be about to come true.'

'Don't start thinking like that. Look, why don't we meet up and have a coffee?'

'Thanks, Mo but I think I'm better off on my own today. Maybe tomorrow or the next day. If that's OK with you?'

'Yes, of course, sure. I'll give you a ring. I'll speak to you soon. Bye.'

Nina had known Mo since they were at art school together. She had recently moved, with her partner and their two girls, Abby and Beth, to live nearby. Mo was always smiling and seemed completely fulfilled by family life. She ran a small business from home making curtains and cushion covers. Her house was chaotic and bright, much like her personality, and always full of children. Nina envied her contentment and her sense of fulfilment. As for herself, she could feel the bank of billowing black clouds threatening to engulf her. She needed to focus her mind on something else; she decided to prove to herself how fit and healthy she actually was. She'd go jogging.

But first things first. Warm-up exercises. A must at her age, she felt. Bending down, knees straight, touching toes. She remembered the days when she could get the palms of her hands to the floor. Her head rolled round to the sound of sinews crunching. She was feeling slightly dizzy. Shoulders up, shoulders down. One arm stretched up to the ceiling and over to the side; she used to be able to get lower. She decided the dismal reality was that she wasn't going to feel any better so she might as well get going. A blast of cold damp air hit her in the face for the second time in as many days as she opened the side door. She realized she'd forgotten her gloves and so, stepping over piles of shoes, she retraced her steps. She also remembered to turn on the answerphone. Gloves in hand, she locked the door once more and put the key in her pocket, underneath a tissue.

I'm pretty sure it's going to be OK; I'm pretty sure the lump's hormonal. But what if I'm wrong? What if I'm wrong? The words throbbed in her head as she placed one foot in front of the other, her eyes locked unfocused on a weirdly jaundiced pavement ahead, the legacy of recently burnt-off yellow lines. It was hard going from the beginning. What if it's cancer? What if it's cancer? She tried to keep her arms pumping at her sides; it was supposed to help. Her breath quickly began to become laboured and her legs felt like lead. What if it's spread? What if it's spread? The sickly sense of gulping for air was the worst. Out of control. Out of control. What if I die? What if I die? In between the waves of panic which rose and fell in her throat, it was briefly possible to think of other things – what to cook for Josie's birthday party, who she had to phone that day, whether there were any letters she needed to write. Even possible to take in the view or the weak winter sunshine on the tiny green shoots which had presumed to poke their heads above the solid ground. She had almost reached the river. She walked for a while; her trainers squelched through a patch of watery mud. What if I have to have chemotherapy? What if my hair falls out? The weakened sun was proving no match against the blackening skies. A man, braving the weather with his dog and umbrella, grunted a good morning. The wind and rain joined forces to slash through the air as

Nina lowered her head to meet them in grim determination. One step, next step, one step, next step. I have to beat this. I will survive. I have to beat this. I will survive.

Suddenly an apparently ownerless bundle of fur hurtled along the towpath towards her out of nowhere. It was a mixed-up mass of legs and tail and lolling tongue and seemed extremely pleased to see her. She had always loved dogs and so greeted this one as she did all dogs with a friendly outstretched hand. Then in the distance there was a whistle and the amenable bundle turned tail and disappeared as quickly as it had come. She was alone. There was momentary relief from the elements as the path entered a small wood. The mud was thicker and gave her a good excuse to walk again. The wind disappeared behind the shelter of the leafless trees and it was very quiet except for the drip, drip, drip of the raindrops from the blackened branches above. Maybe the news will be good. Maybe. Maybe the fear is for nothing. Now and again there was a scuffle as a bird tried to extricate itself from hidden brambles. In the distance, a siren whined above the endless hum of traffic. Nina turned, wet and weary, to make the return journey, all too aware that the exercise had done nothing to quell the rising tide of panic in her throat.

The following week passed slowly. Nina told Malcolm about her visit to the doctor and the proposed mammogram.

He seemed unconcerned, remarking, 'I'm sure it will all be OK. Just a routine check,' before promptly developing a stomach bug and spending the next three days feeling very sorry for himself.

Nina repeatedly asked him how he was feeling in the hopes he'd do the same for her. He didn't. Mo didn't ring either and Nina began to feel as though no one was taking her seriously. I could be dying of cancer here and no one's even asked me how I feel. No one wants to know when I'm going for a mammogram. The letter with the appointment had arrived; it was to be on Josie's birthday. Nina tried to change it but without success. The hours dragged by; the waiting was the worst.

The day arrived at last. She arrived 20 minutes early, hoping to be through with it quickly and out in time to pick up Josie from school. She was too early. There was no one at reception. She sat down and waited. Finally a lady with a loud voice wearing a pink sweater arrived in a flurry of carrier bags and coats. Before Nina had time to put down the letter she was writing and stand up, a queue had formed. Eventually she was given an X-ray form and told to head for the door 'opposite the goldfish pond'. She knew where to go, down the corridor and past the radiator where, ten years ago to the day, she had stopped mid-contraction en route for the maternity unit while Malcolm had been searching for a parking space. Once at X-ray she was told to sit and wait. Again.

'They're just setting up the machine, dear, it will be about ten minutes.'

It might just be the circumstances, thought Nina, but she seems to bear an uncanny resemblance to a member of the Gestapo on leave from the nearest concentration camp.

The whole process that ensued was supremely undignified. First she was ushered into a bare white cubicle and told to undress down to the waist, replacing one garment for decency. Then there was more sitting and waiting before being introduced to a wonder of modern medicine, the mammogram machine. A contraption undoubtedly designed by a man. One might suppose, she thought, that in this age of technology they could come up with something less akin to an instrument of medieval torture. Not only is a woman required to stand with her body and face contorted at an impossible angle but then, to add insult to injury, some stranger manhandles her breast into position. And as if that isn't enough, the flesh is then squeezed and squashed in the vice-like grip of this monster machine for several seconds whilst a picture is taken. The entire process is usually repeated at least four times and, if the woman is lucky, the pictures will be developed successfully and she won't be forced to go through the whole ordeal again.

Once it was all over, Nina was asked to dress and wait. She was then sent back to the clinic she'd started from and told to wait. Again. She settled down to finish the letter she'd started, pleased that the mammogram ordeal was over and momentarily convinced that all would be well. A hormonal benign cyst was what it was; hundreds of women got them; nothing to worry about; the GP had been right. So it was that she was smiling and cheerful by the time her name was finally called.

# Chapter Two

'I'm sorry to have to spoil your daughter's birthday party.'

The smiling lady doctor's voice penetrated the wall of terror which was suddenly amassing itself with alarming speed around Nina as she sat frozen to her chair in the impersonal little consulting room. She struggled to get a grip on what was happening to her as panic rose in her throat, making her feel immediately sick. She was shaking suddenly, uncontrollably shaking from her head to her feet, her left leg in particular took to jigging madly up and down, absolutely refusing to be stilled. Her mouth, which a moment ago had felt perfectly normal, suddenly became incredibly dry. She tried licking her lips, again and again, but to no avail.

'I'll just ask you some boring questions first and then I'll go through your mammogram pictures with you.' The doctor carried on sounding for all the world, Nina thought, as if she were discussing the colour of contact lens on offer.

OK, fine, thought Nina. Questions. Those'll be easy. I can manage those.

She mustered a faint smile as she sat on the edge of her chair, her fingers firmly crossed under the coat which lay across her lap.

'Yes, I have a part-time job. No, I don't do any heavy lifting work. How old am I?' For a ridiculous moment her mind went completely blank. 'I know I was born in 1958... Oh yes, that's right, I'm 41.'

She was beginning to get really worried now, she was beginning to think, only 41, too young to have to travel this road, too young to die.

'If you come and look here, you'll see these tiny specks on your mammogram – white dots. These are very worrying. These are what we are trained to look for. When we see these, we are extremely worried and need to do further investigation.'

'When you say "very worrying", do you mean cancerous?' Nina asked, interrupting the practised flow. There was an ominous pause.

'Yes, I'm afraid so,' came the reluctant reply.

Nina could feel herself going hot and cold now as every last one of the positive thoughts she had entertained only moments before slipped relentlessly through her fingers. Desperately she grabbed at any straws which might keep the whole scenario safe.

'Oh yes. I've just remembered. I don't know if it's relevant, but I do remember bashing myself in the breast just there with my fist years ago when I was trying to start my mother's lawnmower. And another thing, the lump's got smaller – really, not just wishful thinking on my part, but since I saw my GP I've had my period and now it's smaller than it was.'

This brief spurt of verbal diarrhoea was met with a watery smile of uncertain acknowledgement which offered no comfort at all.

'Is the next room free, nurse? I'll do a fine needle aspiration now if that's alright with you. Oh good, the ultrasound scanner's in here too, even better.'

Nina stood up on shaky legs and followed meekly into the next small room.

'Just pop yourself up on there and don't worry about your shoes.'

As she levered herself onto the examining couch, Nina looked at her old boots with their broken laces knotted together and wondered idly if they would leave a dirty mark on the pristine surgical sheets of paper towelling at the foot of the bed. Either way it was not something high on her list of worries. She dragged her errant nightmare-ridden mind back to what the doctor had just said. OK with me? OK with me? Oh God, oh God, no it's not OK with me, none of this is remotely OK with me. Do what? Go where? I'm not supposed to be here. I'm supposed to be in and out of here in a flash, full of reassurances and 'come back when you're 50's. I'm supposed to be picking up my birthday girl from school. She's only ten.

'Just take everything off to your waist and lie back. I'll just scan you to see if this is a cyst or not and then you'll just feel a fine prick. I don't normally use a local anaesthetic as it means two pricks instead of one.'

Nina's mind was racing again. Take it all off? I've only just put it all back on. My breastbone's red, my boobs are bruised and now it's needles! Her heart was racing, pounding uncomfortably in her chest.

'Now you can see this area here,' the doctor was pointing to the ultrasound screen, 'this means it's not a cyst, I'm afraid, no liquid there.'

Nina struggled to absorb this latest bit of bad news.

'Small prick coming now.'

She gritted her teeth and shut her eyes. Her fingers were clenched into fists, one at her side, the other stretched high above her head, leaving the offending breast once more vulnerable to attack. The needle was in now, stinging. She couldn't bear to look but could feel the pumping, pumping of the syringe, sucking out

15

whatever lay within her. On and on it went. Surely it must stop soon. But no. It became harder to hold on. Then at last it was over.

'How was that? Not too painful?'

She struggled to nod weakly. She couldn't speak. Her head felt fuzzy. Too much panic. Pain or no, she couldn't judge it any more. Perhaps it wasn't too terrible, now it was all over.

'Oh good,' came the doctor's unrelenting voice, 'because I'd like to do it all again. I don't think I got enough of a sample that time. Do you think you could bear it?'

Could she? Was there a choice? Would it help? Would anything make any of this any better? She thought back to all the times she'd been told how strong she was, how well she could cope, how independent. She'd always assumed her own pain threshold was quite high.

She heard herself mutter, 'OK.'

'Would you like a glass of water?' The friendly voice of the background nurse interrupted her train of thought.

'Yes please,' her voice wobbled as she spoke. Water, yes, cool, clear, ice-cold water, simple not complicated. The struggle to hold on to reality was immense.

'Hop down then and pop your clothes on,' said the nurse, handing her the water.

'I can't yet. I have to have it all done again I think.'

'Oh dear, no, do you?'

Oh dear, yes.

The doctor was back. 'OK now. Lie down again. Just one more prick.'

It was sorer the second time. The same pumping sucking, pumping sucking, on and on, until finally it was all over once again.

'Pop your things back on and come and sit over here.'

'Here you are, dear, have a chair. It's all too much to

take in, isn't it?' The kindly nurse was all worried and attentive.

It must be bad, Nina thought. I'm being steered towards a chair as though I've aged 40 years in half as many minutes. Demons, demons, gathering in my head. It begins. Will I be allowed to age 40 years? Will I ever see old age? How long have I got?

The doctor was off again. 'Now the best we can hope for is that the lump and the calcification we can see on the mammogram are one and the same thing. Then at least we know what we're dealing with. On the other hand, they may not be connected. The calcification may indicate what we call DCIs, ductal carcinoma in situ, the very early stages of cancer before it has formed a lump. Anyway, the first thing is to get the result of the fine needle aspirations in a few hours. You have two choices. You can sit and wait outside for an hour or so or, if you think you can cope with hearing the news over the telephone, I'm prepared to do it that way. You can go home and ring me later.'

Billowing clouds of black closed in around her. All light was gone, snuffed out by the dark hand of fear. Her little girl was ten years old that day. All she could think of was that she had to be there to light the candles on the cake. She'd prepared her favourite tea. Words swam in her head; this isn't happening to me, this isn't happening to me.

'There are so many maybes, it must be hard for you. Maybe the lump is benign, maybe not. Maybe it is one and the same thing as what has shown up on the mammogram, maybe not. Maybe the calcification is due to other causes, maybe not, I have to say most likely not.'

'Maybe, maybe, no maybe,' was, Nina remembered, the pidgin English translation of 'To be or not to be'. How apt, she thought, how to the point.

'Is anyone with you? Do you have to drive?'

'No ... Yes...'

Nina walked out of the room on legs of rotting cabbage. She walked past the chair she'd so cheerfully sat in barely one hour earlier when her world was the right way up. She turned the corner into the hospital corridor and past the radiator which had held centre stage in another trauma in another life. She retraced the steps she'd blithely taken only 90 short minutes before. In that eternity, reality had been shattered and replaced by a haze of terror which misted her vision and made her whole body shake. She tried to focus on what exactly she'd been told, but there seemed to be no exactly about it. So she tried instead to focus on what she had to do in the next few hours. She had to provide a birthday tea.

She reached her car, drove on automatic pilot through the streets and stopped outside the school, uncertain what to do, uncertain of whether she could face the playground. There was no alternative. So she got out and stood, looking around at all the smiling mothers, ordinary everyday smiles, ordinary everyday mothers collecting their children, and she was consumed with envy. She watched as if from another planet. Oh to be any one of them, with any one of their ordinary healthy breasts. From somewhere she found an ordinary everyday face to wear, collected Josie, together with her best friend Jane, and escaped.

As they walked in through the front door, it hit her that no one was any the wiser, not a soul yet knew of the hell she had entered. For want of something better to do, she put the kettle on. Over the next few hours, she found herself unable to stop drinking tea. There was something so archetypically British about tea in a crisis. She also tried deep breathing for good measure, but it did nothing to help. Somehow she managed to survive the birthday tea, the crackers, the cake and all the jollity. Mercifully it was a small affair as the party proper was to be in two weeks time. She struggled not to cry as she struggled not to wonder how many more parties she would be around for and how many years she would be allowed to be there for the child she had spent so many years waiting and longing to have. The minutes crawled by until she could phone the hospital. She left the girls at the birthday table and dialled with a shaking hand.

'Oh yes, Mrs Hayes...'

Nina flinched. She couldn't summon the energy to explain that she'd kept her own surname so she wasn't Mrs Hayes. Mrs Hayes was Malcolm's mother and she was dead. Anyway, under the circumstances, it all seemed pretty irrelevant.

'Well, the good news is that the test has come back negative so that means the lump is benign. But that still leaves a very big question mark over what has shown up on the mammogram. So you will have to come back in on Friday for further tests under local anaesthetic on the mammogram machine. Your appointment is at 9.30 with Dr Fish.'

Nina put the phone down, not knowing whether she was allowed to feel relieved or not. She went to light the candles on the birthday cake and forced herself to smile and sing 'Happy Birthday'. Irony cut at her heart; terror pounded in her head. Please, please let me be here for all the birthdays to come. Josie, with her best friend for company, seemed oblivious to the phantoms which were threatening to swallow her mother. They pulled crackers, devoured chocolate cake and rushed off upstairs to lose themselves in the computer screen and, for brief interludes, to discuss make-up and 'disgusting' things like snogging.

Nina was left alone to clear up the mess which she did as if in a trance. She worked slower and slower until finally she stopped altogether, coming to rest on a kitchen chair. How long she sat there she had no idea but the next thing she knew was that there was someone at the door. It was Mo. She stood on the doorstep, flanked by two eager young faces, hands clutching brightly wrapped birthday presents.

'Abby and Beth couldn't wait to give Josie her presents. We can't stop though, we're late for...' Mo broke off mid-sentence as she registered her friend's face. 'What on earth is the matter with you?'

'I've been for my mammogram today.'

'Oh God, I'm so sorry, I completely forgot it was today.'

'I've got to go back for more tests on Friday.'

'Why? What's happened?'

While the children rushed upstairs, Nina did her best to make sense of the last few hours. Mo listened intently, her eyes locked on Nina's face. She looked visibly shaken, a fact which didn't exactly inspire confidence in Nina.

Suddenly all four girls were back downstairs and there was noise and wrapping paper everywhere.

'Look, I'm really sorry I can't stay. We're late for swimming lessons. We can't talk now anyhow, with the children. I'll call you later this evening.' With a hurried worried kiss, she disappeared into the late afternoon traffic.

It was a good two hours later when Nina heard the sound of Malcolm's key turning in the front door. Jane had been collected by her rather uninspiring accountant mother with whom Nina had absolutely nothing in common. Josie had taken herself off to soak in a bath, having declined Nina's offer to play a game with her. Nina was on her fifteenth cup of half-drunk tea. This was not going to be easy. Malcolm wearily placed his briefcase in its usual position. He was a tall, thin man who was always immaculately dressed. Even at this late stage in the day there wasn't a single fair wavy hair out of place. He always spoke very quietly, as if afraid that he might be overheard and the balance of the universe disturbed. He was wedded to work, routine was his lifeline and his work the defence behind which he hid from the trials and tribulations of life.

'I've been for my mammogram today,' Nina began.

'Oh yes, how did it go? Everything alright?'

'I don't know... No, I don't think so.'

'What do you mean?'

'Well, I've got to have more tests in three days time.'

'Oh, I'm sure it's just routine, it'll be fine. Where's Josie? I've bought her an extra birthday present. That computer game she wanted.'

He hadn't looked at Nina once during this brief conversation. He'd poured himself a whisky, taken off his tie and was already on his way up the stairs. She returned to her position, rooted to the kitchen chair, cradling her tea, vainly trying to derive some comfort from its warmth, and listening to Josie excitedly opening her present.

He did not notice her as he came down to pick up his laptop before disappearing again into Josie's room to share screens with her. He emerged some time later for some food. Nina could not eat. He made no comment. She went upstairs to say goodnight to her daughter and found herself desperately struggling to hold back the tears welling up behind her eyes. She hugged Josie who struggled to free herself.

'Too hard, Mum!'

'Sorry, darling. Goodnight, sleep well. I love you.'

'Night, Mum.'

It was not Malcolm's custom to climb the stairs to say goodnight to his daughter. They didn't seem to expect or need it of one another, even on a birthday. His head was bent deep into the financial section of the paper when Nina returned downstairs. He didn't look up and he made no mention of her day. The phone rang; she jumped. She felt like a small scared child, completely unequipped to deal with the outside world, and asked Malcolm to answer the insistent ringing. He looked quizzically at her as he reluctantly folded his paper, rose from his chair with a sigh and headed for the phone.

There was a moment's silence and then she heard him say, 'Oh, hello. I'll get Nina for you.' He was a man of little conversation at the best of times.

'It's Mo for you,' he said briefly as he sat down again, already reopening his paper.

She was relieved that it was no one for whom she needed to pretend. She picked up the phone where Malcolm had left it on the table next door and climbed the stairs to slip under the warm covers of her bed.

'Hi, Nina. It's me. I'm sorry it's so late. It's been mayhem in this house this evening with swimming and everything. So tell me all about it. What's happened and how are you feeling?'

'Sick,' replied Nina without pausing to think. 'Scared shitless.'

'What have they actually said?' Mo's voice was steady and reassuring. Nina tried to focus on the few facts she had.

'Well, I'm not really sure. I have to go back for more tests on Friday. There's this lump and something's shown up on the mammogram, calcification, white dots, but they don't seem to be connected because the lump is benign, they told me this evening when I rang.'

22

'Right. Well, that's a good thing anyway. So what are the tests for on Friday?'

'I suppose to find out what the calcification is. It could be ... what did she say ... IDC's or something, intraductal cancer cells. Something to do with cancer cells before they've formed a lump. I'm not really sure.'

'OK. So the lump's not cancerous and there may or may not be other cancer cells present but it's very early days yet. Right?'

'I suppose so,' said Nina wearily, unable to respond to her friend's cheery common sense. She was tired and drained and exhausted by fear. She felt she was clutching at straws again in her frantic efforts to hold onto an explanation, any explanation, that wasn't cancer.

'Look, you're going to be alright. OK? I know you are. I absolutely know it. Are you listening to me?'

'Yes, sorry. I'm just tired.'

'I'm not surprised after today. You get to bed and I'll ring you tomorrow. What's Malcolm said?'

'Nothing. Absolutely nothing. I think he's pretending nothing's happening.'

'Well, you know what he's like. It doesn't mean that he doesn't care. I'll speak to you tomorrow. Goodnight, and try to get some sleep. Bye.'

Nina lay still under the covers for a few minutes, wondering if she could summon the emotional energy to try and talk to Malcolm again. She had long been aware of his inability to engage in anything potentially traumatic. Two miscarriages had taught her that. She decided to get undressed and seek the anaesthetic of sleep. But sleep was a long time coming that night.

# Chapter Three

It was 9.30 in the morning and Nina had just returned from the school run. After wandering aimlessly around the house and staring into each room, half-expecting to be given a reason for being there, she had sunk to rest at the kitchen table, her head in her hands. The sun was streaming in through the window, highlighting on the panes several greasy handprints and one long division sum. The floor tiles seemed to mock Nina as she sat staring at them. Ha! Little did you know how lucky you were! Always thought you had your health, didn't you? More fool you! What now, eh? Now your own body's turned against you? Now the chips are really down? She dragged her eyes from the floor and stared at the breakfast things littering the surfaces; they stared back. She stared at all the different-coloured felt-tip stains on the wooden tabletop. She stared at the floor again. Then, picking bits of candle wax off the table with her nail, she began to think about the last few years of her life and make connections with the nightmare of the present.

For a woman of her age, she had known a lot of people who had died. A spark of glitter flashed on the wall as the sunlight caught the ring she was playing with on her finger; the one Jim had given her so many years ago. Jim, the wild and talented artist, who had swept her out of her safe existence into a mad world of risk during three heady years at art school. Jim, who had left life as he lived it, at full speed. Tears welled in Nina's eyes as the memories flooded back. She had never ridden pillion on a motorbike before or since. On the kitchen windowsill beside her was the plant which her close friend, Jackie, had given her in the days before her pancreatic cancer was diagnosed. She had been given six months to live but had fought on doggedly for two and a half years to die a traumatic and painful death. The night that she had first got ill was the same night that, 700 miles away, Nina herself had discovered she was bleeding during her third pregnancy, a fact which led to her second miscarriage, a baby boy who she secretly named Jamie.

After her miscarriages she had drifted into voluntary work, supporting other women who suffered the same loss. The work filled a gap, it made her feel good, gave her a sense of self-worth and an identity other than that of mother and housewife, the latter being a title she vehemently detested. It had been in an effort to avoid this label that she had kept her own surname when she got married; hence her irrational degree of irritation whenever anyone referred to her as 'Mrs'. She spent days rushing round supporting other people and silently resenting the fact that there was never any time to do the things she really wanted to do. Her career as a sculptress faded further and further into the background. After the birth of Josie, she had simply ceased to try to work. The room which had served as her studio became Josie's bedroom and there was no longer any space in her life for her creativity. She poured all her energies into providing Josie with a brother or sister. Two miscarriages left her a woman in a world of unfulfilled dreams. Meanwhile, the possibility of rekindling her creative fire she consigned to a dim and distant future after Josie'd left home. She began to see that B.C., as she'd decided to refer to her life before cancer, she had never allowed herself time to be creative, possibly because of some unacknowledged block that prevented her getting started, more probably because of fear.

In fact now, many things B.C. acquired a new perspective. She saw herself as superwoman, juggling all the balls, playing all the roles, single-handedly taking everything upon her shoulders, doggedly refusing to listen to any offers of help, believing instead that it was down to her to do it all. It had been true in the outside world and true at home. The feeling fuelled her anger towards Malcolm; he seemed to her to be so useless. B.C. she was unable to see her complete inability to allow him to be anything else. A.D. (after diagnosis), she was left wondering if he were capable of being anything else, even if she was able to allow him the space. The signs were not promising. All in all, it was not a very attractive picture. A woman trapped in a relationship that wasn't working, blocked and resentful at her inability to move on. A pretty good recipe for disaster. A pretty good reason for a physical manifestation of emotional disease. A curtain call for cancer.

At this thought, Nina suddenly realized that she had been sat in the same position for over an hour. Her bottom was numb, her hands had gone to sleep, and she had great red patches on her face where she'd been resting the weight of her head. The sun had moved round the corner of the house and she moved to make herself a cup of tea, not because she particularly wanted one but more because she didn't know what else to do. The sick feeling of anxiety in her throat and chest were back with a vengeance. She tried more heavy sighing to relieve the pressure, it didn't work. Mo rang and suggested she come over. They went for a walk by the river which helped a little.

The subsequent days were spent in a haze of the uncontrolled shaking and sickness that are born of terror. Everyone else's lives carried on as if nothing had happened whilst Nina's had shattered into millions of tiny fragments like the spiteful glass of the Sunday two weeks before. She felt she should make some supreme effort to gather them all together again and reassemble some sort of manageable picture. But it was just beyond her. The shards were elusive and she didn't know what the finished picture was supposed to look like.

She kept going for the sake of her child, and did the daily tasks as if on automatic pilot. The first mountain of each day was getting Josie ready and off to school with all the appropriate components in her rucksack, no mean feat at the best of times, it was nigh on impossible in the current circumstances. Each day Nina would be plummeted into consciousness early, having already been awake several times during the night in varying degrees of cold sweat. The sighing would start immediately in an unsuccessful attempt to stave off the shaking of her leg which threatened to resume within a split second of any conscious thought. It was a monumental effort to get out of bed. She would have to sit on the edge first for several minutes to steady her whirring head before she dared risk standing up on her jelly-like legs.

The daylight hours were spent in an effort to keep at bay the strange wanderings of her blackened imagination. She found herself on one occasion standing in the middle of Josie's room staring at her hamster cage and talking to herself. I mean, how bad can it get? For instance, will I outlive the hamster? Let's see, the average life expectancy of a hamster is two to three years and ours is already one and a half. The bathroom's no better. Is there any point in dental flossing? I might be dead long before I ever see my dentures. Is there any point in moisturizing? She began eyeing up elderly grey-haired ladies in the street. For the first time in her life it seemed such an attractive prospect, such a privilege, to reach wrinkled old age. She also became breast-fixated and would find herself staring at the group of mothers in the playground at school, all with their two healthy bouncing breasts and none, she was sure, with any little white dots showing up on any mammograms.

There were always friends to contend with. Some were worth their weight in gold. Others, caught up as they were in their own fears and anxieties, were not. Nina recalled the joking conversation she had had with a neighbour in the street B.C. They had planned a long walk by the river.

'Yes, Friday will be fine unless of course I've learnt that I'm dying of cancer in which case some exercise would probably do me good anyway – so either way I'll be there!'

Now she found herself knocking on the same front door to break the news that she wouldn't be walking because she'd be undergoing some form of less than pleasant experience at the hospital. Her neighbour's face went ashen. She managed to mumble something about not worrying as they could always do it another time, and that was the last Nina was to hear from her for the next three weeks. Wrapped in her own very personal inability to deal with anything medical, she simply couldn't handle what was happening and was unable to inquire any further. Not so much a case of not caring as not daring. Nina was beginning to realize what strange phenomena occurred when the word 'cancer' was uttered. She found she wielded a powerful wand. Some people froze, she could see the fear rising in their bodies till it reached their faces and coloured the words which emerged.

'Oh God! Oh shit! Oh no! What? I don't believe it! How awful! How are you feeling?'

I don't know, Nina would think, and anyway do you really want to know? How long have you got?

Some people burst into tears on the spot, for her, for themselves, for fear, she could only guess. Some people would launch into explicit clinical questioning, eager to know every last detail and offering to surf the net for more. Perhaps in so doing, exercising some control over the great 'C' and thereby shutting off their own floodgates. After all, if it could be her, it could be them. The tricky ones to handle were the ones who could only stay away and send messages of sympathy from behind closed doors. Behind what they were not saying lurked every demon Nina had ever imagined, screaming back at her with soul-piercing strength. She found it was hard enough to say the words without having to face other people's inability to hear them. 'I have breast cancer' meant accepting the reality of what was happening, it meant public acknowledgment, it meant that the information on the leaflets she saw applied to her, it meant she had a one-way ticket into a world she had hoped never to visit. It meant she was faced with the million-dollar question, 'What are you going to do now?'

Luckily for her, there were a few people there to help her answer that question. As with any trauma in life, she certainly found out who her friends were. They were the ones who turned up at the door for coffee; the ones who asked how she was and were willing and able to listen to the answer; the ones who never once recoiled even when their own fears rose inside their throats. The ones who said, 'Would you like me to come with you to the hospital?' and the ones who said, 'I'm coming with you, I want to be there.' The ones who rang her to check how she was; the ones that didn't stay away.

It was always a relief to get to the evenings, although they did bring with them the trepidation of the night. One evening, Nina was sitting on the toilet seat sharing a rare moment of intimacy with her daughter, who was lying in the bath wobbling the fleshy flawless skin of her newly burgeoning breasts whilst muttering, 'I don't like my boobies, Mum, I don't want them to grow. Aren't they a nuisance? Don't they get in the way?'

What could she say? She smiled at her daughter as her heart broke and her mind raced. Will I be there to support her if she grows up to inherit this nightmare? Will I be able to be living proof that she can beat it? Will she know it can be a beginning in her life and not an end? Looking deep into her daughter's eyes, she disappeared into thought. Will I be here to watch her life develop? Or will I be forced to leave her forever, this precious child? Imagine not seeing how that plot turns out. She vividly remembered the day it all began.

# Chapter Four

It was a brilliant blue sun-drenched morning. The whole day stretched ahead of her as she slid the pregnancy testing kit from its packet. She read the instructions and followed them carefully. She left the kit in the bathroom and went to climb into her paint-spattered overalls. She had thrown herself headlong into the decorating of the Victorian terraced house that she and Malcolm had just moved into. It represented a blank canvas on which she was free to create her nest. She was revelling in newly married life. It meant freedom and a new direction. It meant release from the pressure of earning a living as a struggling sculptress. Freedom from the anxiety of competing with colleagues, all of whom seemed to be moving on to greater and better things. Freedom from constant doubt and rejection: was she good enough? Did she have what it took to succeed? Was she even talented? Achieving fame for her work mattered to Nina; she'd never really thought about why. Maybe it had something to do with her family, the fact that her mother had never truly acknowledged her achievements, but then Nina's family was another story altogether. In any event, the need to be recognized was a great pressure; the thought of failure scared her. Then it had happened; an escape route had opened up before her and she had grabbed it.

She was living in a small flat in south London with a

cat called Charlie and a lot of unsold sculptures. She had a part-time job at an arts centre, a shared studio space and numerous waitressing commitments which filled her evenings. A typical resting artist. There were a couple of local craft shops which sold her work and she had once had a write-up on the arts and crafts page of a women's magazine which generated a short-term but lucrative interest in what she was doing. She was living a rather isolated life, fearful of relationships, struggling to make ends meet and determined not to approach her family for help in the face of her mother's unspoken disapproval of her lifestyle. It was six years since she had left art college, six years since Jim had died, six years of striving for independence, when the letter arrived.

*Dear Ms Salis,*

*We have been offered the use of a prestigious West End gallery for two weeks in September due to the generous sponsorship of Harcouts & Co., accountants. We write to ask whether you would be interested in mounting an exhibition of your work together with a group of ex-students. Please let us know your response as soon as possible.*

*Yours etc.*

Nina's heart leapt; this was the chance she'd been waiting for, the chance to exhibit somewhere where it mattered. She lost no time in selecting her pieces and in contacting the other ex-students involved. She worked hard with new-found vigour putting the finishing touches to pieces she had long since abandoned. It reminded her of the unadulterated days and nights of creativity which she and Jim had shared. The mad times spent in the early hours, experimenting with clay and paint and colour and shape. She missed him and wished he were there to share in her good fortune. Her flat suffered, as did Charlie; there was rarely any food in the fridge, but she didn't care. She was happy, in her element, working with a purpose again.

The opening night arrived and her heart was beating somewhere near the base of her throat as she and the others waited in the eerie stillness of the empty gallery for the first guests to arrive. Harcouts & Co. in their white-collar benevolence had provided champagne; the glasses sparkled in neat rows on a white tablecloth just inside the door. Slowly the gallery began to fill. Suited businessmen feigned interest in individual works and tried to talk as if they knew all there was to know about contemporary art. Nina hovered, willing them to pick her work to adorn their expensive London lobbies. Monied wives arrived, dripping jewellery, immaculately manicured.

Through the hubbub, the clink of glasses and the rising levels of inane conversation, Nina became aware of one man standing stock still in front of one of her sculptures. He had been there for a good 15 minutes. It was her 'Seagull and Sea' which had captured his attention. Nina was intrigued. This was her favourite piece and the one she was most proud of. It was also her most costly. Without thinking, she moved through the crowds to stand just behind him. He sensed her presence and turned.

'It reminds me of all the childhood holidays by the sea I wished I'd had,' he said. He smiled as he spoke and his whole impeccably turned out exterior seemed to warm. 'I'm Malcolm Hayes.' He put out his hand in typically British fashion.

Nina took it and shook it. She was in two minds as to whether to give him her name in return. She was rather enjoying the opportunity to discuss her work in anonymity. She smiled and said nothing. They stood in silence for a few moments.

'I collect works of art by unknown artists; it's a sort of hobby of mine.' He spoke without taking his eyes off the sculpture.

A surge of excitement rushed from Nina's toes up through her legs, round her body and filled her head with a dizzy pleasure. Yes, yes, yes! she screamed in silence, surreptitiously punching the air at her side. This is it! I've been discovered! I'm on my way to fame and fortune! He's obviously got money. He's obviously fascinated by art. He's going to buy all my work and make me a household name.

Suddenly worried that her sudden joy might be a trifle too transparent, Nina asked nonchalantly, 'And you like this piece?'

'I do, yes. It's perhaps a trifle naive but I like the movement in the waves and in the gull's wings.'

Nina managed not to hear the slightly patronizing tone in the reply, swallowed up as she was in the deliciously warm feeling that comes to the artist with the knowledge that their work has touched another human being.

She was enjoying herself and becoming more daring. 'I have a feeling this artist will be very collectable one day,' she responded in as off-hand a tone as she could muster, suppressing the broad grin which was threatening to break out on her face at any moment.

Malcolm was now looking at her and she noticed he had piercing blue eyes. 'So you recommend this piece as a good investment, do you?' he asked, smiling again.

'You never know, anything's possible. Would you excuse me please.'

Nina beat a hasty retreat at this point, unsure of

whether she could keep up the subterfuge, and lost herself in the crowd. She found a glass of champagne and a corner to hide in, and watched the proceedings from a safe distance. She noticed that more and more 'Sold' stickers were appearing on the works around her. Her fellow artists all seemed to be throwing themselves into the thick of things, chatting away and making, Nina was sure, all the right noises to all the right people. Networking. She cringed at the thought. She was much happier in the isolation of her studio, fired with excitement and secure in the act of creation. She knew she should be out there selling herself, but she just couldn't bring herself to do it. Her train of thought was unexpectedly interrupted by a voice, the voice she had just been speaking to.

'I wondered if er ... er ... well, I was wondering if you might like to have dinner with me one evening. That is, of course, if you're not too busy.'

Nina was so surprised by this sudden invitation that she couldn't speak. On the one hand, she couldn't think of anything worse than going out for the evening with a man her mother would clearly approve of; on the other hand, she mused, it might be interesting to see how the other half lived and it would at least be a free meal. She heard herself stammering, 'Yes ... um ... yes ... yes, I'd love to'.

'Great! That's really great! Good! Right, well, all I need then is your phone number and I'm sorry but I don't think you gave me your name.' He seemed genuinely pleased and quite surprised that his invitation had been so readily accepted, and was smiling the same warm smile again.

Now it was Nina's turn to smile. 'You'll find my name and address on the back of your programme,' she said, 'I'm one of the artists exhibiting here. In fact,' she added with a broader grin, 'the "Sea and Seagull" you were looking at is mine.'

For a moment he appeared somewhat taken aback. 'Well, how extraordinary! What a coincidence! Actually it's not yours any more, it's mine. I've just bought it!'

Nina could have kissed him. She felt like jumping up and down for joy and flinging her arms round this stranger who had just proved to her beyond all shadow of a doubt that he valued her work. She managed to control herself, however, and say in a restrained tone, 'Oh, have you really? Well, that's marvellous. I'm so glad you like it.' As an afterthought, one of which she was quite proud later, she added, 'Perhaps I could have your name and address for my records as I like to invite people who've bought my work to future exhibitions.'

He reached into his inside jacket pocket and handed her a gold-edged business card with the words 'Harcouts & Co.' in bold type in the centre.

'I'll be in touch soon,' he smiled as he put his half-empty glass back on the edge of the table and disappeared into the evening air.

The rest of the evening went well. Business was good. Many of the works were sold. To her amazement, Nina discovered that her mystery date had bought two of her pieces. She went home on a high and sat up late into the early hours of the morning conjuring up images of exhibitions in New York, commissions from the rich and famous, large flats and airy studios.

Consequently, the days and weeks that followed were a bit of an anticlimax. Commissions did not come flooding in, no big company hammered on the door demanding works to adorn their prestigious reception areas. In fact, nothing much happened at all. Normal life resumed for Nina, her evenings filled with waitressing, her days with shifts at the arts centre. She spent less time in the studio, disheartened. It was several weeks later when, late one Sunday afternoon, the phone rang.

'Hello. Er... Nina? It's Malcolm Hayes here. From the gallery? I'm so sorry for not getting in touch sooner but I was unexpectedly called away on business. I've been in Germany for a month.'

'Oh hi,' said Nina, rather than what she was thinking which was, 'Oh my God, I'd forgotten all about you!'

'I was wondering if you'd still like to come out to dinner. That is, of course, if you don't have other plans.'

It wasn't clear to Nina whether he meant for that night or for every other night in the foreseeable future. In any event, the opportunity to be waited on instead of doing the waiting was too good to miss.

'Oh, I think I could possibly squeeze you in to my busy social schedule,' she laughed.

'Oh, er ... um ... er... good. Right. What about this Friday?' He sounded hesitant, unsure of whether she was joking or not.

'Fine.'

They made arrangements to meet and said their goodbyes.

All the men Nina met in her life as a waitress tended to be several years her junior and generally held little attraction. Her days were usually spent with Charlie in her studio, her love affairs confined to whichever piece of work was currently in creation. So the smartly dressed, well-heeled business man with the warm smile she remembered from the exhibition was a new kettle of fish altogether. As she thought about him over the next few days, his image conjured up for her a picture of 'normal' life, of a house and children, of safety from the harsh struggle to achieve. She was intrigued at how attractive a prospect that seemed, intrigued to find out where a relationship with such a man would lead.

Eighteen months later and she had found out. It had led to a new home, to a sun-filled bedroom where she stood in paint-spattered overalls waiting for the results of a pregnancy test. Events had moved very swiftly. That first dinner date had led to others. Nina had been swept along into a world far removed from her rather shabby little flat. There was money to spend, there were meals in smart restaurants to be eaten, there were trips to the theatre and there were days out in the countryside. Malcolm, it turned out, was the head of his department at Harcouts & Co. Nina never did work out exactly what it was he did but he knew a lot about computers and balance sheets. The job paid well and it was secure, two phenomena rarely encountered by her or any or her artist friends. As the weeks went by, and almost without her noticing it, Nina began to see less and less of her friends, and her cat. She continued to work on her sculptures and she continued to go out with Malcolm. She gave up her waitressing jobs. She returned home later and later at night.

Finally the evening came when Malcolm cautiously and very politely suggested that she might like to stay at his flat. They made love by candlelight, Nina's suggestion. She carried the heavy silver candlesticks into the bedroom from Malcolm's dining table where they had sat, she suspected, since the day they had been bought. Afterwards she carried them into the bathroom and had a bath. Sex with Malcolm was not exactly passionate – if she was honest, it wasn't even particularly exciting. But it felt safe, it felt planned, like so much in Malcolm's life she was to realize.

Once they were sleeping together, it wasn't long before Malcolm booked a table at a very expensive restaurant and produced a very expensive ring between the main course and pudding on the assumption that Nina would

38

agree to marry him. Caught up as she was on this new course in her life, and with the possibility of realizing her lifelong wish to have children, she accepted immediately. Her family were over the moon. Malcolm was everything her mother despaired of Nina ever having. He had a proper job, he was respectable, he had money. He would make it possible for Nina to settle down and do what her mother had devoted her whole life to doing – bringing up children. Nina's sister, Isabel, who was already a long way down that road, was also pleased. She had harboured a secret envy of her sister's artistic lifestyle and had always wondered if she was missing out. The wedding day came and went, an event which had little to do with what Nina would have chosen and everything to do with what her mother felt was appropriate. Malcolm was an only child and his parents were elderly. They kept a discreet distance. Nina tried to get to know them but made few inroads into the cold exterior she was presented with. Shortly after the wedding, the newly-weds moved into the terraced house which Nina was now decorating.

She suddenly remembered the pregnancy test and rushed into the bathroom to see the result. There it was, as clear as day, a neat blue circle. That proved it. The miracle had happened. She was to become a mother.

Seldom had a child been so eagerly awaited. Nina's whole being buzzed with the things she would share with her unborn daughter. She was sure that it was a daughter. They would go for walks, feed the ducks, play in the playground, explore the world. They would make dens and cakes, build Lego machines, play aliens and fly kites. Then later they would go shopping, visit art galleries, have coffee together and exchange secrets. They would make a great mother and daughter team. They would share so much. Her daughter would be creative like her. They would enrich each other's lives in ways she'd not even dreamt of.

And Malcolm, Nina thought, where would Malcolm fit into all this? She rushed downstairs and dialled his number. It was his voicemail. She decided against entrusting such momentous news to the discretion of technology and rushed back upstairs to look again at the pregnancy test. Yes, the result was still the same. Excitement coursed through her veins. She wanted to run, she wanted to shout, she wanted to tell someone, but who? Lotty and Mo were the two names that sprung immediately to mind. Lotty, like Mo, was a friend from art school days. The three of them had remained close although they didn't see much of each other. Lotty had become a graphic designer and had never shown any interest in marriage or motherhood. She was already a partner in her own firm and doing very nicely for herself with a spacious garden flat in Hampstead and a very healthy bank balance. Mo had continued to produce bright and vibrant materials, have lots of boyfriends and live in Hackney.

Nina chose to dial Lotty's number first. The response was typical.

'Oh my God! Well I trust you won't be expecting me to change its nappy! Ring me again when it's about seven years old and I might come and visit!'

Nina smiled. 'I'll take that as a "no" then to the invitation to be present at the birth!'

'What?!' came a strangulated gulp from down the other end of the telephone line.

'Only joking!' laughed Nina, taking pity on her friend.

'You had me worried for a minute there. No, seriously, it's great news. Let's go out for a meal to celebrate. I'll give you a ring from home and we'll fix a date. I'm really pleased for you. I hope you'll all be really happy.'

# Chapter Five

Happy. 'I hope you'll all be really happy...' Long-lost words echoed in the grey semi-consciousness of Nina's brain as she surfaced slowly from a fitful, fidgety sleep. Had she ever been happy with Malcolm? Had Josie filled her life with the sunshine she half remembered from that jubilant day ten years and nine months ago? How different to the one that now dawned. It was Friday, the day of the tests. Once again she struggled out of bed, still on legs that seemed to belong to someone else, and did her now well-practised impersonation of an organized mother in total control of preparations for school.

She hadn't a clue what she was in for, all she knew was that further tissue samples had to be taken, this time on the mammogram machine and under local anaesthetic. So, she'd reckoned it up – one jab for the local, one for another fine needle aspiration and one with a bigger needle which she wouldn't feel thanks to the anaesthetic. Three jabs, no picnic but manageable.

Josie was being taken to school. After she'd left, the house seemed ominously quiet. Nina paced the downstairs rooms. The doorbell rang. It was Lotty. Lotty, who hadn't flinched once since being hit with the news. Lotty, who wouldn't hear of Nina going to the hospital on her own. Lotty, who had told Nina she would be there for her.

'Chauffeur at your service, Madame. It's my job to make you laugh today!'

'Trust you to take the easy option!' Nina smiled, gathering money for the car park, and turning on the answerphone as they left.

Twenty banter-ridden minutes later they were sitting in the same waiting room Nina had last sat in a lifetime ago, three days before. There she was, back at the mercy of the concentration camp commandant. The individual who Nina had met on her previous visit appeared to have washed her hair and actually raised a sympathetic smile as she passed her by in the corridor. It was a 'we're old buddies now' sort of look which did nothing to boost Nina's confidence. The condemned woman and her companion didn't have long to wait before they were ushered round the corner to the cold and clinical, bare white changing cubicles where, once again, Nina stripped. She began to feel the degradation setting in as she relinquished control over her body and the medical machine took over. She sat down close to Lotty's warmth and tried to absorb her life-giving energies. She was shaking again. The next moment she was called in to the room where, beside the giant mammogram machine, a different doctor, female and very precise, offered her a repeat explanation of what was about to happen to her and why. Nina tried to take in what she was being told and, as the child within her ran screaming for the door, she wished she'd asked for a grown-up to be present.

Somewhat ominously, the doctor repeated the words 'Don't worry, we won't do anything without first telling you what it is we're going to do.'

Clearly not a barrel of laughs, thought Nina, as she was made 'comfortable' in an enormous old-fashioned wheelchair which looked as if it had been specially reclaimed from storage for the occasion. On her lap were placed several layers of white surgical paper. The staff, of which there were three, another bad sign Nina felt, were unceasingly informative. Then it began. There seemed to be endless injections, computer readouts and programming of digits. Then there was the pièce de résistance, the tool which extracted the core samples.

The doctor explained, 'I'm just going to let you hear the sound this makes. I think it would be better if you didn't look.' At this point, from somewhere behind Nina's left shoulder, there was a click and a sound like a staple gun going off. 'It's a bit of an awful noise, isn't it?' The doctor smiled almost apologetically.

There followed several more shots of local anaesthetic and six staple gun explosions deep into Nina's crushed and abused right breast which all this time had been sandwiched unceremoniously between the cold hard plates of the mammogram machine. The rest of her body meanwhile was twisted and contorted around the machine, her arms held up in an unwieldy embrace.

After what seemed like an eternity, and seconds before she was about to faint, Nina heard the doctor say 'I think we'd better stop now.'

Still in the giant lumbering wheelchair, she was laid back while a nurse pressed down hard on her bruised and battered breast.

'I have to warn you that we may not get a result from this and you may have to have a small operation to see what bigger operation needs to be done.'

The disembodied voice of the doctor pierced Nina's consciousness as she lay reeling from this latest ordeal and caused tears of despair to spring up behind her closed eyelids, trickle quietly down her temples and run into her ears.

'You cannot be serious!' she wanted to scream, McEnroe-style.

As she was helped to sit up and told to put on her clothes, she noticed deep circles of blood all over the sheets of paper on her lap. There seemed to be a degree of frenzied activity going on in an effort to arrange an appointment for her with the consultant as soon as possible. Through the haze of her befuddled brain, she realized there could be little doubt about the negative outcome of proceedings so far. She decided to risk asking.

'Is there any chance that the results from today could be good news?'

'No, I'm sorry,' came the bleak reply.

'OK. So what does that mean will have to happen, surgery?'

'Yes. You'll have to come in as a day-case patient, in and out in the day, perhaps one night's stay. The surgeon will remove the intraductal cancer cells.'

'What about radiotherapy and chemotherapy?'

'Oh no, you won't need either of those. Now we need to arrange a time for you to ring me on Tuesday for the results.'

The doctor handed Nina a piece of paper with a phone number on it, told her to wait outside for an appointment time to see the consultant, and wished her goodbye. Nina struggled out of the door and sank to rest beside Lotty. It had only been 40 minutes but it felt like four hours.

'How was it?'

'Well, at the risk of putting off any poor unfortunate creature who is forced to travel in my footsteps, "barbaric" is the word that first springs to mind!'

'That good, eh?!'

'Well, it's cancer. They've said there's no chance it can be anything else.'

At this, it was Lotty's eyes that welled with tears as she put an arm of comfort round Nina's shoulders. Nina was moved at her friend's spontaneous reaction, but also taken aback at what she took to be the implicit strength of her despair. Finally, an appointment materialized for the following Tuesday. The consultant would see her and explain everything. The subdued duo left for the car. Nina desperately needed to hang on to the arm Lotty offered her. She felt as if she'd been abducted, assaulted and dumped beside some anonymous motorway of speeding traffic; trapped in time, battered in body and ice-cold in mind.

'See that bag on the floor?' asked Lotty as she swung the car out of the hospital car park and into the late morning mayhem in the centre of town.

'It's a present. Go on. Open it.'

'Thank you,' said Nina bending down and reaching into the footwell to retrieve a Waterstone's carrier bag. She felt inside and pulled out a large paperback book called *The Artist's Way*.

'It's been recommended to me by several people and it occurred to me that now would be a good time for you to read it. It's all about how to unlock yourself as an artist. I've haven't finished it but two things stick in my mind – "morning pages" and "artist's dates". The morning pages are about making a deal with yourself to write three A4-size pages of stream-of-consciousness thought before speaking to anyone in the morning. The pages go straight into a brown envelope or drawer, definitely not to be re-read or shared with any unsuspected critics. Hard for you, I know, to do first thing, but you could always do them later in the day. Anyway, the artist's date is something special you do entirely for yourself once a week. It could be buying yourself a present, it could be a walk in the sun or the rain, it could be a massage, it could be time to do something you enjoy but haven't done for ages. What do you think?'

After the last two hours, Nina was incapable of thought, but her frozen soul began to stir as she listened. It struck her that Lotty was talking about the future, a future she had to find a way of believing she had. She looked out of the car window at the trees lining the park and wondered how many hundreds of years they had stood sentinel-like beside the road. She knew that many women survived breast cancer and lived into ripe old age. As the streets and the houses and the shops and the people flashed by, she made a pact with herself that, whatever it took, she was going to be one of them.

With Friday and the tests over, the weekend hours dragged by in a semblance of normality. She tried not to focus too closely on her extremely painful breast which looked as if it had just done ten rounds with Mike Tyson. She tried not to think about having to tell her parents the joyous news but, by Saturday evening, she felt she could put it off no longer and forced herself to dial their number.

'Hi, Mum. It's me, Nina.'

'Oh Nina, darling, how nice to hear from you at last.'

Dierdre, Nina's mother, always made a point of making her daughter feel as if she should have rung more often.

'I'm afraid I've got some rather bad news,' said Nina quickly as if in a rush to get the words out before her courage failed her and her mother dragged her off into some irrelevant conversation. 'It seems as if I've got breast cancer.'

There was silence at the other end of the line. 'Mum, are you there? Did you hear what I said?'

'Yes, yes, darling. I am sorry but I'm sure there's nothing to worry about.'

'Mum, it's breast cancer,' Nina half-smiled and then added miserably, 'I don't see how you can possibly say there's nothing to worry about.'

'Perhaps they've made a mistake. Have you had any tests?'

'Yes. I've had biopsies taken and there's no mistake. I see the consultant on Tuesday and he'll tell me what happens next. I think it probably means going into hospital for a day.'

'Oh, not too bad then. I'm sure you'll cope wonderfully, you always do.'

For a split second, Nina considered letting her mother get away with this, but quickly decided not to.

'I don't feel as if I'm coping at all at the moment actually, Mum. I feel terrified.'

'Yes, well, darling, I'm just off out for bridge. You know, it's one of my usual nights so I'll have to go. Would you like to speak to your father?'

Nina sighed. Her heart longed for her mother to be able to offer her the support and love she needed, but it was not to be, nor ever had been. Her father, however, was a different matter. The years had bound them close. She had watched him become more and more self-effacing as nothing he did ever seemed to satisfy; quieter and quieter as his wife's demands became louder and louder. While she became caught up in a swirling social vortex of bridge parties, better gardens, bigger cars and immaculate houses, he retreated further and further into a solitude of his own. There was a brief muttered conversation in the background as the phone was passed from one to the other.

'I'm so very sorry, darling. What terrible bad luck. Tell me what's happened so far.'

Nina did her best to fill her father in on what she understood her situation to be. He listened without interruption.

47

'Do you think this consultant knows what he's doing? Has he got a good reputation?'

'I don't really know, Daddy. I haven't met him yet but he seems very highly thought of locally.'

'Well, if there's anything I can do to help, anything at all, you just let me know. Tuesday you say is when you see him?'

'Yes.'

'Will you ring us on Tuesday evening, then?'

'OK.'

'Keep your spirits up, darling. I feel for you. I know you can get through this. It won't be easy, but I know you can do it.'

'Thanks, Dad.'

He was gone. Nina put the phone down, feeling all of ten years old. Bereft. She was suddenly not at all sure she could get through it. What if she was going to die? What about all the things she still wanted to achieve in her life? What about seeing her child grow up? As if on cue, Josie's head appeared in the doorway and caught her mother standing motionless, gripped in the claws of yet another rising panic.

'What's the matter, Mum?'

'Nothing, darling.'

She hated lying to her but couldn't tell her anything until she knew what it was she had to tell her. By Tuesday evening, she thought, I'll be able to answer the questions she will ask. Her mind wandered to the expensive skiing holiday they were supposed to be going on with Mo and her family in a couple of weeks' time. Would they be able to go? Or would that be yet another disappointment to add to the trauma? She knew that life was unjust and there was little to be gained from dwelling on 'Why me?' What she couldn't help asking was, 'Why my child? What has she ever done to deserve all this?' Needless to say, the walls of the house supplied no answer.

'Are you sure, Mum? You don't look as if there's nothing the matter.'

'No, honestly, darling, I'm fine. What are you up to?'

'Dad and I are trying to work out this new computer program. It's really cool. Can I have something to eat?'

'It'll be supper time soon. I'm just about to do it but you can have some fruit if you want something to keep you going.'

'Oh Mum, can't I have a packet of crisps? Please? I'm really starving.'

'Oh, go on then.' Nina hadn't the energy to argue. And anyway, one packet of crisps was hardly likely to hurt a child who had inherited her father's slimline proportions. Josie grabbed a packet and raced back upstairs. Nina moved into the kitchen and began cutting up vegetables like a zombie.

The following day was Sunday and she wondered about going to church. She had hardly been since Josie's christening and wasn't sure why the thought occurred to her on this particular morning. Possibly it had something to do with being made to face her own mortality. And in facing it, daring to disbelieve at her peril. She wasn't sure. She certainly wasn't a believer in any conventional way, but she had long sensed the existence of a power greater than the individual beings she saw around her. It might have been their collective energy, or perhaps it was Nature herself, the power of the wind and the tide, the thunder and the sun. On reflection, a visit to church seemed a little over the top. Malcolm and Josie were as usual closeted around a computer screen; instead she left the house quietly and headed for the river, walking not running this time.

It was a still, quiet, lying-in type of morning. The only early risers were a few fishermen and the odd sweaty jogger. The rain had swollen the river, giving a sense of urgency to its flow and sharpening the quality of the smells in the early morning mist. It was not as cold as it had been; there was a distinct promise of spring in the air which Nina tried her best to absorb into the heart of her being, frozen as she still was in an icy grip of fear. She walked until the houses left her and there was a respite of green. She stood at the river's edge and stared desperately into the murky water like a fortune-teller into a tea-cup. There was a splash to her right and she just caught a glimpse of a water vole's tail-tip as it disappeared into the weeds at her feet. The river flowed on regardless, just as it had done, Nina thought, for hundreds of years. Human life, her own in particular, seemed suddenly dwarfed into a flimsy insignificance. She shook her head in a fruitless attempt to shake off the demons and turned to retrace her steps along the path.

# Chapter Six

It seemed as if Tuesday would never come. Nina was amazed that life appeared to carry on regardless. Malcolm came and went as usual, not wishing to know any more than Nina managed to tell him. In fact she felt he would rather have known less, preferring instead to believe nothing out of the ordinary was happening. Finally, Monday's night-time hours dragged themselves into day. Nina hauled her weary limbs from her bed; battle fatigue seemed to have seeped into her bones. Much to her own surprise, she spent the morning very positively, laying out ingredients for cakes for the forthcoming birthday party. Josie had chosen a trip with a few friends to the Museum of the Moving Image. Nina was by now well into Lotty's book, and had even managed to overcome her inner resistance to writing the 'morning pages'. On this particular morning she found herself furiously scribbling the same sentence over and over again ... 'I will beat this. I will beat this. I will beat this.' What the hell, she thought. On an impulse she decided to copy out some quotes from the book and even derived some pleasure from finding coloured card to write them on. A simple task that occupied her hands and didn't tax her brain. Once she'd finished, she sat at the table, not quite knowing what to do with them. It all seemed a bit daft and irrelevant.

Then it struck her that what she needed was a space, a

space for herself. Not herself as mother, not herself as wife, just herself; perhaps even herself as sculptress. They had a spare room which was used as a general dumping ground and it occurred to Nina that there was nothing to stop her claiming this room for her own. The only person to use it on a regular basis was the ageing Charlie. It was quite a revolutionary thought to Nina that there might be some way to resurrect herself as a creative being within the family home. She gathered her little coloured cards together and went to stand just inside the door of the room. There were piles of old newspapers, magazines and Malcolm's old work papers littering the floor. The picnic bag left out from the previous summer stood alongside an old second-hand exercise bike which neither she nor Malcolm ever used. The sofa bed was hardly visible under piles of discarded clothes which had come to rest there on some forgotten journey to the Oxfam shop. In the midst of the pile lay Charlie, quietly snoring. The pictures on the walls, the lampshade and the old armchair in the corner were all items left over once the rest of the house had been decorated.

Nina surveyed the scene with new eyes. There was possibility here. There was promise. This room could represent her future, the one she was trying so hard to believe in. In a frenzy of activity that belied her earlier weariness, she fetched a roll of black dustbin bags and started shovelling in debris from the floor. Charlie watched her sleepily but didn't bother to move. Before she knew it, she had filled three bulging bagfuls. Then she suddenly remembered the time. Time to dial the dreaded number.

The receptionist asked if her call was expected. She said 'Yes' and was told to hold while they found the doctor. She waited and waited. She shook. Finally there was a voice at the other end of the phone.

52

'Yes. Mrs Hayes. I have your results. I'm afraid it does show cancer cells and it shows that they have spread outside the ducts. This means you will have to spend six or seven nights in hospital and have lymph nodes removed as well to see if it has spread any further.'

There was an interminable silence while Nina desperately struggled to take in this stark and shocking piece of news.

'I'm sorry, I always seem to be giving you worse news. Are you on your own, Mrs Hayes? Is there anyone with you?'

Nina's head was spinning. She wanted to shout, 'Yes, yes, I'm on my own and that's not my name and no one told me you might be giving me this much bad news. I thought you were going to confirm I had intraductal cancer cells. I'd only just got my head around going into hospital for one day, and now it's worse, much worse. Who said you could move all the goal posts?'

The doctor's voice wafted back into her consciousness, 'So you will see the consultant tonight and he'll explain everything to you then and tell you what he's going to do.'

The doctor apologized again, said goodbye and put the phone down, escaping as she did so from the need to acknowledge that she'd just pushed Nina's world over the edge of yet another precipice in just four minutes flat.

Nina sat staring at the floor in front of her. She couldn't move, she couldn't speak. She could hear herself whispering over and over again, 'Oh God, oh God, it's getting worse and worse, oh God...' She tried to think who she could ring. She knew she needed to make human contact to avoid slipping over the edge into a black abyss but she couldn't think straight, she couldn't think numbers, she couldn't think who.

Then a voice broke through her numbness. 'Call me any time. I'll be at my desk, whatever, just call me if you need to.'

Lotty. She would call Lotty. She was shaking so much it was hard to dial.

'Hello.'

'Hello, it's me.' She was barely audible. 'I've just had the results. It's got worse, much worse. I don't know where it's all going to end. It's spread, I don't know how far. I've got to have a much bigger operation.'

'What shall I do?' Lotty asked immediately. 'Shall I come over? I could come right away, I'd be with you in an hour. Shall I do that?'

'No, I'm fine,' Nina managed to mutter. 'There's no need for you to do that.'

'Well, will you ring Mo then? Promise me you'll ring her? You mustn't be on your own.'

Nina promised and put the phone down. She dialled Mo's number straight away because she'd promised, and in case all resolve to do anything left her. All she got was the answerphone. She wasn't sure why, but she tried Malcolm at work; he wasn't in his office. She put the phone down again and froze. She simply couldn't believe this was happening to her. She was completely unaware of how many minutes had passed when the phone rang, piercing the icy silence and making her jump. It was Mo. As soon as she heard the news, she offered to come at once. Nina replaced the receiver and froze again.

After a few minutes she got up and wandered into the kitchen where she stood staring at the cake ingredients. She'd forgotten all about them. As if in slow motion she began to put two and two together, telling herself that she might as well be doing something as sitting rigid waiting for the axe to drop. She beat the butter and sugar together and wondered whether she'd be able to beat anything after her operation. She beat the eggs and wondered how many more times she would be able to make birthday cakes for her child. She sieved the flour and weighed it, even managing to remember the baking powder. Very slowly and very methodically she began to add first one and then the other. Mo arrived just as she was about to put the mixture into the little paper cases which were all lined up pert and neat in ordered rows acting for all the world as if nothing had happened. Nina filled them, put them in the oven and made coffee. She told Mo over again what she had just been told, trying to absorb the information, trying to feel it somewhere in her body but she felt nothing. She felt no different, no iller, no sorer, no pain, nothing.

Their conversation was interrupted by a strong smell of burning. King Arthur-like, she remembered the cakes. She removed the blackened offerings from the oven and put them straight outside the side door where they sat in smouldering indignation, their little paper cases now looking a great deal less smug. She returned to sit at the kitchen table, her head in her hands, trying to sip coffee and trying to communicate. She couldn't remember from one minute to the next what had been said. After a while Mo suggested that they go for a walk, and Nina remembered noticing earlier what a lovely clear, crisp, bright, sunny, full-of-life sort of day it was. Walking seemed like it would be a tremendous effort but so did sitting, thinking and watching the demons gather, so she agreed.

They set off for the river, following the same route Nina always took. Ironically she was the fitter of the two and naturally walked faster. They passed rows of streets and cars and houses, rows of people going about their ordinary everyday lives completely unaware, it struck

Nina, of the hell she was experiencing or even that she existed at all. The world kept turning without so much as a hiccup to register that hers had stopped dead still. They soon reached the river which sparkled in the winter sunshine. They didn't go far along the towpath.

Mo chattered away in a desperate attempt to lighten the atmosphere. 'I bet in a few months time you'll be showing off your prosthesis to me without so much as a second thought.' Almost before the words left her mouth, Mo wished they hadn't. Nina felt a wave of horror well up inside her.

'Hopefully I won't have to have one. I don't know yet.'

'Sorry, sorry. That was a really stupid thing to say. I'm such an idiot.'

Nina forgave her immediately. What mattered much more than what she said was the fact that she was prepared to be there, with her, standing on the edge. When they got back inside the house, Nina attempted to warm up bread and soup. It required an even bigger attempt on her part to eat it. There was a lump in her throat which seemed to be growing daily. All she could do was wait for the 5 o'clock appointment with the consultant, the fount of all knowledge.

Somehow she managed to pick up Josie from school. She stood in the playground and smiled innocuously at the other mothers arriving for their daily rendezvous, every fibre of her being wanting to shout 'You bloody happy healthy breasted women! Have any of you any idea how lucky you are? Have you got a clue what you could be going through? What I'm going through?'

A lone dad passed her on some steps, 'Cheer up! It might never happen!'

'Oh God, oh God,' she wanted to scream, 'it already has.' She smiled and nodded. Josie came bounding

56

down the steps full of the joys of spring and asking if she had bought her the latest magazine on computer games. Nina apologized. She hadn't. Failed again. She dropped Josie off at her chess club and then returned home to waste some minutes aimlessly wandering again from one room to the next, seeing nothing and not sure where she'd come from or where she was going next.

At last it was time to pick up Malcolm from the station and head for the hospital. The doctor that morning had warned her not to expect to be seen at 5 o'clock as it was a very busy clinic. She had to be on time though, just in case, as the great man was never obliged to wait. She drove to the station, parked and waited, wondering if Malcolm would appear or whether there would be a last-minute call on the mobile to explain which unavoidable meeting had prevented him being there. The minutes ticked by; the appointed train came and went. She was on the verge of giving up when, much to her surprise, a reluctant and harassed-looking Malcolm appeared at the station entrance. He placed his briefcase carefully on the back seat and climbed in beside her.

'Well, I'm here!' he announced almost as if he expected a medal.

Predictably he didn't ask her how she was feeling and they drove in silence for a few minutes. Nina was rehearsing in her head how to tell him what she'd learnt that morning. Why was it that it felt such an effort to talk to him, whereas she always found her close friends so easy to communicate with?

'I had to ring the doctor this morning, to get the results...' she began.

'Oh yes.' Malcolm was reaching round to the back seat and trying to extract some papers from his briefcase.

'It wasn't good news,' Nina went on, putting her foot

suddenly hard down on the brake to stop at some lights which had spitefully turned red on her approach.

'Oh shit!' exclaimed Malcolm as his open briefcase slid off the seat onto the floor scattering its neatly documented contents everywhere.

'Yes, to put it mildly, that is what I thought,' said Nina.

'What? Sorry, I meant my briefcase, I didn't hear you.'

Didn't want to hear me, more like, thought Nina, taking a deep breath, sighing a deep sigh, and starting again.

'I said that the news the doctor gave me this morning wasn't good. In fact it's getting worse and worse. I now have to go into hospital for a week, have a bigger operation, and they don't know how far it's spread. I guess it means the holiday's off.'

Her voice came out louder than she intended. It did the trick. Malcolm stopped scrabbling to retrieve papers off the floor of the car and sat motionless, staring out of the windscreen ahead of him.

'I tried to ring you but you weren't there.' Silence. 'Well, say something.'

'Er, I don't know what to say, there's not much I can say, we'll just have to wait and see what the consultant says. I'm sure it will all be OK.'

'What do you mean, it will all be OK? How can you possibly say that? I don't see how.' Nina pulled sullenly into the hospital car park and took a ticket from the machine at the barrier.

They got out of the car in silence and walked in silence to the clinic where only one short week before, an eternity ago, Nina had sat writing a letter as she waited in cheerful anticipation of being told everything was alright. The nurse confirmed it would be a long wait and so they went off in search of a cup of tea. Nina knew her way around the bowels of the hospital having visited numerous patients and staff there in her role of befriender. Her role from another life where she was the successful provider of moral support for all. Not this life, on this day, when she could barely walk unaided, when her fear was so big it threatened to suffocate her in its airless embrace. They managed to find a cup of tea. It tasted strange to Nina, whose mouth had been permanently dry for a week and whose lips needed licking constantly. They sat strained and tense in the big hospital staff cafeteria which was virtually empty, peppered only with one or two couples in earnest conversation. There was nothing for it but to return to the crowded clinic where they sat again and waited. And waited and sat.

After about 20 minutes, Nina became aware of a very loud conversation going on at the other end of the waiting area. A brash, very overweight young man, who looked at first sight as if he might be a woman, was holding court, regaling those sitting around him as well as those some distance away with the details of his diagnosis and treatment. He wore a tent-like T-shirt and matching leggings; it was hard to say which were the louder, them or his voice.

'I don't talk about it much. I felt this lump, see, in my chest. Well, I was told not to worry, it was a cyst. Then I got called back two days later. Bit of a shock it was. Come and see me urgently, the doc said. Then they told me I was one in a thousand, a man with breast cancer. I was told it was incredibly rare. Of course I would have to have it in both breasts. So that was it basically, had to have surgery, no choice. A double mastectomy. And all the radiotherapy stuff and all that. And here I am, back for my regular check-up. Course it's a bit nerve-wracking. Will I, won't I be alright? But I don't let it bother me. No, it don't bother me. I'm fine now.'

This intrusive speech, which in other circumstances Nina might have found entertaining, was mercifully interrupted by a summons for the unfortunate man to enter the lion's den. He disappeared behind a closed door amid murmurs of comment from the assembled crowd. Malcolm glanced up from his paper long enough to grunt relief that semi-silence had been restored. Sixty long minutes ticked by. Doors opened and closed. Various white-coated registrars appeared and disappeared accompanied by assorted nurses as if engaged in some sort of macabre Jack-in-the-box dance. Once, a dark-haired bespectacled man in tie and shirt emerged as if in a hurry. Various members of staff orbited round him as he took four strides between one closed door and another. Nina reckoned he had the air of a consultant but he was gone before she could register his appearance. A moment later, the overweight young man in brightly coloured leggings came crashing out of the room that had swallowed him up, eyes down, completely silent, ashen white, and made a hasty exit, deaf to the goodbyes from his erstwhile audience. Speculation shivered around the waiting crowd as everyone exchanged worried glances. Just how bad had his news been? One by one, patients and their carers retreated into their own emotional traumas, eyes fixed on the floor.

Nina's leg began to shake: it was nearly always her left one. Her heel would lift from the floor and her knee begin to jig up and down at alarming speed. She could stop it if she really wanted to by pressing her heel hard down into the floor. Mostly she didn't want to stop it because it provided some degree of release from the dreadful tension which had gripped her heart over the past few days. Sometimes, if things got really bad, both legs would go and then her whole body would be plummeted into a frenzy of manic jigging. She risked another look around the waiting area and noticed for the first time what was showing on the television screen suspended from the ceiling. 'Your Horoscope,' it read, and then proceeded to flash up one after another, Aquarius, Taurus, Libra, Cancer. Interestingly tactless choice of programme under the circumstances, thought Nina. She watched banal predictions blink monotonously out into the ether as life and death hovered on uncertain edges. Another hour ticked slowly by. Suddenly, out of nowhere, a round and very smiley woman wearing a pleated skirt and homely twinset appeared at Nina's side, knelt on the floor beside her and put a familiar hand on the side of Nina's chair.

'Hello,' she said in an extremely cheery sort of way. Nina tried to respond. 'Now, let me see, who are you?'

'Nina Salis,' came the shaky and rather miserable reply.

'Oh yes, I know. It's a very worrying time isn't it? Well, don't you worry. I'm Doreen, the breast care nurse and I'm here to look after you. Don't you worry, we'll take good care of you. Now have you been told about Mr Hawkes?'

She didn't wait for a reply but carried on regardless, whether or not her information was welcome. 'He's excellent. You couldn't be in better hands. He doesn't pull any punches. He'll tell you exactly what's what and I'll be there to explain things to you afterwards. It won't be long to wait now.'

She drew breath, waiting for some sort of grateful response. Nina offered none. 'Don't you worry, once we've got hold of you, we don't let you go.'

With this deeply unreassuring parting shot and a

sympathetic smile, she disappeared as fast as she'd appeared, on a quest to home in on some other poor unsuspecting victim. Nina wasn't sure how much of this exchange Malcolm had heard, but he made no comment. She was left to wallow in her horror at being now and indefinitely the property of the breast care nurse. The woman's admonitions not to worry had, if anything, the opposite effect. It was an hour later, on her now-familiar jelly-like legs, that she and Malcolm were finally ushered into a small consulting room. At last, privy to what had remained behind closed doors for the past three hours, they were greeted by the bespectacled young man Nina had noticed earlier, Doreen, another nurse, and a very young-looking round-faced medical student who hovered nervously behind the desk.

The bespectacled young man spoke first: 'Right, come in, sit down. I'm Mr Hawkes.'

As Nina and Malcolm sank into the two proffered chairs, he half-rose to lean across the desk and shake hands, as if impatient to get this time-wasting formality out of the way.

'Let's just check a few things. You're forty-one. You have one child. You were on the pill for ten years approximately. You do some voluntary work from home. You have no history of breast cancer in your family. You presented with a lump. I'll need the mammograms.'

He spoke fast as if time were running out or he was late for dinner. The last in this barrage of statements was addressed to the nurse who moved swiftly, murmuring that she wasn't sure where to look so she might be some time.

'Not to worry, Captain Oates!' came the unexpectedly witty reply.

'I need to examine you. Off with your things please. Up on the couch. Lie down. Arm above your head. This is a medical student. May I have your permission for him to examine you as well?'

Nina found herself stripping off yet again in a room full of strange men and women. She wanted to say she did mind very much if one more stranger poked and prodded her but then she thought how else is he going to learn and one more wouldn't really make much difference.

'I suppose so,' she said resignedly as she lay back and gritted her teeth.

Mr Hawkes was very gentle. His minion was not. Meanwhile, 'Captain Oates' had returned with the mammograms. The great man glanced at them and sat down. Nina was dressed again by this time.

'Right. I'm going to put forward a plan of action, tell you what I propose to do, and you're going to tell me whether that plan suits you as an individual or whether it doesn't. OK?'

Nina nodded. She didn't see Malcolm's response.

'You have a Grade Two cancer on a scale of One to Three, so not the best but not the worst. We have some calcification we can see on the mammogram pictures. So I propose to remove the area of calcification together with the palpable lump, leaving a one centimetre-wide margin of safety all the way round. I also propose to remove some lymph nodes in order to determine whether the cancer has spread any further. Prior to this you will have a sentinel node scan whereby an amount of radioactive liquid is injected into the breast and photographs taken at intervals. This enables us to target the lymph nodes most likely to be infected by showing us the direction of flow from the cancerous area. Doreen will explain this in more detail to you. I can't promise to cure you, but I can promise to do everything possible to give you the best chance of recovery.'

He stopped, looking for affirmation, and suddenly there was silence. Nina could manage nothing more than a nod.

'Now, I'm not sure when I'll be able to do this for you. Pass me the black book please.'

Great title, Nina thought. She waited for him to suggest a date as he flipped impatiently through the pages.

'It looks like four weeks next Tuesday is the earliest I can offer.'

Nina found her voice and, thanking her lucky stars that Harcouts & Co. offered their employees family medical insurance, asked what would happen if she went privately.

'Well, this is what medical insurance is for. And you would free up a place for the next NHS person. In that case, I would hope to operate a week today in the morning or one evening that week. I take the operating space wherever I am offered it.'

Nina pushed the all-important signed insurance form across the desk and asked, 'Is there any advantage in my having a full mastectomy now at the outset? Would it improve my chances of survival?'

As she heard herself utter these unbelievably bleak and unremitting words, she was aware that her advocate was stifling a yawn, but the clear matter-of-fact voice continued, 'No biological advantage at this stage. Your chances of survival are dependent on the type of cancer as much as on the size of the tumour. There are many different types of cancer cell, some more aggressive than others. Of course, if you particularly wish to consider a mastectomy, I will listen.'

Nina felt she had little choice but to trust this man whom she didn't know from Adam and into whose hands she was relinquishing her life. He was fast assuming god-like status. With instructions to ring his secretary for an operation date, he ushered them out, obviously eager to bring to an end a clinic he had begun some six hours earlier. No sooner were the beleaguered pair out of one door than Doreen was on hand to push them in through another. She seemed eager to be plied with questions. Malcolm continued to be silent and Nina's only thought was to collect Josie. Far from being nonplussed, Doreen announced that she would be in contact and, much to Nina's dismay, reiterated her earlier comment, 'Don't you worry. Once we've got you, we don't let you go.'

Nina couldn't wait to get out of the hospital. She walked as briskly as her shell-shocked legs would let her and Malcolm followed close behind. He too seemed shell-shocked and struggling to take in the enormity of what was happening, a reality which he had hitherto successfully managed to block from his mind. He had few resources with which to support his wife. He mustered an unconvincing, 'I'm sure you're going to be alright,' and then fell silent again.

Mo had collected Josie from her club and fed her. When they arrived to pick her up, they were met with a melee of different children and a mother Nina recognized from school. She was a beautiful woman with long blonde hair and lovely cheek bones, so healthy-looking, laughing and joking with her children, not a care in the world. The hilarity was too much for Nina. There were too many children. She had to escape.

Several hours later, after Josie had gone to bed and Malcolm had retreated to the safety of his computer screen, Nina sat alone. Tomorrow she would have to tell Josie that her Mum had breast cancer and needed to go into hospital for an operation and that she wouldn't be able to go on her long-awaited skiing holiday. She would have to tell Mo, too, that the holiday was off. Tears of fear and regret began to trace slow paths down her face as her mind drifted back to long-lost holidays from the past.

# Chapter Seven

Josie was 18 months old. It was their first holiday since she had been born and they weren't confident enough to venture out of the country. They had hired a cottage on the outskirts of Lyme Regis in Dorset or Devon, depending on which half of the town you were standing in. Except that when they arrived, it wasn't a cottage with the picturesque roses round the door and pretty garden which Nina had imagined, it was a rather soulless modern bungalow, very clean, very cold and almost clinical. The walls were uniform magnolia and there was a lot of plastic furniture. It had taken them four hours to get there; Josie had slept for one of them and objected loudly for the other three. Malcolm had considered the driving his domain and consequently had shown no interest in entertaining his daughter. Nina emerged from the car with a stiff neck from having spent more than half the journey twisted round in her efforts to amuse Josie. She was irritated that Malcolm seemed to consider their child her sole responsibility. In 18 months she could count on the fingers of one hand how often he had changed a nappy or administered a meal. It was slowly dawning on her that he liked the idea of a family but was unable to engage in it as a reality. As she unpacked their optimistically flimsy summer clothes and folded them into the ill-fitting MFI chest of drawers, she wondered what on earth she was doing being pregnant again. It was eight weeks now and she had told no one, only Malcolm. She felt trapped and chained.

Before she had time to dwell on the thought, Josie suddenly let out a piercing scream from the living room area. Nina dropped the pile of clothes in her hands and ran. Malcolm was just looking up from his tourist's guide to Lyme Regis to see Josie reach up and pull over a newly opened bottle of milk. The bottle rolled off the table and bounced off Josie's head before continuing to weave a course around the living room floor, spewing milk as it went. Josie, the carpet, the table, the floor, two armchairs and a box of groceries which Nina had painstakingly packed early that morning were all saturated with milk. Malcolm didn't move at first. Nina picked up the screaming Josie and cuddled her, soaking her own clothes with milk in the process. She headed for the bathroom and sat Josie in the bath as milk and tears together dripped off the end of her nose. Her hair was sopping. Nina ended up having to give her a bath and then wash all the clothes they were both wearing. When she returned, some 30 minutes later, Malcolm had made an attempt to clear up. The contents of the box of groceries were sat in little individual pools of milk on the table. He had found a washing-up bowl and cloth and was squatting down trying to mop up the worst of it, being careful to avoid contact with any of it himself. Nina sighed loudly at the inadequacy of his efforts and took the cloth off him.

'Give it to me, I'll do it. You look after Josie, if you think you can manage that.'

She swallowed her anger and frustration and began scrubbing the floor as if it were somehow to blame. It took her the best part of an hour to clean up. It was not an auspicious start to the holiday.

By the time they were ready to leave the house to

explore, it was late afternoon and dark grey stormclouds had rolled in off the sea bringing in their wake a fine, damp sea mist which settled like a silent cloak over everything in sight. Nina was exhausted from the car journey, the clean-up operation, the unpacking and the anxiety over whether the entire bungalow would for ever stink of sour milk. Her main thought was to buy some bicarbonate of soda; the only saving grace in the whole affair was that most of the furniture was made of plastic. She put Josie in the buggy, packed a bag of emergency supplies and set off at a brisk pace down the street as if by walking faster and faster she could dissipate her anger. Malcolm almost trotted at her shoulder. They reached the steep hill of the High Street and began walking downwards towards the sea and the gathering mist. Rather disgruntled fellow holidaymakers stood in groups deciding whether to put on their plastic macs or pretend that the mist would soon blow away and reveal blue sky and sunshine.

Malcolm, Nina and a now peacefully sleeping Josie reached the bottom of the High Street. There was no beach to speak of but a wide promenade led off to the right towards what looked like the Cobb in the distance made famous by Meryl Streep's double in *The French Lieutenant's Woman*. They trudged on in silence, Malcolm nonchalantly now pushing the buggy, acting as though he did so every day of the week. Nina was still angry; he hadn't even helped to unpack never mind clean up the milk properly. She'd only left him for five minutes to look after Josie. It just proved her point that he was incapable and that it was all down to her; she had to do everything. Amidst her frustration she reminded herself that this was the beginning of a week's holiday, a family holiday, a supposedly happy event.

She slowed her pace and joined Malcolm, placing a

hand lightly on the buggy. It was the nearest she could bring herself to be to him. Josie was beginning to stir and Nina suggested that they go down the stone steps in the wall to the beach. Malcolm reluctantly agreed; he didn't like sand in his shoes. By the time they'd carried the buggy down the steps, Josie was wide awake and straining to get out. Nina took her hand as a pair of determined unsteady legs made a beeline for the sea which was quietly lapping tiny waves on the shore. Her red wellies were still in the back of the car and so the next half an hour was spent in a tireless effort to distract her from her determined intent to test out the water. Malcolm gathered some stones and started arranging them in patterns on the sand. This fascinated Josie, who took to picking them up as fast as he put them down and alternately throwing them or putting them straight in her mouth. Far from clearing, the mist seemed to be rolling over them in thicker and thicker blankets. It hugged the harbour walls and then licked at the base of a line of huge stones massed higgledy-piggledy along one side of the beach like so many cobbles long ago abandoned by an anonymous giant. As it slunk across the sand, they decided to call it a day and head back to their newly acquired home, via a supermarket, where they bought some bread, some more milk and a tub of bicarbonate of soda.

By the time they'd reached the bungalow, they were all decidedly damp and yet another change of clothes was in order. Malcolm settled into an armchair surrounded by piles of local guides and maps. Nina set about moving breakable items from Josie's reach; she checked the cupboards for child locks; one good thing, she thought, she didn't have to worry about stairs. Once she'd satisfied herself that Josie was in no immediate danger, she set about preparing her some tea. After she'd fed her, she decided to give her another bath, more to pass the time and for its entertainment value than because she felt her daughter was particularly dirty. Malcolm had not looked up or stirred from his chair except to make himself a cup of tea and to offer Nina one. The other rooms seemed cold to her when she emerged from the bathroom and she went to put on the one thick sweater she had brought with her. She found one of Josie's favourite books and plonked it and a pyjama'd Josie into Malcolm's lap, stating that she couldn't prepare supper and read to Josie at the same time. Malcolm was only too happy to oblige – reading was an activity he felt at home with, the words were there in front of him, he didn't have to invent anything, it was all done for him. Josie snuggled happily down against his chest and sucked her thumb. Nina glanced back at them as she headed for the kitchen and smiled. She thought that after all everything might be alright.

The next two days passed reasonably happily. The sun shone and whilst it wasn't ever boiling hot, at least there was no rain. One day they visited Charmouth, the next bay to the east. Equipped with a picnic lunch which Nina had prepared, and plenty of snacks, they left the car in the car park and set off across the little wooden bridge which spanned a small river as it made its way out to sea. Already, several noisy boys in rubber boats were shattering the peace of a small family of ducks who lived on the pond a way upstream. They beat their oars down onto the water and shouted dares to each other. Josie was squirming to be allowed down to run on the green cliff base through which the path trailed to the beach. They made slow progress until Malcolm tired of it and swept her back up onto his shoulders. They managed to make it past the beach café without succumbing to demands for ice cream, past the bouncy

71

castle and on along the beach through the massed British holidaymakers in varying stages of disarray. The cliff face rose to their left in a bank of black volcanic mud interlaced with golden fingers of sand which snaked down from above as if pointing towards the treasures beneath. Whole dinosaur skeletons had been found here, bared to the world each time another swathe of Dorset countryside slipped onto the beach below. The cliffs were always on the move; the houses on them perched precariously on borrowed time. The tourists climbed them at their peril. Many a shoe or worse had been sucked down into the muddy depths of the grey ooze which bathed the bottom of their slopes.

During the day Nina and Malcolm watched the tide complete its outward journey and they saw it devour the beach on its return home. Nina expended vast amounts of energy building a giant sandcastle, more tiny pebbles than sand, for Josie to stand on as the water washed in. During its construction, Josie was more interested in transporting parts of it to other spots on the beach. Once finally finished, she delighted in standing on the top and kicking down the sides. Consequently, by the time the sea actually reached the castle, there was not a great deal of it left to be washed away. The beach was not Malcolm's favourite venue; the sand in his sandwiches irritated him. He had risked bringing his laptop with him and continually became extremely agitated if Josie and her sandy little body looked like coming anywhere near him or it. It fell to Nina to distract her. They paddled, they gathered seaweed, they dug, they moved copious amounts of sand around in small buckets, they fished for crabs in the little pools that revealed themselves at low tide.

When Josie had tired of all the activity, Malcolm suggested a walk along the beach. He had read that there were plenty of fossils to be found; the beach was famous for its ammonites and belemnites. He and Josie set off and for 20 glorious minutes Nina lay on her back staring at the clouds as they skidded across the pale blue sky. No one made any demands of her. No one talked to her. In the silence, her imagination soared; she saw all sorts of life forms in the shapes adopted by the scurrying clouds; she began to think how she would sculpt them, what materials she would use. Her face relaxed and she wallowed in the momentary freedom she had snatched. Far too quickly, it was over. A very sandy little bottom landed heavily on her tummy and all her emotional energies were once again focused on one tiny demanding scrap of humanity.

The brief interlude of good weather didn't last and, typically of most British seaside holidays, the rain returned. They tried to visit local landmarks but were forced to spend much of their time in the car. Josie didn't take kindly to the plastic hood which fitted over the back-carrier and would complain loudly every time they tried to take a walk in the wet. They drove inland one day to visit Ham Hill, a curious collection of assorted hillocks, the result of years of quarrying for the local golden hamstone. On a kinder day, there would have been an impressive view from the top. In the event, all they saw was a sea of grey. On another day they drove a little further west and took a ride on a tram which ran from Seaton inland for a mile or so. It was on the tram that Nina became aware that she was bleeding. In a darkened toilet in the pub where they'd stopped for lunch, her heart lurched as she saw the dark red stain on her knickers. Tears sprang pricking to her eyes. Please no, please let this not be happening. She felt immediately guilty that the pregnancy had made her feel trapped. She didn't know what to do. She shuffled back to Malcolm in an instinctive effort to keep her legs close together and so somehow prevent more of her baby from dropping out.

'I'm bleeding. I think I'm having a miscarriage.'

Malcolm looked up from his map. 'Oh. I'll ... er ... get you a drink.'

'Did you hear what I said?'

'Yes, I heard. I'm sure it's nothing to worry about. Women bleed in pregnancy sometimes, don't they? And if the worst comes to the worst, we can always try again. Give it a day and I'm sure it'll stop.'

But it didn't. The rest of that day, it was the same. Nina began to put off weeing, frightened of what she might find. She had no tampons, no sanitary towels, and was forced to make a miserable trip to the chemist. Into the night, it continued. She couldn't sleep. In the early hours of the morning she sat on the plastic toilet in the plastic bathroom of their plastic holiday home and passed a large amount of blood. She knew that all there was of Josie's brother or sister was now gone.

The next day she made an emergency appointment to see a local GP. He was too busy and preoccupied to do anything other than to quote statistics at her and suggest she see her own GP when she returned home. When she emerged from the surgery, deflated and exhausted, she went and stood on the seafront and watched the relentless to-ing and fro-ing of the waves as she tried to make sense of her feelings. The surge of the tide seemed to mirror the surge of sadness she felt at the loss of the life within her. She had an overwhelming urge to try again, to be pregnant again. She didn't really understand the need to provide Josie with a sibling; it wasn't as if the marriage was a happy one and she knew that children very rarely cement relationships. The waves offered no resolution so she turned away and headed back.

It was the last day of their holdiay and they decided they should brave the beach once more. The rain had cleared. As she had done every day during the week, Nina prepared a picnic. She packed a bag full of all the spare clothes and other essentials required by a restless 18-month-old on a day out. Sighing heavily and loudly as she went about these tasks, she tried in vain to release some of the welling sorrow within her. In the face of her grim determination, Malcolm would retreat. So by the time they were all strapped into the car, she was feeling miserable, hard-done-by and exhausted. She returned from her holiday with a bag full of fossils, an aching heart and a determination to make her marriage work.

# Chapter Eight

Nina slept little during the night after the visit to the consultant. She lay curled up on her right side, her back turned toward the sleeping Malcolm, and she rehearsed in her head the words she would use to tell Josie what was happening. She blinked and blinked unseeing at the dark. The blackness in the room seemed to creep into her heart as she willed herself to sleep through the long hours of the night. She returned to consciousness in the morning with a dull ache behind her eyes and a much sharper pain at the base of her throat. Her leg started to shake almost immediately. Panic, her constant companion for the last few days, rushed in on her like the seventh wave in a storm. She dragged her rag-like limbs from the bed and wobbled downstairs to make Josie's breakfast and packed lunch for school. She had decided at around 2.30 a.m. to talk to Josie at the end of the school day rather than the beginning. Father and daughter left the house an hour and a half later, each with their own separate agendas, each in their own ways oblivious to the hell in which Nina was struggling to survive.

There was just under a week to be got through and Josie's birthday trip to the Museum of the Moving Image to be managed. Nina had a second attempt at baking cakes for this event, more for something to occupy her hands than because she seriously believed the effort would be appreciated. She could have just bought packets from Tesco's had not some deep-rooted sense of duty prevented her from doing so. This time the cakes survived. Mainly due to the fact that, once they were in the oven, Nina stood guard over them, having slid down to sit on the kitchen floor, her back against the cupboard door and her feet wedged at the foot of the cooker.

Having managed to stir herself enough to open the oven at the appropriate time, she then wandered upstairs as if in a trance and found herself again sunk to the floor, this time in the spare room which she had begun clearing out only the day before. It seemed like much longer ago. The three black dustbin bags sat exactly where she'd left them like grumpy tramps. She sat beside them. Charlie slunk in and curled up quietly on her lap. They all shared the silence until it was abruptly shattered by the ringing of the door bell. Nina crept down the stairs reluctant to face the outside world.

She opened the door to be greeted by Lotty's beaming smile. 'I've given meself the day off work. I'm here and I'm all yours to command! The world is our lobster! What do you fancy doing?'

Nina smiled despite herself. 'I don't really know, to be honest. I was just looking at the room I thought I might turn into a space for me...' Her voice trailed off as it retreated back into the panic-filled well inside her.

Lotty was already halfway up the stairs. 'Great! Come on, show me what you've done. I'll help.'

Nina followed her friend up the stairs and stood beside her just inside the doorway.

'Well, the first thing we need to do is clear out everything that you don't specifically need in here. We're going to need more bags, nurse ... sorry, a joke in bad taste in the present circumstances.'

The two women set to work, silently making piles for

the tip, the charity shop, other corners in the house. Slowly a space began to take shape within the long narrow room. Nina's mind was occupied, organizing what should go where, and for two whole hours the anxiety in her chest abated.

'Right! Luncheon is called for I think!' Lotty announced as she tied up the tenth black bin bag. 'And what we need is pictures. You need a picture in this room that you really like. Let's go picture shopping!'

Nina hadn't the energy to make decisions or to gainsay anybody else's. They set off in Lotty's car to a favourite local gallery of Nina's. The young girl who ran it was happy to let them browse. As Nina fingered through the stacks of prints in their different boxes, she could feel the cold finger of fear return to the base of her throat. Desperately she searched among the pictures for an escape. And she found it. Right at the back of the final box she looked through.

In the foreground was a dark shadowy archway which led onto a sunsplashed passageway at the base of some stone steps. There were yellow flowers in terracotta pots lining the steps and the promise of a view at the top bathed in Italian sunshine. Nina could feel herself in that moment standing in the dark archway, yearning to be in the sunshine and climbing the steps. She did something she'd almost forgotten how to do; she acted totally on impulse and bought the print. Lotty insisted on paying to have it framed. They had lunch in a little café round the corner, Lotty's treat. Nina managed to sip a bowl of soup and nibble at some bread. It occurred to her that she had hit upon the ultimate diet, if only she could patent it. Guaranteed to produce amazing weight loss! A stone a week! A diagnosis of breast cancer!

It was soon time to collect Josie from school and the

horrible reality of what had to be said hit Nina with a sickening thud. She said goodbye to Lotty and thanked her for being there and for the day they'd had together. As her car drove away, Nina felt frighteningly alone. She decided to walk to school so that she could talk to Josie on the way back. She arrived at the playground ten minutes early and looked around for somewhere to sit so that she wouldn't have to engage in conversation. Josie was first out, and not impressed to be walking home. She automatically dumped her bag into her mother's arms and Nina debated whether to tell her to carry it herself because her mother felt too weak to do it for her. She thought better of it. They walked off in silence. Nina started the conversation several times in her head but no sound came out of her mouth. Finally she managed to speak.

'Josie, I've got something I have to tell you. It's not good news I'm afraid.'

'Oh, Mum, not my party! You're not going to say I can't have my party!'

'Oh no, darling, it's nothing to do with your party. I'm afraid the doctors have found a lump of tissue in my boob that will make me ill if they don't remove it. So I'm going to have to go into hospital to have an operation which means that we won't be able to go on our skiing holiday I'm afraid.'

'What sort of a lump? What's it made of? Why's it there?' The questions were fired like bullets from a gun. There was a glint of fear in Josie's eyes as she stopped dead in her tracks to look up at her mother.

'I don't know why it's there, darling. It just appeared and it's made up of cells which aren't like other cells in our bodies; they will make me ill if they're not removed.'

'Is it cancer? Are you going to die, Mummy?'

This last question hit Nina like a punch in the stomach.

79

For an instant, it winded her and she found herself taking a deep slow breath in an effort to hang on to some sort of control. She knew it was important to give Josie an honest answer.

'Yes, darling, it is cancer and no, I have no intention of dying. '

'But Nanny died of cancer.' The colour drained from Josie's face as she stood stock still in the middle of the pavement looking suddenly for all the world like a toddler who had lost her mother.

'Yes, darling, that's true but there are lots of different kinds of cancer and lots of different parts of the body that can be affected by it. Nanny's was much more serious than mine.'

Nina was really struggling now. It was quite true that Malcolm's mother had died of cancer but it was pancreatic cancer and it had spread quite extensively before it was diagnosed. There was, however, as she realized to her cost yet again, only the one word to describe so many situations and that word yielded such power. Cancer. Her heart went out to her daughter.

'I'm going to be alright, darling. Come on, let's get home and have some tea. Would you like some sweets from the corner shop?'

Josie's face brightened a touch and she started walking again. She chose a sherbet dipper and a packet of Maltesers and didn't ask any more questions until they were inside the front door.

'Will you have to go into hospital? What will happen to me? Who will look after me?'

Nina hung their coats up, took another deep breath and sat down on the bottom step of the stairs. Josie stood looking down on her.

'I will have to go into hospital and I'll have to stay in hospital for about a week so that's why we won't be able

80

to go on our skiing holiday this year. We'll try and book it up again, though, for next year. And Daddy will look after you.'

Josie was silent. 'I'm very sorry, darling.'

'I'm really worried about you, Mum.'

Josie stepped towards her mother and flopped down beside her on the stair. Nina put her arms around her, and for a gloriously warm and totally unexpected few moments, they hugged each other. Josie was not a child who liked to be hugged or kissed, much to her mother's disappointment. So this was a treat indeed, but what a price to pay for it, thought Nina. It was not to last. Josie was on her feet again almost immediately.

'What's for tea, Mum? I'm starving!' she said as she disappeared into the sitting-room where she threw herself onto the sofa and switched on CBBC. There were no more questions. Later, after Josie'd eaten, Nina heard her footsteps going up the stairs, and moments later the unmistakeable sounds of computer games came filtering down through the floorboards.

Nina finished clearing up, made herself a cup of tea and slumped onto the nearest kitchen chair, drained by her efforts to put on a brave face for her daughter. She had no idea how much time had passed when the sound of Malcolm's key in the door snapped her back into reality.

'I'm back,' Malcolm placed his briefcase neatly on the floor by the front door and hung his jacket on a hanger.

Why, oh why does he always have to state the obvious, thought Nina. She would have felt irritated if she had had the energy. She didn't move to greet him. She heard father and daughter talking in low tones to each other at the foot of the stairs. She heard Josie's voice and the words 'holiday' and 'hospital'. Malcolm was saying very little. He came into the kitchen, poured himself a whisky and came and sat down beside her.

'Have you had a good day?'

Oh yes, Nina wanted to scream at him, oh yes, I've had a brilliant bloody day, sitting here panicking about whether my body is riddled with cancer and how many months I've got to live!

'OK, thanks. Lotty came over. We've been clearing out the spare room.'

'What for?' Malcolm asked absent-mindedly, his attention focused on a stain he'd noticed on the sleeve of his shirt.

'I thought I might turn it into a space for myself, somewhere I could work, a studio.'

'What for?' Malcolm repeated. 'You don't work any more.'

'Well, I thought I might try to again, once the operation is over.'

'Do you think you'll be fit enough then?'

'I don't know, I don't know how I'll be.' Nina could feel the groundswell of panic over the uncertainty of her future. 'But I've got to have something positive to focus on.'

She looked at Malcolm, who was staring unseeing at the surface of the kitchen table. She knew she wasn't an easy person to support. She knew he was struggling, and felt a moment's pity for him. His whole safe, secure, ordered way of life was toppling on the edge of a precipice and he had no idea how to stop it. It wasn't long before he had disappeared to the sanctuary of his computer screen.

At bedtime that night, Josie had more questions. 'Will you have to go into hospital soon? What about half-term? What will I do while you're in hospital?'

'Well, perhaps Daddy will take a day or two off work and Mo will do things with you. Maybe you'll go swimming. And Lotty's offered to take you to see a show in the West End. Would you like that?'

Josie didn't answer. She seemed to be processing this information with the same quiet reserve with which she approached most of her life. Nina ached to be able to get closer to her but she'd never been able to find a way in.

'Will you have to go into hospital soon?'

The fear hit Nina's throat again as she envisaged all that was in store for her once the hospital doors closed behind her.

'Yes, darling, it will be soon.'

# Chapter Nine

The first day in hospital dawned not so much bright as early. Very early. At 6.00 a.m. sharp, a sound akin to the engine room of the Titanic kicked into Nina's consciousness. She had been awake every two hours, irritatingly on the hour, throughout the night and had just sunk into an exhausted state of semi-consciousness when the hospital air-conditioning revved into action. She strongly suspected it was this that was responsible for the niggling sore throat which had developed apace since she walked through the front doors late the afternoon before.

She had spent most of the previous day in the brand new Cancer Centre being 'sentinel node mapped'. This she understood was a relatively new procedure; the first hiccup in which had proved to be the injection. The nurse, it seemed, was unsure of her capabilities in this area and had to call for adult help.

Nina lay on the uncomfortable couch listening to the airport-like 'bing-bonging' of the Centre's intercom system, a cross between 'Avon calling' and 'Your flight is now boarding'. She thought of Mo sitting outside in the waiting area where they'd been forced to part company. Good old dependable Mo, desperately trying to lighten the leaden atmosphere of the day. She had insisted on coming with Nina when it transpired that Malcolm, much to his relief, had an important meeting that morning. There was a ceiling tile missing and the dark guts of the grim bright building were clearly visible to Nina as she lay spread out on the slab. It reminded her that tomorrow she was heading for the operating theatre where her own insides would be similarly exposed. Her morbid imaginings of unforeseen complications and death on the operating table were interrupted by a cheery 'Hello there! I'm Doctor Barpin. How are you?'

Several expressions sprung to her mind. Limp lettuce on legs. Jelly en croute. To name but two.

'OK, I suppose,' she said weakly.

'You don't sound too sure. Now don't you worry. I'll try not to do to you what I did to one patient I had. Gave him an injection and put him to sleep for four days! Total accident. He had some sort of allergic reaction to the drug and the next thing he knew it was Friday.'

Nina couldn't help smiling. The voice belonged to a warm and gentle round-faced man in his sixties, she guessed. Despite his opening gambit, he exuded quiet confidence. She felt as safe as it was possible to feel in a purpose-built Cancer Centre on the eve of an operation for breast cancer.

'This will soon be over. Let me see, ah yes, here's the lump. Now, you'll just feel a small prick... That wasn't too bad, was it?'

On a scale of one to ten, with events on the day of the core biopsies scoring ten, it did indeed rate extremely low.

'We will meet again, no doubt.' The kindly round face smiled and disappeared.

The nurse asked Nina to position herself under a plastic monolith of a machine which was programmed to chart the progress of the deadly dye. Five minutes later and she was being asked to wait once again, this time in a little area just outside the door. There was the obligatory pile of magazines for company. She idly picked one up from the top. A shapely blonde-haired model beamed out from the cover page. *'Find a Bra for the Way You Are!'* read the somewhat inauspicious headline. Nina wondered how many women en route for double mastectomies or worse had been forced to stop off here before her and read what she was reading. A morbid fascination forced her fingers to turn to the relevant pages. Beautiful double-breasted women sporting bras of every shape, size and colour grinned inanely out at her. Another of life's little ironies, she thought, as the nurse reappeared to suggest that she go and find a coffee and come back in an hour.

She and Mo made their way to the next floor in search of the Cancer Centre coffee bar. They found it perched on the corner where several corridors met. There were about half a dozen small tables, and most were empty. Nina came to a halt at the nearest one while Mo went to buy two very indifferent coffees which tasted mostly of the inside of the machine in which they had been made. Nina's leg began to shake and Mo took her hand. They sat in silence and watched the world of cancer go by. Opposite the coffee bar was a reception desk, at the foot of which was a large weighing machine. As they checked in, each victim was made to make the pilgrimage onto the machine and off again while their degree of emaciation was recorded without comment. First they came with thinning hair, then they came with baseball caps, and finally they came with bold bald shiny heads, men and women and a child of about eleven in a wheelchair.

Nina's eyes glazed over as she fell further and further into the possibility that this was her future. Mo had exhausted her supply of cheerful comments. Their silent reverie was abruptly cut short by a group of large people, seven in all, none of whom seemed to have the smallest shred of spacial awareness. Their intent was to sit at the next door table. First, the back of Nina's chair was thumped by one of them, an overweight woman wielding a large shoulder bag which caught her on the back of the head as the ample torso of its owner leant forwards. Next, two of her equally weighty companions pulled out chairs, making it impossible for Mo to go on sitting where she was. The table screeched in protest as they pulled it across the floor to accommodate their collective presence.

'We're just looking for somewhere for him to take his 11 o'clock dose!' volunteered the woman next to Nina in a booming voice which could be heard down the length of all the adjoining corridors. Nina managed a weak smile at both the woman and their elderly companion who was confined to a wheelchair which they clearly intended to position at the table as well.

Mo and Nina decided in unison and without conferring that it was time to leave. They returned downstairs, mustering mild amusement at the scene they'd just witnessed. Before long they were sinking into the silence of the general waiting area once more. Not one person was daring to look around, every single head was buried in a magazine; even Mo succumbed to the pages of *Hello*. An eerie atmosphere of tension seemed to settle on the shoulders of everyone who waited. It wasn't long before Nina's name was called and she found herself once again sitting alone with only another pile of ancient magazines for company. This time it was Princess Di who caught her eye, a smiling radiant young woman with tanned legs enjoying a holiday somewhere hot. A far-flung image from the pictures of mangled car wreckage in a Paris tunnel. Nina shuddered at the uncertainty of anybody's future and threw the magazine face down on the table. She counted floor tiles till the nurse appeared and ushered her back into the same little room to lie under the same piece of high-tech equipment. A couple of minutes and it was all over, and she was free to go. She and Mo walked briskly side by side along the bright corridors, past the pictures of flower arrangements and peaceful country scenes and out into the grey drizzle of the day.

It was still drizzling 19 hours later when Nina awoke to the sound of the boilers. She struggled into consciousness as her mind skimmed back over the previous two weeks. How had she, a fit and healthy woman with no painful symptoms, come to be lying in a hospital bed facing surgery and death? The door banged open, heralding the arrival of a nurse in the sort of sensible shoes that squeak noisily on the polished floors of hospital corridors.

'Oh, Mrs Hayes, I wasn't going to wake you if you were still asleep.' Nina could only admire the sparkling irony as she glanced at her watch. It was 7.15 a.m. 'Mrs Hayes' again. She was just about to explain when the nurse, who was trying to draw the curtains without using the pulley, said 'Have you seen this?'

The world outside was white and silent. It was drizzling snow. Nina's mind immediately turned to her other life, the one before Josie's tenth birthday, the one in which she was off on a skiing holiday, when she had been worried about sitting on an aeroplane for seven hours. Ha, what a joke, she thought! Today she'd willingly swap a million long-haul flights for the journey she now found herself forced to travel.

Breakfast was non-existent. 'Nil by mouth' read the foreboding notice above her bed. So there was not even that diversion to pass the time. She wondered if Malcolm was managing to get Josie off to school. She envied all the unseen people in the houses in the streets outside her window who would be getting ready for another normal day. She wondered if she should get out of bed and sit in a chair while she had the chance. After all, the rest of the day and all the coming night she would be compelled to spend motionless and gathering bed sores. She thought about trying to jog round the room to get the old circulation going. She realized how reassuring it was, the knowledge that you can move about unaided, and how little time she spent appreciating the fact. Not so, not now, as the minutes ticked ever closer to the general anaesthetic. As if to prove a point to herself and hoping that no one would come in and catch her, Nina began to jog on the spot and then back and forth along the length of one wall like a hyperactive lion in a circus cage. On the twentieth circuit she stubbed her toe on the bed leg and decided to give up. She collapsed into the chair and closed her eyes.

Pictures of blood cells coursing round her body made her think of the books she'd read about visualization techniques. Ever the sceptic, Nina wasn't convinced, but she'd found herself in the last few weeks in the unusual position of feeling so out of control that she was prepared to try anything. After all what did she have to lose? She vaguely remembered reading about seeing pictures of big brave healthy cells locked in battle with nasty negative little cancer cells. Sitting, out of breath, in her hospital room on the eve of surgery, consumed as she was with fear, she wasn't sure she could muster the necessary blood-curdling spirit. It was as much as she could manage to see her healthy cells shepherding the truant cancer cells into a tight little ball which could then be surgically air-lifted by her trusty surgeon in shining armour and dumped in the nearest incinerator. It wasn't half hard work though, trying to think positively. At every corner, the demons lurked.

She moved to the window and leaned on the sill, her arms folded. She looked down at the patchwork quilt of snow on streets and rooftops. She saw the sun glinting in the whiteness and imagined dragons' lairs stacked high with sparkling diamonds. She looked up at the pale blue cloudless sky as the sun rose on another day, and watched as a lone seagull soared its way towards an unseen sea. If the gull can, so can I, thought Nina as she turned away and the door opened.

'Good morning, Mrs Hayes.' Here we go again, thought Nina, visions of Malcolm's mother crowding in on her. 'I'm Mr...' His name went straight in one of Nina's ears and out the other. 'I'm the anaesthetist. Your surgeon tells me he wants to remove a little bit of you.'

Nina's smile was as pale as the sky she'd just been staring at. She thought, I'm sure he doesn't. I'm sure he'd rather be out playing golf. But, yes, you're right, that is what he's going to spend this snowy morning doing, removing lumps. I'm number three on the list so let's hope three is a lucky number.

'Have you had any operations before?'

'Only a "d and c", once, after my second miscarriage.' When my second beautiful baby died and I could do nothing to stop it happening, she thought, but refrained from adding.

Her reply elicited not a flicker of sympathy. He moved straight on. 'And that was under local anaesthetic?'

Nina's mind went blank, shrouded suddenly in the memories of those miserable days. She nodded.

'Would you say you were a fit and healthy young lady?'

For the first time Nina registered a hint of warmth in the eyes behind the gold-rimmed glasses. After all he had just referred to her as 'young'. She struggled to remember back before all the panic and the trauma and the heartache and the sickness and the shaking. Yes, she thought, she did feel fit and healthy. Bizarrely, despite facing the diagnosis she was facing, nothing had changed. She didn't feel any different physically, nothing had stopped working, nothing was hurting. Not yet, anyway. The pain, she knew, was on its way.

'Afterwards you will be sore. Not so much the breast but under the arm. It's the arm that moves and the movement that makes it sore. The physio will come and tell you that you have to do all sorts of painful things like brush the back of your hair. So I'll give you a little machine and you can press the button when you need pain relief. Wait four minutes and if nothing's happened, you can press it again. And again. And again if necessary.'

Oh God, thought Nina, not a syringe driver. That's what dying people have.

'Don't worry, I will have programmed the machine so you won't be able to overdose yourself in your hazy post-operative state!' He chuckled as he left.

Oh alright then, thought Nina, so much for that idea. She watched him go, all smiles and smart suit and tie; not an egg stain in sight.

During the course of the morning it transpired that the theatre staff had been late getting in. It seemed the unbidden snow had succeeded in bringing all traffic to a standstill within a 10-mile radius of the hospital. The morning's operations were to start late. Nina would have to wait. She had two visitors. First Malcolm. Having succeeded in getting Josie to school, he had forced himself through the front doors of the hospital. He was trying his best, although every sinew in his body strained to reach the sanctuary of his work. He sat awkwardly at Nina's side. She could see what an ordeal it was for him. He didn't stay long, promising to return that evening. Soon after he left, Mo arrived. She, too, had just

91

completed the school run and Nina ached with envy at the normality of her world. She brought a magazine. Nina was pleased to notice no advertisements for bras and no in-depth articles about cancer. Their friendly chat was interspersed with long periods of silence when Nina struggled not to lose herself in the pit of panic that hovered always inches from her feet. Eventually she found herself alone with nothing left to do but wait.

She wandered into the toilet, locked the door and took her sweatshirt off, then her T-shirt, then her bra. She looked down at her breasts. She looked up and caught sight of herself in the mirror. She tried to say goodbye to her body as she knew it, as she had always known it. She tried to absorb the fact that it would never be the same again. She stood frozen in time.

There was a knock on the door. The noise made her jump.

A voice called out, 'Mrs Hayes, the lady before you has gone down. Would you like to change now please.'

As Nina snatched her T-shirt from the toilet seat she felt like a medieval peasant bound for the torture chamber. It was time to struggle into her excessively attractive surgical stockings and the equally fetching hospital gown. Top of the bill though were the surgical knickers. These were made of paper-thin material attached to stringy bits of elastic and designed to fit a medium-sized rhinoceros. Let's hope, Nina thought, no gust of wind catches me on the way to theatre or I'll be last seen floating off over snow-capped roofs, bloomers inflated, like some lopsided hot-air balloon.

She was left alone again to wait. Every time she heard the squeak of nurses' shoes or the roll of trolley wheels, her stomach lurched. Was her time up or was some other poor victim being wheeled away? Or was it the tea trolley and the biscuits? And where were the instructions?

Nina was sitting on the bed, surgical stocking in hand. The toe and heel looked fairly straightforward so she heaved those on and then pulled hard. She stood up, one fingernail broken and the others throbbing from the effort. Hello, what was this sort of gusset-like structure which had ended up shining out like a beacon on the front of her upper thigh? And why was the elastic not continuous around the top of the stocking? Something was definitely wrong. It's no good, she thought, she would have to call for adult help.

Several minutes later and the mystery was solved by a willing young auxiliary. The gusset apparently was designed to go on the inner side of the thigh where the elastic split. To achieve this, Nina discovered, required precision twisting and pulling, too little and the gusset ended up at the front, too much and the devious thing ended up round the back.

Once the auxiliary left, her mission accomplished, Nina paced the wall again savouring her last moments of pain-free exercise. Christopher Reeve popped into her head from nowhere. What must it have been like to wake up to his new world of total paralysis? She could not begin to imagine. She wondered at the courage of men and women who survived great traumas to go on and inspire others. She wondered if in her small way she would be able to do the same. Would she be able to make this a new beginning? Would it be a different Nina who survived?

# Chapter Ten

She woke on the morning after her operation feeling as if her right shoulder had been mangled by a combine harvester. She didn't dare look in the mirror. The previous day and night were a blur of semi-consciousness and unanswered questions. 'Would you like the injection for sickness in your bottom or your leg?' 'This is to stop your blood clotting – would you prefer it in your tummy or your arm?' Actually Nina would have preferred not to have it in any part of her anatomy.

When she finally came to, the first thing to catch her eye was an aeroplane trail sparkling in the sunlight in the clear morning sky like a giant shooting star. She began to take stock. The effects of the general anaesthetic were still very much in evidence, bringing with them recurrent waves of nausea which threatened to engulf her. The cannula in the back of her left hand was turning the skin around it red and sore. She had a drain, a plastic tube, which emanated painfully from somewhere underneath her right arm. It led, via some sort of weird suction device, to a disgusting looking plastic bag which she found discreetly hidden inside a cotton fabric cover. The whole contraption was then hung onto a little plastic stand which stood about 2 feet high off the ground beside the bed. This, of course, she had to carry around, in the absence of any obliging gnome to do it for her. Given that there was no chance the entire paraphernalia could be ignored, she decided to give it a name. For no apparent reason, 'Doris' sprang to mind.

By 8.00 a.m. she had managed to sit up, stand and even use the commode. Each task took twice as long as the day before, necessitating a one-handed approach, the hand on the 'bad' side being unable to weight-bear and the one on the 'good' side being occupied ferrying 'Doris' around. Welcome the 99-year-old geriatric cripple! Undaunted, however, she was in the process of awarding herself ten gold stars for achievements when breakfast arrived.

'I ordered you tea and toast. I thought that was all you would feel like this morning,' smiled a friendly nurse as she stood waiting for Nina to clamber back into bed and prop herself up on the numerous pillows.

Breakfast in bed, what a treat! Or it would have been if not for the untimely interruption of a very sweet and very nervous student nurse who came and hovered over her, regaling her with the minute details of her freezing cold bike ride into work, how icy her fingers had become and how much they hurt her. Not content with this, she then homed in on the collage in the photo frame by Nina's bedside. There were pictures of Josie at different ages, a picture of Malcolm, and in one corner a tiny scan picture.

'Oh, I do love your picture. What a pretty dress. And is this your little girl before she was born?'

'No, that's one of my miscarried babies. I've had two.'

'Oh, I'm sorry, I shouldn't have brought it up. I guess you must really need the picture. Is it upsetting? I suppose you don't have to have it out all the time. I shouldn't have said anything. I'm sorry.' She finally faltered to a halt.

Between mouthfuls of toast, Nina reassured her that it

was OK, she wasn't about to burst into tears and, yes, the picture was important to her.

'I'll leave you to get on with your breakfast then,' the little nurse smiled uncertainly and scuttled off.

Hallelujah, thought Nina, as she sipped her tea in peace at last, momentarily secure from further attempts at pastoral care. However, the respite was short-lived. She had barely swallowed her final mouthful when she noticed a decidedly grey hand appearing round the edge of the door. It was followed several seconds later by an equally grey face which blinked repeatedly at her like an elderly mole, just surfaced after years underground.

'Er ... um ... er ... I'm just going to the chapel to celebrate Holy Communion. Would you like me to ... er ... bring you communion afterwards?'

Nina was at a loss for words. Wouldn't be much point, she wanted to retort. The mole was undeterred by her silence.

'Or ... er ... would you like me to give you a blessing or shall I ... er...?' He stopped as if searching for further suggestions.

'Perhaps some thoughts for me in your prayers,' Nina managed to mumble in an attempt to be polite, her voice verging dangerously near hysterical laughter at the sight of this creature struggling to manage the harsh reality of day. He seemed satisfied with this, blinked more frantically for a moment, and crept off.

Nina shuffled slowly to the shower room and locked the world away. Should she have been more honest and told him straight that she was a devout atheist? And anyway, was she? She stared at her drawn face in the mirror, half-expecting someone from the other side of the glass to answer. But no guardian angel appeared. No blinding flash of light. In fact nothing happened. As she made half-hearted attempts to wash herself, she wondered if it was possible that this was her body swathed in bandages, that this was her in hospital with cancer and not some figment of a dream-like imagination. Weren't two miscarriages and an unhappy marriage sufficient? Why all this as well? Again in the absence of any likely answer, she wished for herself a rainbow in the clouds.

At this point she caught sight of her sleep-stained face again. She stared deep into her own eyes and found herself repeating 'I will survive, I will survive, I will survive. Josie will not become a motherless child.' Slowly seeds of realization were beginning to grow. She knew that she had to find some good out of this nightmare and direct it towards herself, her soul. She had for so many of the past few years put herself on hold that it would be hard to kick-start the process of her life. But there in that hospital shower room it broke upon her with the relentlessness of an incoming tide that the road to survival lay in her ability to change.

'Do you need any help?' The hesitant student nurse was back. Nina jumped.

If you only knew; she smiled wryly from behind the closed door and heard herself reply, 'No thank you, I can manage.'

Ten minutes later she and 'Doris' emerged into the public glare of her room. The coast was temporarily clear and she sank thankfully to rest in the chair beside the bed. She closed her eyes and let her mind escape, filling it with images of the studio she would create for herself at home, the studio in which she'd exhume herself, the sculptress, once again. Rebel-like, she planned. The sofabed would stay, on it she'd read or contemplate her latest piece of work. It would have a vibrant cover and wild and wacky cushions in clashing colours and she wouldn't care that Malcolm wouldn't like them. The floorboards would be glossy white and there'd be shelves on which to display her finished pieces. The bricks from the garden would do to build bookcases for her favourite books soon to be salvaged from the boxes in the roof. It dawned on her just how much of her former self had been neatly tidied away to make space for Malcolm and their unborn children. There had to be pictures on the walls too, not just leftovers from elsewhere in the house, but special pictures that she would chose herself, like her Italian steps. She'd need a good strong table to work on with more shelves above it for materials. That would be something to shop for once she got out of hospital. Slowly, images began feeding her future. She saw herself looking out of the window over the rooftops to the line of trees that marked the winding passage of the river in the distance. She imagined herself drinking strength from the sky, the sun, the wind, and the river, from the continuity of it all. She would tap into the energy of creation and it would make her well.

There was a timid knock on the door and a soft padding of feet heralded the arrival of their owner before Nina had time to leave her imagined world and open her eyes. This face was one she recognized, one she had last seen just before her operation. The name badge confirmed it, another member of the pastoral care brigade. She had appeared unbidden the day before, muttering words about the weather and God's blessing, reminding Nina of every film she'd ever seen in which the condemned prisoner gets a last visit from the priest. She could only assume that the entire pastoral team were trained to respond like vultures the minute any patient survived an operation. This fragile, pale-faced woman who never bothered to introduce herself walked straight to the bed and sat down. Much too close for comfort.

'Do you like to read? Such a good way of passing the time I always think. Would you like me to find you some women's magazines? So much easier to read than a book, they don't require so much concentration do they? Oh, and I see you like music.' She pounced on Nina's Walkman like a twittering bird upon a worm. 'I've a CD player you could borrow and some CDs.'

No, no, no! Nina wanted to yell. She dutifully answered the banal questions in monosyllables, hoping this would encourage the woman to vanish. Finally she seemed to take the hint and padded out, leaving in her wake the pungent sweet smell of cheap talcum powder.

The rest of the morning passed uneventfully, mercifully without any more unwanted visitors. Shortly after a distinctly indifferent lunch of insipid fish in a watery sauce followed by cold custard and lukewarm jam tart, guaranteed to do nothing to improve the health of any convalescent, Mo arrived bearing grapes and a bar of organic chocolate.

'How are you doing?'

'Oh, marvellous, marvellous! No, not too bad really. I'm just terrified about Friday.'

'Why? What happens on Friday?'

'That's when I get the results from the lab. When they tell me whether it's spread to my lymph nodes and beyond. When I find out whether I have to go for liver scans and brain scans and God knows what else.'

'Right. Well, I'm sure it won't have spread. You've got to keep thinking positively.'

'Yes, I know but it's hard work. I can't help being afraid of the worst.'

'I know but hang on in there. You're doing so well. I saw Josie and Malcolm arriving at school this morning. They looked very organized. Have they been in to see you yet?'

'No, not yet. They're coming in after school today, that is if Malcolm gets back from work in time.'

'Oh God, I didn't know he was going in to work today.'

'Yes, you know Malcolm. I think it's one of the few things keeping him going at the moment. He's trying but he's just not cut out for this.'

The two friends chatted on comfortably for over an hour until Mo realized it was nearly time to pick up from school. She promised to return the following morning. Another hour passed, Nina wasn't sure, she might have slept for a few minutes. The next thing she knew a ravenous Josie flopped down onto her bed, shedding school bags as she did so. Malcolm followed a pace or two behind, looking nervous of what he might find and somewhat flustered.

'Have you got anything to eat, Mum?'

'Hello, darling, how are you? Yes, I think there's a packet of biscuits in that cupboard.'

Malcolm laid a light hand on Nina's shoulder and kissed her briefly on the forehead.

'How's your day been, darling?' Nina addressed her daughter's hunched back.

Josie was too busy rooting in the cupboard to turn and answer so Nina turned her attention to Malcolm.

'How are you doing?'

'Oh, OK I suppose. Bit of a rush to get back from work but no major disasters so far. We're alright, aren't we, Jose?'

'Yeah, we're fine, Dad, except you forgot to put in my snack for school this morning and I was starving by lunchtime!' As she spoke, Malcolm produced a pen and notebook from his inside jacket pocket and began writing something down.

'Sorry. Won't happen again.'

Their lives, Nina realized, were being run with mathematical precision in her absence. She longed for a chink in the armour, a hint that all was not well, a sign that they were struggling without her. Josie's long lanky body was stretched out full length on the bed, she was flicking through the television channels, the remote control in one hand, a chocolate digestive in the other.

'All baby stuff. Why's there nothing good on?'

'Have you got any homework to do? Maybe I could help you,' Nina offered.

'No thanks, Mum, it's maths so I think I'd better do it with Dad later on.'

There was no use arguing with this; it had been several months since Nina felt competent enough to contribute on the maths homework front. Figures had never been her strong point and they had always been Malcolm's world; it looked as if they were going to be Josie's too. There was silence for a while, apart from the inane banter of the children's television presenters. Finally, Malcolm appeared to have summoned up enough courage to speak.

'How are you?'

'Not too bad. Not looking forward to Friday. But otherwise OK.'

'Do we know what time he's coming on Friday?'

'No, but I'll ask him today. I think he's coming in today.'

Malcolm nodded, silent again. Josie watched more television and ate more biscuits until it was time to leave. Nina ached to be going with them.

'Why do you have to stay in here, Mum? Why can't you come home now? I don't like it when you're in hospital.'

'I know, darling. But it won't be for much longer. I'll soon be home.'

Josie made a face as she gathered up her bags and headed for the door with her father. Nina desperately didn't want to say goodbye. She sat motionless, trapped in a ghastly microcosm of a scene she prayed she'd never have to play. Spectres stirred and gathered strength as the film ran in her head. She struggled to change the reel as the door closed. She began talking to herself again. No, I will be a grey-haired octogenarian climbing steep Italian steps in the Mediterranean sunshine; I will live to see my daughter grow up.

There was a hurried rapping on the door which catapulted her back into the present.

'Just checking that you're here. Mr Hawkes is on his way.'

Where else would I be, mused Nina, Outer Mongolia perhaps or the Great Barrier Reef? But this was obviously a serious business. The great god of gods, the consultant surgeon, had arrived on the ward and the royal household was temporarily thrown into a state of turmoil. Patients were hurriedly ushered back to their beds, temperatures were taken and drains checked, notes were hastily scribbled up. As the great man swept tornado-like into the room, Nina realized she was shaking from the waist down and totally unable to speak. That is, she would have been even if she hadn't had her lips closed firmly round the thermometer which had just been thrust into her mouth by a nervous nurse. Mr Hawkes grabbed her notes as he swept past the end of the bed and tossed the unread thermometer at the nearest nurse, discarding it as if it were a piece of chewing-gum he'd discovered on the sole of his shoe. With hardly a pause for breath, he began ripping off the wide, white, sticky bandage which swathed Nina's chest. He was smiling.

'Well, it's all gone according to plan. You might find you have a down day tomorrow and you will be tired. It's alright. You can look down. It's not too horrific a sight.'

Nina was just plucking up the courage to do as he

said, when he swept out as suddenly as he had swept in. His whirlwind appearance left eddies of aftershock in its wake. One of the attendant nurses breathed a sigh of relief as she stood clutching a bra and a bra extender, a strange-looking extra section of strap.

'You'll have to get used to putting your bra on round your waist, doing it up in front and then twisting it round and up.'

Nina didn't like to admit that she'd never been able to put on her bra any other way. This, at least, did not come as a huge readjustment. After all the panicked flurry, there was sudden calm. She was left alone to contemplate in terror the next time the great man would make his entrance. Would he come as the executioner with axe in hand? Or would he be the bearer of glad tidings? One day at a time, she knew, one step at a time. But sometimes the steps came tumbling in on each other, like waves on a shore.

Hours slipped by; night fell. She was feeling sick. No one had ventured through the door for some time. She had tried the telly. She had tried reading. She had listened to her tapes, painstakingly recorded for her by Lotty, but these, too, in the end had failed her. She sat on the edge of the bed with the blue vomit bowl in front of her and remembered her friend Jackie's last few days. She remembered the bowler hat-shaped bowl made of egg-box cardboard which Jackie would clutch. Every so often her hands would go into spasm and her nails would play a demented tune on the surface. Three days more and the pancreatic cancer had won; she had died. Nina's demons gathered ever closer and the sickness threatened to overpower her. Eventually rousing herself from a frozen state of miserable indecision, she rang the bell. When the nurse finally arrived, the solution came as no surprise.

'Can you bear being stabbed again? It will only be a little one and it will make you feel much better.'

Wearily Nina rolled over to expose her bottom. It hurt. It hurt because everything hurt. It hurt because it was last thing at night. It hurt because she was scared. When it was over, she lay on her back on her clinically prepared pillows and the tears ran down the side of her face and gathered once more in her ears.

# Chapter Eleven

The night was better than the one before. The injection had worked and Nina dreamed that World War Three had been declared, America having blown some small unsuspecting country off the face of the Earth. The dawn found her unable to sit up unaided. Her first attempt left her with a sharp, stabbing pain in the centre of her chest. The thought occurred that she was now about to have a heart attack, a little something extra to add to the already substantial list of worries. On balance, though, she decided the pain was more likely to be caused by the removal of lymph nodes. Either way she had no choice but to ask the first nurse who appeared to help her sit up. The news on the standing and walking front was more encouraging; the trip to the bathroom and back was far less laboured. Rumour had it that she might even get a hoist bath, the promise of which on the previous day had been withdrawn due to an insufficient level of recovery on her part. Another failure, she felt.

Breakfast was once again interrupted, this time by an anonymous soft-shoed lady wielding a watering-can. 'Ooooh, you wouldn't want to be out there this morning. Bitter it is. Much nicer in here.'

Nina wanted to chuck her toast and tea at her. If one more well-intentioned idiot tells me I'm better off here than somewhere else, I'll scream. Did it not occur to any of these jaunty conversationalists that she would cheerfully sell her mother in order to be anywhere else but where she was?

'Have you been in long? When are you leaving us?'

Oh if only it was that simple, thought Nina enviously. If only I could just forget about tomorrow and leave today. She wondered if the little flower-watering lady had any inkling of the significance of the one more day that she had to face. From where Nina was standing, or rather sitting in the hard-backed plastic-covered chair, it felt like the difference between life and death. Not for her the sort of operation that can be had and then forgotten as normal life is resumed. Not for her the carefree tripping off home once the surgery was complete. No, she couldn't escape being told what she longed not to hear. Would it be Mount Everest she'd be forced to climb or only the Ben Nevis she was already half way up? The sick finger of fear rose in her throat once again as she took the easy option and replied, 'Saturday I think.'

'Oh, home for the weekend! That'll be nice then,' said the flower lady, taking her leave.

Ten minutes later and the promise of the bath materialized in the shape of the nervous student nurse from the day before. First Nina was ushered into a small room dotted with various items of medical cleanliness. The bath towered above and around the assembled group; a nurse and now two hesitant students. Nina was made to strip off completely and left to stand shivering on the hard bare floor. She was asked to sit on a damp cold seat while a general discussion ensued over which hydraulic switch to press first. Finally lift-off was achieved. The seat went up, the bath went down, the seat went down and the bath came up. The first five seconds were blissful but the cold quickly seeped in. The jacuzzi button stubbornly refused to function and Nina declined the offer of being left for a soak, fearing that by the time anyone remembered to return, rigor mortis might have set in. Seat up, bath down, seat down, bath up and she was out on dry land again, cold but clean.

'Er ... were you kindly going to wash my hair?' The question set the cat firmly amongst the pigeons.

'Oh, I'm so sorry, I completely forgot. I would have done it in the bath. Er ... perhaps I could manage it in the basin with a cup if you were to lean back, but then that might be painful.'

Never mind painful, thought Nina, I'd need to be a limbo-dancing contortionist given that no basin in the building was more than about two feet from the floor.

'Maybe it would be better if I leaned over the side of the bath and you could use the shower head.'

This suggestion was greeted with smiles of relief all round. Five minutes later and the task was accomplished.

The student nurse's gratitude seemed unbounded.

'Thank you for being such a good patient ... and so patient.' She dared a little laugh at her own joke. 'I'm afraid I feel like I'm bumbling a lot of the time. Like when I had to take your cannula out yesterday, I was so afraid that I was going to hurt you that I fiddled around far too long.'

Nina adopted her most reassuring tone. 'Most people feel like they're bumbling most of the time, some are just better at pretending they're not. Just be yourself and I think you'll make a lovely nurse.'

It did the trick. The young girl hurried off with a spring in her step, and a broad grin on her face, and Nina was free to return to her room.

It was to be a day of visitors. These fell into several different categories. First to arrive was the 'I'd rather be anywhere else but here but I felt I ought to come' variety. A mother from Josie's school came bearing magazines and chatted away about anything and everything other than what Nina was going through. The look of fear in her face spoke volumes. She didn't stay long. Then there were the 'I too have brushed with death' variety keen to drag a reluctant Nina into their exclusive club. There were the ones who came, quietly supportive, bearing armfuls of positive energy, exuding the fact that they cared about Nina's future, exuding the belief that she had one. Last but by no means least were the family, the ones you are stuck with for life, the ones you cannot choose, the ones that come with trunk-loads of emotional baggage.

'Hello, darling, how are you? We've had a terrible drive. Well, poor Izzy has, she's done all the driving. Two accidents and endless tailbacks. Such a nuisance or we'd have been here much sooner. We've brought you some grapes.'

Nina's mother placed her cheek against her daughter's and kissed the air, an accustomed greeting practised to perfection. She perched on the edge of the chair which Nina (and 'Doris') had vacated on their arrival. Nina kissed her sister and the two women sat side by side on the bed.

'Oh, I'm sorry. Well it's nice of you both to come and see me.' Nina paused, assuming that her mother didn't really want an answer to the question she'd asked as she'd offered no opportunity for a reply. 'How's Dad?'

'Oh, he's alright, moping about with a bit of a cold so I told him not to come. Don't want to give you any germs, do we?'

'I should think I get enough of those from the nurses so it wouldn't have mattered.' Nina was good at masking her disappointment. 'Give him my love, anyway.' Her father was the only family member who might have guessed what she was going through. She had been looking forward to seeing him.

Her mother carried on regardless. 'How is Josie and how is poor dear Malcolm managing? I spoke to him on the phone the other evening and he did seem to have a lot to do. Pity it's that bit too far for me to come and help every day. Still, I expect the poor man will cope.'

It amused Nina that her mother referred to everyone in the immediate family as 'poor' – everyone, that was, except herself and her father. As far back as she could remember, her mother had never had much time for him. She treated him very much as a waste of space except for the fact that he brought in money and was useful when things needed mending around the house. Despite his not inconsiderable position of authority, she had always regarded his work as an irritating distraction from the jobs she needed him to do at home. She seemed to blame him for not being there when he was at work, and would think nothing of interrupting an important meeting with a phone call to say that a tap was dripping.

Isabel, Izzy for short, had followed their mother into a familiar lifestyle. She'd married young and began having children immediately. In fact, she'd gone on having children till she wasn't so young any more. Her marriage to Julian, the estate agent, had so far survived the birth of four of them. They lived a boxy sort of life in a modern boxy sort of house in the heart of suburbia, ten minutes drive away from both parents and parents-in-law. It was all very cosy.

'Julian and the children send their love. It's a bad day for Amelia at school today. Ballet and French! So she was not in the best of moods this morning.' Izzy was trying to look cheerful but the corners of her mouth gave her away. She kept crossing and uncrossing her legs, each time pulling her skirt down around her knees, as if in the hope of finding a comfortable position.

'Poor Amelia,' butted in Nina's mother, 'it's such a shame. Does she have to do ballet and French, darling? Couldn't she give them up if she doesn't like them? I don't suppose either are going to do her much good in everyday life.'

'Oh, she'll be alright, Mummy.'

Izzy had never once in her life stood up to her mother. She had left school with six indifferent 'O' levels and followed her mother's advice – a brief cooking course and then a secretarial course. She worked for a while in a solicitors' office before getting a job in the largest estate agents in town. There she had met Julian, and the rest was history. She had never ventured down a road her mother didn't approve of and had never seen the necessity to slip the maternal reins.

'So what happens next?' asked Izzy, attempting to change the subject from Amelia's traumas.

'Well, I think you should insist that she give up one or the other. No point forcing the poor child to do things she has no interest in.'

Nina smiled at her mother.

'To answer your question, Izzy, I wait. Till tomorrow. That's when I get the results of the histology report. When I find out whether it's spread or not. Whether I have to go on to have bone scans and liver scans and God knows what other scans.'

'Oh, I'm quite sure it won't come to that, darling,' their mother interjected confidently, 'you've got to have a positive attitude. You've got to be your usual strong self. You'll be alright. You've always been a coper.'

A flicker of pain rose in Nina's eyes as she acknowledged the emotional miles that separated them.

'I am trying to be positive, Mum, but it's not always that easy.'

'Well, keep your chin up, darling. Poor Izzy's had a terrible time recently, you know. Julian's been away on one training course after another and left her to manage the children entirely on her own. It's so lucky you've got Malcolm at home when you need him. Anyway I'm afraid it's time we were making a move. We have to get back for picking up from school, don't we, Izzy?'

They rose in unison as if eager to leave the room before Nina exhibited any further signs of weakness. The traditional air kissing was repeated and Nina stood as the door closed behind them. She sank back into the plastic chair, suddenly overwhelmed with a rush of sadness. Sad that her mother had never been able to see the frightened lonely child within her who needed hugging. Sad that her sister was locked into a preplanned way of life from which she was unlikely ever to escape. Sad that her father wasn't there. Sad that they would remain forever incapable of giving her the support she'd always craved.

After they'd gone, she lay on the bed and switched on the Walkman she had borrowed from Josie. She slotted in one of Lotty's tapes and floated away on the words of songs and the sounds of instruments. It was balmy and it was peaceful; for a few moments the anxiety subsided and she relaxed. She slept. And then she dreamed.

# Chapter Twelve

'But art school, darling! Are you really sure? I mean it's not as if it's going to lead to any sort of proper job, is it? And in London too! Goodness knows what will happen to you there. For one thing, it's going to be very expensive finding anywhere to live. I just don't think it's a suitable career, you wouldn't be happy, you'd always be penniless and what a waste of all your exam results. Why not do a good secretarial course at the tech, you could go on living at home. You could get a good job I'm sure.'

Dierdre drew breath. She glanced at her silent husband and then fixed her 19-year-old daughter with an appealing stare, confident in the belief that she could persuade her to see sense. Nina turned to her father for help.

'What do you think, Dad?'

Her mother ploughed on regardless. 'Your father agrees with me, darling. Much more sensible to do a secretarial course like Izzy did or maybe even a cooking course. There are lots of restaurants springing up all over the place and anyway people are always willing to pay someone to cook special meals for them if they're entertaining. That's right, isn't it, Peter?'

There was a silence which seemed to Nina to last forever. She shifted on the edge of the sofa but never took her eyes off her father. It was crunch time, close your eyes and jump time, now or never time. Throughout her childhood she had acquiesced in her mother's controlling strategies. She had always been there for meals, right on time three times a day, every day; she had always done what she was told; gone to school, worked hard, done her homework, even gone to family functions at her mother's insistence, the words 'You'll enjoy it when you get there' ringing in her ears. But this she knew was different. This was spiritual life or death to her and she had to make a stand. But she desperately needed help.

'I think, my dear,' said her father, 'that if it's really what you want to do, then you must do it.'

He spoke very quietly, a soft smile played around his lips and he looked at his daughter with great love. She, in turn, was awash with affection for him and eternal gratitude for his understanding. It was not the first time he had taken her side.

'Thanks, Dad.' She longed to bound across the room, fling her arms around his neck and hug him but the icy look her mother was giving him somehow made this impossible.

In any event, before she could move, her mother stood up, said in a very grey voice, 'Well, thank you so much for your support,' and left the room, banging the door shut behind her.

Nina sank back into the cushions of the sofa and sighed. 'I wish she could understand how much it means to me. I'd die a daily death if I was a secretary. I'd poison people if I was a cook. I need to choose my own way. You understand, don't you Dad?'

'Don't worry about your mother. She'll come round. It's just that she has no knowledge of the world you want to enter and she finds it threatening. She'll get used to the idea in time.'

'I wish I had your confidence. I don't think I've ever

fitted into her picture of what a daughter should be. Not like Izzy. Just because Izzy did all those things, it doesn't mean I can. I'm not like Izzy, however much Mum wants me to be.'

'Well, it's your life, sweetheart, and you must do as you think fit.' With that he rose and followed his wife into the kitchen to try and make the peace.

Nina lay where she was, sprawled across the sofa, while her mind wandered back over the past 19 years. Her earliest memory centred around a birthday party in the park. She couldn't remember whose party it was, but she remembered the identical pink and white lacy dresses with full skirts and flouncy petticoats that her mother had insisted she and her sister wear. Izzy's, of course, remained pristine clean; even at so young an age, she recognized what was important to her mother. Nina, on the other hand, had gone tree climbing and pond dipping; she had fallen from one into the other and was a slime-green dishevelled mess by the time their mother came to collect them. Dierdre was mortified and, once in the privacy of the car, furious with Nina.

'Look at you! What do you look like! What on earth will people be saying about you? Don't you ever consider me and what people will think? If only you could be more like your sister!'

Ah, those words rang clarion clear in Nina's ears down the years. 'If only you could be more like your sister!' She had tried, for many years she had tried. But she had never quite managed it, nothing she did ever seemed quite enough, or so it felt to her. She took sanctuary in the company of her father who had always seemed to have a deeper understanding of human emotion than his wife.

He was a small trim man with abundant fine hair which he used to keep in place through the liberal use

114

of gentleman's hair oil. Nina loved the smell of it. He worked for a local family firm and was very popular amongst the employees; he was the one they would always go to if they had a problem. From quite an early age, Nina would walk to meet her father on his way home from work. She would pretend to hide when she saw him coming and he would pretend to get a fright when she jumped out at him, a broad grin across his face. In the few minutes they shared, they would exchange news from the day and plan their next fishing trip. There was a large lake nearby and there was nothing her father liked better than to sit in the quiet stillness at the water's edge, staring out across the reeds and willows. And there was nothing Nina liked better than to sit with him. Sometimes she would read, sometimes she would play about with the little fishing rod he'd given her, often she would draw. She filled notebooks with sketches of the minutiae of lake life and the nature that surrounded it. She climbed the oaks that stood guard around about and copied the patterns in the bark and the shapes the sunlight made on the dappled ground. She developed a feel for the forms she saw which was to feed her work in years to come.

And she forged a special bond with her father which was to become the basis of a split which gradually developed within the family. Her mother, anyway, seemed to side with her sister, a trend that was compounded by the hours Nina spent with her father. Meaningful glances would be exchanged at mealtimes which only Izzy and her mother were privy to, trivial secrets manufactured out of nothing. They would titter and giggle together like schoolgirls, leaving Nina and her father to make their own attempts at serious conversation. They sought refuge in each other's ways.

In the early years, Izzy had not been altogether

comfortable with her mother's endless comparisons with her sister, always in her favour. As time went on however, she grew accustomed to the status quo and, almost without knowing it, grew slowly into a clone of her mother. Being the eldest, she of course did everything first. Or not, as in fact it turned out. Dierdre steered her daughter mercilessly along the tracks she considered suitable. Izzy lost any ability she might have had to deviate. It was therefore left to Nina to break all the rules. And break them she did. It was almost as if she was driven by a compulsion to crack the mould, perhaps because the mould was so strictly imposed, perhaps because she was more her father's daughter. In any event, the two sisters grew further and further apart; sometimes Nina would be sad at the loss of what might have been between them. Most of the time, however, her energies were taken up in fighting the teenage battles never engaged in by her sister. There was one in particular which she never forgot.

'You will be back in this house on the dot of eleven. Not a moment later, young lady!' Dierdre was standing between Nina and the front door, her husband hovering in the background.

'But Mum, it's New Year's Eve. The party doesn't finish till after midnight. I just can't leave before that.'

'Oh yes you can! Or else you can choose not to arrive in the first place. It's entirely up to you.'

'Mum, this is totally unfair. Everyone else is staying to the end.'

'What everyone else might do is no concern of mine. I'm your mother and what I say goes. You're far too young to be out all night at parties.'

'But Mum, it's New Year's Eve.'

'Nina, I don't care what it is. You are to be back home by eleven. You are only thirteen, may I remind you.'

Nina couldn't believe her mother was being so unreasonable. None of her friends had a mother like hers. She sat down hard on the bottom step of the stairs, folded her arms and stared miserably at the pattern on the carpet.

Dierdre took her silence as an opportunity to hammer the nail in harder.

'You don't see your sister demanding to stay out all night at parties and she's two years older than you.'

'Oh, I wondered how long it was going to be before you brought perfect bloody Isabel into the conversation!'

'Nina! Please don't swear! It's most unladylike!'

'Bloody, bloody, bloody hell!' yelled Nina, standing up and for the first time in her life, letting her temper rip at her mother. 'Bloody bloody bloody Izzy! Bloody perfect Izzy! Bloody "I can do no wrong" Izzy! Bloody "Yes Mummy, no Mummy, three bags full Mummy" Izzy! Hello? I'm your daughter too or had you forgotten that?'

'No, I hadn't and believe me, sometimes I wish you weren't!'

An uneasy silence froze in the air. Both mother and daughter were equally taken aback. Both had said more than they meant to. It was Dierdre who gathered the reins first and assumed control. She was almost purple with rage and at her most awesome. She stood over her daughter shouting and pointing upstairs with a shaking arm.

'Go to your room at once, young lady! I will not have language like that spoken in this house!'

Nina was crying with indignation and anger. She realized she'd overstepped the mark and wasn't sure how to return. She desperately wanted to go to the party and saw the likelihood of that happening disappearing fast behind her mother's furious face. She turned, ran up the stairs and into her room, slamming the door as hard as she could behind her. She threw herself on her bed and beat the pillow with her clenched fists. It wasn't fair, it just wasn't fair. After about half an hour, there was a quiet knock on Nina's door. Her father's voice was calm and measured.

'Your mother and I have discussed the situation. You may go to the party and I will walk round at eleven to collect you.'

Nina heard his footsteps on the stairs; it was a statement obviously not open to discussion. She dried her eyes, re-did her hair and left the house without a word. When her father arrived to collect her, he was immediately invited in and offered a drink. The two of them arrived home about 20 minutes after midnight. Nina's mother was in bed. She remembered how they were all made to pay over the next few weeks while Dierdre maintained her 'silent treatment'. She spoke only when absolutely necessary and then only in monosyllables. A heavy pall of retribution spread around the walls of the house.

Nina remembered the New Year's Eve battle as if it was yesterday, as she made her way into the kitchen to offer to help prepare lunch. No one spoke. Her mother was banging plates and knives and forks onto the table, slamming cupboard doors, and on one occasion kicking the cat which had inadvertently wandered across her path. Her father was quietly preparing a salad in the corner. Nina's 19 years had taught her to know better than to try and reason with her mother. She knew they were now to be subjected to the usual 'silent treatment'. It might last hours, it might last days. The one who would bear the brunt of it was inevitably her father. And bear it he did. He, like his two daughters, rarely challenged his wife for fear of the price there was to pay.

'Can I do anything to help?'

The hard-edged tension in the room was broken only by the chop-chopping of raw carrots in the corner.

'I'll come back some weekends, Mum. It's not as if London's that far away.'

Nina might as well have not wasted her breath. Her mother was in no mood to be humoured, in fact she was not a woman who could be humoured. When Nina looked back on this day many years later, she could see that it wasn't the fact that she was leaving home which bothered her mother nearly so much as the fact that she was choosing a road which formed no part of her mother's plans for her. Dierdre had her daughters' lives all mapped out in her head. She also knew exactly where and how she wanted herself and her husband to fit into these plans. Any deviation posed an unacceptable threat. However, all the 19-year-old Nina knew was that, once again, she had disturbed the status quo, got her father into trouble, and let the family in for days of living with her mother's displeasure. They sat down and ate lunch in angry silence.

# Chapter Thirteen

Day three in hospital dawned early again as the boiler rooms of the Titanic kicked in at 6.30 a.m. sharp. She tried to turn onto her side, remembering too late the drain. 'Doris' squeaked in brief protest as she was dragged along the floor beside the bed. The noise reminded Nina of a bad dream she'd just had about giant drain tubes being dragged relentlessly from her body. As she began to surface into consciousness, the realization hit her that this was D-day. Gone was the buffer zone of another night's sleep. Today she found out whether she lived or whether she died. She felt sick. She swallowed, and realized she had a sore throat again.

Struggling out of bed, a feat she could now manage on her own, and clutching 'Doris' for company, she made her way into the bathroom and gargled with salt water. It had always worked B.C. and there was no reason to suppose it wouldn't work A.D. Probably just the dry hospital air anyway, she thought, screwing the top back onto the bottle and looking at her world-weary morning face in the mirror. Without thinking she began her chant, 'I will survive, I will survive, I will survive'. The face in the mirror stared back at her, clearly not completely convinced.

She and 'Doris' shuffled back to bed and waited. It seemed like a long time till breakfast, which she ate but didn't enjoy. It felt much like munching cardboard. Soon after, a visitor arrived, the mother of one of the boys in Josie's class, she worked at the hospital. Nina knew she'd been quite ill recently.

'How are you my dear? You look fine.'

'Oh OK, I suppose, not looking forward to getting my results this evening.'

'The thing is to keep positive. You're going to be fine, I'm sure. Live for today because tomorrows are a luxury that may or may not happen, that's what I've learnt.'

She took Nina's hand and squeezed it between both of hers. The physical warmth unleashed a flood of emotion. Tears welled up behind Nina's eyes and spilled out onto her cheeks, running silent rivulets through the moisturiser she had just applied. Where were all the guarantees of yesterday? What had happened to the certainties? What had she done to deserve all this? And where was it all going to end?

'Don't you worry. You're going to be OK. Look at me, I'm still here aren't I?'

Nina nodded silently. She sat motionless for some time after her visitor left, muddled thoughts milling in her head. She imagined Josie arriving in the classroom amidst a flurry of books and bags, putting her things away, chatting. Then the picture blackened. She saw a silent Josie, creeping, a child with trauma in her face, a child with no mother. She saw her standing alone, shunned by classmates and wary teachers alike, the scattered eggshells of her life around her feet. With a supreme effort, Nina pulled her mind back to the present and vowed to herself through her tears that she would stop that happening. Whatever it took.

The morning dragged wearily on until lunch arrived. A tuna sandwich and an orange; one of the healthier alternatives from an uninspiring menu. Nina picked up a paper which had materialized out of nowhere and began idly leafing through the pages. Without conscious thought, she found herself staring at the obituaries and reading '*Death of young cancer campaigner*'. She read on, expecting – or perhaps it was hoping – to see pancreatic cancer or liver or lung cancer but no, inevitably, she read '*breast cancer diagnosed four years ago*'. This enterprising young woman had apparently set up a charity to offer support to younger women with small children. '*Despite being seriously ill, she worked tirelessly for the charity*'. There was a picture of a smiling lady in her thirties looking for all the world as if she had her whole life ahead of her. Nina found herself inexorably drawn to read every last sad detail.

She felt herself standing on the very edge of a thousand-foot drop. Below the sheer cliff face lay unforgiving, wave-wracked rocks. Grey stone, grey sea, grey sky. Invisible hands pushed her ever nearer a point of no return. She became dizzy with the height of it and her legs, both her legs, began to shake. Darkness fell, except for one small point of light far in the distance, one small voice which kept repeating 'You are not her. Step back. Step back. Face it 40 years from now. Step back.'

Nina tried to imagine a time in her old age when she might embrace the no returning, and greet the edge like a safe old friend. She tried to see an eccentric octogenarian sculptress living for her work, mounting exhibitions to widespread acclaim. She closed the paper, folded it, threw it to the end of the bed and made herself finish her sandwich. She decided to walk, first back and forth across the room, then out into the corridor, up and down, up and down, running the gauntlet of inquiring smiles. Exercise, she reasoned, was a reinvestment in life. And she had to pass the time until the great man arrived with her results.

When she got tired of dragging 'Doris' around, she returned to her room and tried to listen to some music. But the lyrics were no match for the demons of the day. They gathered, rumbling into her head, barging past each other in their quest to conjure up the worst. The cancer's spread, it doesn't look good, you're going to die. Prepare your husband, support your child, tell your family. Let go the things that now you will never do. Nina hit the stop button on the tape and forced her eyes wide open; she tried sighing out the mounting anxiety. She got off the bed and began to pace again. The minutes ticked grudgingly by until finally there were 45 of them to go. A reluctant Malcolm arrived, looking harassed.

'Hello. How are you? Any sign of him yet?'

'You must be joking. We've got 45 minutes yet. He's hardly likely to be early.' The words came out more harshly than she intended.

Malcolm poured himself a cup of tea from the pot which had been left sitting on the bedside table. He didn't seem to notice it was cold as he sipped in silence, saying nothing.

'Josie alright?' inquired Nina for want of something better to say.

'Mmm, yes, she's fine. Going to do her homework at Jane's. I said I might be late picking her up.'

'Not too late, I hope. I can't bear this waiting. I just want to know, one way or the other.'

'I'm sure you're going to be alright.'

Malcolm put his cup down on the table, got up and moved to look out of the window. Nina wished he sounded more convinced. She felt like she was waiting for the jury to come back in, for the judge to put on his black cap, for the sentence to be passed. Like waiting for the next hostage to be pulled out of the room as the gunshots from outside echoed in her head. Like hell on earth. Each minute was excruciating, each second a heartbeat hammer in her chest. She looked at Malcolm's back and wondered what they were supposed to do. What they needed was a 'Beginners Guide to Waiting for Death'. Should they try and read the paper, play cards, watch the television, make conversation, drink tea, take deep breaths, sit and shake, stare into space? The choices were endlessly unattractive. Supper came and went. Cardboard and watered milk would have been as appetizing as the fish in white sauce on offer. She forced herself to eat it nevertheless. Her body needed all the help it could get if it was to fight. The minutes ticked on. It was now well past the appointed time.

'His operations must have taken longer than he anticipated or some poor patient somewhere must be waking up in a much worse state than expected.'

Either way it meant more waiting. Malcolm suggested walking in the corridor. Nina tried. She took his arm and wondered when the last time was that they had walked arm in arm. She was now utterly terrified. If the Grim Reaper appeared now, bursting from the lift with his hellish host in tow, she knew she would collapse in a heap at his feet, so she persuaded Malcolm to return her to the sanctuary of her room. Locked in an atmosphere of sharpened dread, they tried to play cards. Nina kept losing; not a good sign she decided. Lotty had brought her a jasmine plant; it filled the room with the scent of summer meadows. Each time a wave of panic rose in her throat, Nina breathed deep, drinking in the sunlit smell, trying to imagine her whole body filling with positive energy. They turned the television on and attempted to watch it; there was a programme about abandoned gardens. She was shaking all over now, unable to summon the energy to quell her quaking limbs. Her whole body ached with the mounting well of terror which rose ever upward in her throat. Suddenly, finally, the door swung open and he was in the room.

'Sorry it's a bit late. How are you?'

'Terrified,' she answered weakly.

'There's no need to be that terrified.'

He sat on the bed, throwing a pile of files across the sheets as he did so. What does he mean '*that* terrified'? Does he mean there's a need to be less terrified? What's he going to say?

'Can I see the drain reports, please?' He turned to one of the nurses in attendance, holding out his hand as he spoke as if expecting to be given the information without having to ask for it.

Nina was beside herself, struggling to breathe now. Oh God, oh God, why isn't he saying something? Why doesn't he just say 'Well, it's good news' or 'I'm afraid the news is bad'. He was fumbling with some notes from the top of the pile.

'Are these your notes?'

Oh God, he doesn't even know whose notes he's got.

'Now the aspiration showed we had a Grade Two cancer and that is indeed what we have – at level seven which is the higher end of Grade Two but still Grade Two. The important news is that the lymph nodes were all clear. The type of cancer shows positive for hormone receptors. We would guess it's been there for some time, the deposits of calcium indicate that. Therefore we would suppose it to be a slow-growing cancer. So as to further treatment, we go as planned. Radiotherapy to the rest of the breast for six weeks in approximately three weeks time, once the wounds have healed sufficiently. You will be on Tamoxifen for five years and then we review the situation because it is not without its side effects. You have about an 80 per cent chance of long-term survival. Any questions?'

'What does it mean when you say positive for hormone receptors?'

'It means any remaining cancer cells will be severely frightened by the Tamoxifen. Would you like to go home tomorrow?'

'Yes, please.'

'Right, then. Drain out tomorrow afternoon and I'll see you in a week. You may get a build-up of fluid under your armpit once the drain's out, but don't worry, I can just drain it off for you. Goodbye.'

Quite frankly, Nina thought, she hadn't the energy to worry about anything past that exact moment in time. He could have told her that her left foot was likely to drop off next week and she'd probably have thought it a small price to pay for being told that the cancer hadn't spread. She was aware, though, that it was not all wine and roses. All the while that the great man had been holding court, 'twin-set and pearls', the breast care nurse Doreen, had been making cooing noises in the background about what wonderful news it was and how they should break out the champagne. There was nothing Nina felt less like doing. The minute the entourage had left and the door closed, she burst into tears.

Malcolm came and sat close to her; he held her hand and waited. Her other hand lay limp in her lap, cradling a crumpled tissue which caught the tears as they ran down her cheeks and dripped off the end of her nose. She didn't know if she was crying from relief or disbelief. Her mind was racing again, trying to process what she'd just been told. She knew it was good news compared to what she might have been told, but she found it hard to think of anything that had happened as good. Maybe the news hadn't sunk in, maybe it felt like tempting fate to be too confident. The only thing she knew for certain was that the whole experience felt like an enormous trauma. She knew recovery would not be easy. She saw a long road stretched ahead. But she would recover, she promised herself. Of this she was certain. Exhausted though her body and spirit were from the past few weeks, she resolved in that instant to come out fighting. She owed it to herself, to Josie, to Malcolm and to all the people who cared about her.

Much later that night, long after Malcolm had gone and the nurses had left, she reached in her drawer and drew out the Chinese symbol for trauma which Lotty had given her on the day of her biopsy. She turned it over and over in her hand in the semi-darkness and read, 'Opportunity riding on a dangerous wind'. And what a wind it was proving to be! It whipped her up to heights others only dream of, she saw sights beyond the clouds that others couldn't see, she saw how far it was to fall. That night she'd been given the chance to fly. Could she, would she, find the strength to do it?

She sighed long and hard as her lids finally closed on a day she hoped never to have to live through again.

# Chapter Fourteen

The next thing she knew it was morning. Not even the boilers had managed to penetrate her post-traumatic exhaustion. She woke on her final day in hospital dreading the drain being removed. During the silent morning hours which were unperturbed by visitors, memories seeped into her mind of another drain, another hospital, another occasion, when what was left of Josie's little miscarried brother was surgically removed. She remembered the same sense of being out of control, the lack of information, and she remembered the overwhelming sadness which threatened to engulf her over the months that followed. And here she was, eight years on, once again at the mercy of the medical machine, once again struggling to stay afloat.

The sound of the door opening broke her train of thought. It was Poritia, a nurse from Zimbabwe.

'Going home today I hear?'

'Yes, that's right, but not until I've had my drain out which I'm not looking forward to at all.'

'Don't worry, it shouldn't be too painful. What you need to do is take some deep breaths and we can gently remove the tube, as you are breathing out. Would you like me to do it for you?'

'Oh yes, that'd be great. If you don't mind. I know it's no big deal but it brings back bad memories.'

'Well, don't you worry. It'll be fine.'

Poritia was holding Nina's wrist, taking her pulse, when her eyes fell on the ring which Jim had given her.

'That's just like my mother's engagement ring. How lovely! I've never ever seen one like it anywhere else before. That's a sapphire, isn't it? And it's square cut, just like hers. So pretty.'

For a few moments Nina watched her eyes drift a thousand miles away to some treasured childhood moment in an African landscape.

'Go with the flow and all will be well. Go with the flow and you will be fine.' She spoke gently with great conviction and then she left. Nina looked at her ring and her mind welled with memories of Jim and the waste of his death. Poritia returned a few minutes later to say that she wouldn't after all be able to remove the drain as she was needed to escort a patient to another hospital. She seemed genuinely disappointed. She handed Nina some painkillers and said goodbye.

About half an hour later the door opened and a pale-green-coated medic appeared. 'Going home today, I hear. I've come to give you some advice about your arm.'

Nina deduced from the label on her ample bosom and the colour of her uniform that she was a physiotherapist.

'Now it's going to be stiff, and it's going to be sore.'

Nina smiled wryly. Since the operation, she wouldn't have guessed that anyone had been rummaging about inside her breast were it not for the cacophony of colours it was displaying again, yellows, blues, blacks, reds and purples. What she had noticed was the pain in her arm and shoulder caused by the removal of lymph nodes; the little buggers were certainly making their absence felt. The whole of her upper arm felt as if the top layer of skin had been grazed off leaving an open sore. Meanwhile every tendon and muscle seemed to have clenched itself into one massively tight fist.

'I'm going to give you some exercises to help. We find some ladies like to do these exercises for the rest of their lives.'

How incapacitating could the loss of a few lymph nodes be? By the time her humourless companion had gone on to outline the dangers of sustaining cuts that become infected leading to the development of lymphoedema, resulting in the need for rehospitalization, Nina had heard enough.

'I presume that some women never go on to develop any of these things?' she asked, falsely cheerful.

The thought was obviously a novel one. 'Er, yes, that is true but it's always a good idea to take a supply of antibiotics with you if you go away on holiday.'

Nina spent the next ten minutes listening obediently to instructions.

'Your arm's surprisingly mobile so soon after the operation.'

'Well, I've been doing exercises already actually.'

'Oh, I see. Right. Well then...'

She was left with an instruction leaflet and an invitation to return for more 'treatment'. The latter she vowed not to need. She read *'Do wear rubber gloves when cleaning basins and baths.' 'Don't prune the roses.' 'Do apply suntan lotion liberally.' 'Don't lift heavy shopping bags.'* She folded the leaflet and tucked it away at the bottom of her drawer.

She waited. An hour went by and no one came. Her lunchtime sandwich came and went. It was 'rest' time. Another hour and a half and still no one. She tried to relax and lose herself in her music. So much of the whole experience had been about waiting. Waiting for the unknown. Waiting to see what lay around the corner.

Waiting for the axe to fall. Waiting for the bomb to drop. Finally an unfamiliar face appeared. She removed her headphones.

'Right! Shall we have this drain out then?' The voice was brusque and business-like. Nina turned obediently onto her side and tried to breathe deeply. 'Now this may hurt a little.'

She struggled to stay in control. The staff nurse pulled hard as she was breathing in. Quickly Nina sighed her breath out, took another short breath in and breathed out again long and hard. It was over. Not the most pleasant of sensations but neither was it the awful pain she remembered from eight years before. She and 'Doris' bid their silent farewells.

'There, that wasn't too bad, was it?'

This seemed to be a favourite gambit of the nurses and doctors she encountered. How the hell did they know? Jabbing, cutting, slicing and syringing. She smiled weakly, replaced her headphones and sank in a wash of sound waves and sadness. She was still intact. She had a future.

Later she spent a leisurely hour rejoicing in her freedom of movement without 'Doris' and packing her few possessions into the bag she had arrived with what seemed like a lifetime ago. On the dot of 4 o'clock, as previously arranged, Malcolm and Josie arrived to take her home. Josie was excited; Malcolm was nervous. Nina sensed that he wasn't sure how to manage this surgically altered woman, his wife. Or was it that Nina herself felt that she was changing? Even in the midst of all the trauma as she still was, she knew that she could not return to life as it had been B.C. It was frightening, but no more frightening than living with the unwieldy spectre of cancer itself. She took Malcolm's arm and made her way along the corridor, into the lift, out of the front door and into the car park. Josie was on her best behaviour, all smiles, carrying bags, opening doors, repeatedly asking her mother if she was alright. The blast of cold air which hit Nina's face as she stepped into the outside world took her breath away. She noticed the remnants of the snow which had fallen briefly at the beginning of the week. The nooks and crannies in the nearby buildings were splashed with greying white. Walking from her room to the car felt like running a marathon. She resolved to get fit.

'We've done all the washing up, Mum. And the house is really tidy. I tidied my room today too.'

'Well done, darling.' Nina smiled and wondered if it had really mattered to her that much B.C. It seemed such an irrelevance. She resolved to let things go more. She breathed the icy air deep into her lungs and sighed it out again. If she was to stop cancer reincarnating itself somewhere else in her body, she was going to have to banish blocks, she was going to have to change. She sang in her head as they drove the short distance home. 'Banish blocks, banish blocks.' And there had been a lot of them. She drank in the sights of the everyday Saturday world as they passed, striving to feel a part of it all again. Josie was out of the car almost before it had stopped.

'Come on, Mum!'

'I'm coming, darling.' She struggled out of the car and looked up with new eyes at the house on which she had expended so much time and energy, creating the perfect home for Malcolm and all the children they were going to have. She felt slightly other-worldly as she walked the few steps to the front door. She remembered the day she'd chosen to paint it bright red in contrast to the safe white windows. Malcolm had been horrified. Once inside, she was thankful to collapse into the nearest armchair.

'Come and see my room, Mum. Come and see how tidy it is.'

'I'll come up in a little while, darling. I just need to sit here for a few moments.'

Josie went to help her father carry the bags upstairs and the flowers into the kitchen. For the first time in several years, Nina looked at her living room. The walls were white, shadowy white in the corners; it was years since she had painted them. The floor was carpeted in a practical plain blue-grey. The Liberty pattern on the chairs and sofa had been muted by the sunlight over countless summer months. She realized that all the art on the walls was very safe, still life, pictures of Malcolm's from his art collecting days. Nina struggled to her feet and looked out of the window at the small patch of green and border which made up their garden. A robin landed on a lilac branch near the house, cocked its head on one side and stared back in at her. There was a thunder of feet on the stairs and Josie reappeared.

'Dad says do you want a cup of tea?'

'Oh yes, please, that would be great.'

'Will you come and see my room now?'

'Alright, darling, I'll try.'

Nina used the banister to half pull and half support herself up the stairs. She was wary of using her right arm; it hurt when she tried to straighten it out in front of her and she kept being reminded of the gloomy warnings of the physiotherapeutic pessimist. She stood for a moment at the top of the stairs, silently attempting to reassure herself that her arm was not going to swell to the size of a barrage balloon overnight nor was she going to need to be doing exercises for the rest of her life. She took a deep breath and followed Josie into her room.

'Wow! That's one tidy room!'

Josie sat swivelling herself round and round on her desk chair, beaming. She was clearly pleased with herself. All her CD roms were neatly stacked on one side of her desk, her CDs on the other. Her computer sat in the middle, ready for action. There were pencils and paper, books and computer magazines, all in neat piles. Most of the room was taken up with bunk beds, the top one of which was home to all Josie's soft toys. One of her few concessions to childhood, eleven years worth of collecting, they piled one on top of each other in a dishevelled mound of fur and plastic eyes.

'Do you want me to bring your tea upstairs?' Malcolm shouted from the kitchen.

'No, it's OK. I'll come down. Well done, darling, that's a fantastically tidy room.'

Nina was suddenly swamped by a rush of tenderness for her daughter.

'Give us a hug, darling.'

'Oh Mum, don't be so silly,' Josie didn't move from her chair. She looked slightly awkward, grinning sideways at her mother. She was indeed her father's daughter.

'Josie, where do you want your drink?' Malcolm called again.

'I'm coming, Dad.' She rushed out of her room and down the stairs before Nina had time to speak.

Nina stood for a moment and then moved to perch on the warm edge of the seat Josie had just vacated. She stared at her bed and wondered at the child she had produced. Whatever had happened to the soulmate she had envisaged having during those sunny summer months of new pregnancy? Where was the artistic child who was going to bounce along at her side into art galleries and theatres and exhibitions? When did they ever fly kites? And who was this child whose first love was computers and whose favourite subject was maths?

The child who had plenty of brains but not many friends, who liked nothing more than to be at school. The child who found it hard to hug her mother.

'Your tea's getting cold.' Malcolm was calling again from downstairs.

'I'm coming.'

# Chapter Fifteen

Bowels were the order of Nina's first full day at home. Never in her whole life had she been gripped by such chronic constipation. She felt as if she had a barber's stock of razor blades stuffed up her bum and was about to spontaneously combust at any minute. It was difficult to walk. She didn't know whether to confine herself to the bathroom, lie down on the bed or try to keep moving. The brief respite of the day before was all too quickly forgotten. Beyond her control again, she was delivered into the vice-like clutch of medication, her system jammed solid, all her bodily functions suspended.

From her vantage point on the toilet seat at the bathroom window, where she was forced to spend most of her day, she watched the ordinary people in the street below going about their ordinary business and she ached to be one of them. An ordinary Sunday person who cleans their car or goes for a walk or nips into Tesco's or cooks a meal or reads a paper. Instead, here she was, a crone-like cripple forced to walk with her legs apart and her right arm locked tight against her side, slingless and bent. Once again the tears began to trace their weary tracks down her cheeks. Self-pity had set in with a vengeance. She felt as if she'd been drugged, subjected to ECT and systematically abused for a second time. Lonely and isolated, she had no resources left with which to fight.

The hours dragged on. In desperation she phoned the

surgery. The duty doctor, whom she didn't know, was unconcerned. He told her it was a common side effect of painkillers and suggested 'Lactulose' and glycerin pessaries.

Malcolm went to get them and then took Josie to the cinema. Nina found the file for their skiing holiday and returned to the bathroom. Papers flew as she sat on the toilet. Did she have cancer when she was paying that invoice? Or when she received that statement? She wondered what would have happened if, on some instinctive whim, she had insisted on a mammogram then. The phone rang. Fortunately she'd remembered to take it with her into the bathroom.

'Hi, it's Mo. How you doing? I didn't ring yesterday. I thought I'd give you a chance to get settled in at home. How's it going?'

'Not brilliant. Chronic constipation. I'm sure I'm about to explode!'

'Oh God, poor you! How ghastly! Is there anything I can do? Have you got anything to take for it? Do you want me to come over?'

'No, thanks. But thank you for the offer. I'm not great company right now. You'd have to sit in the bathroom and anyway I'm not a pretty sight! I've got some medicine which will hopefully start working soon. Either that or something's going to rupture in the not too distant future! Just another of the little joys of cancer treatment!'

'Are Malcolm and Josie there?'

'No, they've gone to the cinema. I'm not sure Malcolm quite knows what to do with me or how to treat me. You know him, he's not said anything. This whole thing has really got to him I think and he's just not capable of talking about it. To be honest, it's better that they're not here because I don't have to pretend for them.'

137

'It's hard for you, though, not getting any support from him.'

'Uh, nothing new there then. We've hardly been bosom buddies for a long time now. Come to think of it, I'm not sure if we ever were.'

'You sound really fed up. Are you sure you don't want me to come over?'

'No, honestly, thanks Mo, but there really isn't any point right now.'

'OK. Well, if you're sure. I'll ring you tomorrow. Keep smiling. You're going to be alright. I know you are.'

'Thanks. Bye.'

Nina pressed the button on the phone and sat nursing it in her hands, unable to summon the energy to do anything else with it. Mo's cheery optimism warmed her soul and filled her eyes with tears again. At the same time, gremlins started hammering at the door. How does she know I'm going to be alright? How does anybody know? What if she's wrong? What if it comes back? What if it's spread and no one's picked it up? What if I die? What about all the things I still want to do in my life? What about Josie? This was getting tedious. First things first. She resolved to stop taking all the painkillers. It seemed like a fair swap; agonizing armpit for spontaneously combusting bottom. She decided to risk leaving the bathroom to wend a snail-like trail around the house. As she crept from room to room, as if inquiring from each one why she was there, she was reminded again of eight years before. The same silent house. The same frozen state of trauma. The same emotional exhaustion. The tears. The struggle. And the flowers.

Nina had been inundated with flowers in hospital; some she had brought home, some she had left for the nurses, some for other patients. But still they came.

Flowers of every imaginable size, shape and colour. Some arrived unannounced in humble terracotta pots or tied in simple posies; other presented themselves proudly in gigantic cardboard boxes or strange white polystyrene coffin-like containers. She was even beginning to receive flowers from people with names she didn't recognize. Who were they and why did they feel compelled to send her bouquets of pink flowers? She was running out of vases and she was running out of surfaces on which to put the vases. Anyway, she'd always thought there was something slightly funereal about a house full of flowers. She remembered the Interflora labels which had arrived after her miscarriage – if you turned them over they read 'Send flowers, send happiness'. It was not to say that she didn't appreciate the flowers that came, multicoloured, multi-shaped. Lotty's jasmine plant sat on the chest of drawers in her bedroom. Now as in hospital, its pervading sweet smell poured into the room, becoming an almost tangible focus for the positive energy in the air. Whenever the panic rose anew in her throat, whenever the dark midnight hours stretched on indefinitely, she would drink in that smell of jasmine and feel reassured that she was not alone.

Loneliness was, it dawned on her, a powerful adversary. On the one hand, she had names of people she did not know who had walked this road before her, names provided by her GP, by the hospital, by well-intentioned acquaintances, and support groups. She could ring them. But none of them would be her. Their cancer would be theirs, not hers. On the other hand, there were her friends. Friends who could never completely understand. She now had one foot on another shore, a shore they could know nothing of. She was caught between the devil and the deep blue sea. And the beach she stood on was a lonely one.

Malcolm and Josie returned from the cinema in time to produce some soup for her supper. She knew she had to eat, and eat well, but it was a struggle to bombard her beleaguered stomach with anything in the way of food. Malcolm disappeared for the evening to immerse himself in work. He was unhappy about the amount of time he had been forced to take off and was eager to catch up on what he'd missed. Mother and daughter sat and watched the mindless rubbish Sunday viewing afforded until Josie took herself off upstairs to read before going to sleep. It was much later, after eleven, when Malcolm reappeared to find Nina standing in the middle of the kitchen, frozen to the spot, tears dropping off the end of her nose once more. Gone was the high of the results two days earlier. Gone was the relief at having a body which had ceased to be the property of the medical profession. Gone was the triumph of leaving hospital. In its place stood a terrified woman with breast cancer. Too scared to think of herself as a woman who had had breast cancer. Too scared to step forward to the light. Malcolm did his best to help. He tried to comfort his wife's undamaged side. He told her she must think positively. Nina knew it to be true, she knew she could. But just not this night, so late, after so much pain, as blackness gathered. She was shaken from her thoughts by Josie's cry. Nina dragged herself upstairs to find a tearful child, clearly quite attuned to her mother's state of mind, lying on a moist pillow.

'I can't stop crying, Mummy, I don't know why.'

I know, thought Nina. She rubbed her daughter's face and stroked her arm. 'You're just tired, darling. Your body's had enough; it needs to sleep.'

'I can't get to sleep. I've been trying for ages.'

'Everything always seems worse late at night. You'll feel better in the morning. It's half-term, remember.'

140

Nina listened to herself and wondered who she was trying to convince. She blew her nose.

'Have you been crying too, Mummy? Or are you just blowing your nose?'

'Yes I have, darling. I think I'm just tired too. What do you say we both try and get some sleep?'

In a rare moment of intimacy, they kissed each other goodnight.

Nina decided to have a bath. Under normal circumstances, a soak in a steamy scented bath would have helped. But first she had to undress and face her battered body. She was luckier than many she knew. She'd got cancer in her larger breast and it was still larger than the other one despite the surgery. But it was a mess. Criss-crossed now with 3-inch-long scars and peppered with yellow, black and blue bruises, it was topped with a strange pert dark pink nipple that looked as if it was suffering from its very own personal trauma. Nina told herself it would all heal eventually; the bruises would fade, the scars would settle comfortably into the fabric of her flesh. In time, in time. They'd become beacons to remind her in the future of a past she was unlikely ever to forget. She sighed, lit her candles and turned off the light. She took off her bra and lay awkwardly in the warm water, twisted to one side, propped up on her left arm. The flickering light lulled her into a false sense of drowsiness and it took a monumental effort to climb out and dry herself. By the time she had struggled into bed, she was wide awake again. The panic was back in her throat, and her heart was thumping in her chest. At 1.00 a.m. Malcolm came to bed; she listened to his laboured breathing for several hours before she finally fell into a brief and troubled sleep.

# Chapter Sixteen

Nina was glad when the morning came. She had spent the witching hours convincing herself that the dull ache in her left leg was a thrombosis and that death from a pulmonary embolism was imminent. If by some miracle she escaped this, then the other sharp stabbing pain in the centre of her chest undoubtedly heralded a heart attack that would finish her off by morning anyway. As she still appeared to be alive when it became light enough to read, she reached for the one piece of paper which the hospital had sent home with her. *'Beware of pains in the legs, especially in the calves. Contact your doctor immediately.'* There it was in black and white. Proof that it was serious; another trauma in the offing. As she lay there in the cold dawn, she marvelled at how readily the medical profession had relinquished its responsibility. One minute the minutest details of her bodily functions had been common knowledge, the next she simply ceased to exist. She could be dying and not one of them would be any the wiser.

There was just a hint of suspicion tucked at the back of her mind that the pain might not be as serious as she imagined, that it might actually have more to do with the surgical stockings she was still wearing. These extremely attractive Nora Battyesque garments resolutely refused to stay up around the top of the thigh, preferring instead to roll up upon themselves and work their way downwards so creating a circulation-crushing mass of elastic stocking in the restricted area of the knee joint. It felt like trying to walk with a couple of koala bears strapped to your knees. As if this wasn't bad enough, the hole at the bottom, which was designed to lie under the toes, had a nasty habit of working its way backwards up the foot and embedding itself in the scanty flesh on either side, so creating great red weals which later developed into ripe blood blisters. Several times even before the pain in the leg, Nina had considered abandoning the ghastly things. She wasn't quite confident enough, however, to disobey instructions.

Pathetic was what she felt in this cold grey dawn. She resented having to take things slowly. She was annoyed that her arm was stiff and sore. She hated her body for being a mess. She felt chewed up and spat out and it wasn't fair. She decided tea would be a good idea. Gingerly running the gauntlet of her stabbing chest pain, she inched her bottom up the bed until the bedhead supported her weight sufficiently to enable her to sit up. She wrapped her dressing gown tightly around her, folded her arms for added warmth and tiptoed her feet into sheepskin slippers. Their softness was reassuring. She crept downstairs, avoiding the step that always creaked, careful not to do anything to disturb the early morning silence of the house.

Once in the kitchen, she switched on the kettle and lit one of the gas rings for extra warmth. She was shivering in the anxiety of the day. She pulled a kitchen chair over to the cooker, lit the oven and sat beside the open oven door cradling a hot mug of tea in her hands. In black and white films, she thought, it was always brandy and hot sweet tea. No one was more surprised than her that she hadn't hit the bottle. B.C., she had been accustomed to reaching for a wine glass every evening at about six, even counting down the minutes on particularly bad days. A.D., she had felt so sick and light-headed with fear that alcohol had seemed a totally inadequate means of transport out of the all-engulfing horror in which she'd found herself.

Lurking too was the notion that her besieged body needed all the help it could get. It was bizarre, this diagnosis of life-threatening disease when she felt no pain, no dysfunction, no sign whatever of ill health. Once the facts began to seep in, as she had to suppose the cancer cells had already done, it became increasingly important to her to detoxify her body, to rid it of anything unhealthy, be it cancer cells or alcohol. In fact, it occurred to her that if she lumped them both together, she had a halfway decent chance of shrinking the larger threat to a manageable size. Was it six months or a year it took for every trace of alcohol to leave your system? Perhaps the same was true of cancer cells. Of course all this supposition might well have been utter rubbish, but she felt she had to believe in the power of positive thought and the illusion of control even if illusion was all it turned out to be.

It was a knotty dilemma. If you have a 'problem' with alcohol which, as any self-confessed alcoholic would admit, is potentially life-threatening, you stop drinking, the alcohol leaves your body and if you can keep it up, you're on the road to recovery. If you have a 'problem' with cancer cells, what can you stop doing to make the difference? According to the consultant, his patients always asked what they had done to cause the cancer. The answer was invariably 'Nothing'. So positive thinking was the only medicine left within their control. Whatever happened, Nina resolved to hang on to the fact that she would get better, the great 'C' would not return, she would survive. But the good old gremlins begged to differ. They swam through that early morning kitchen, niggling threads of blackness whispering of sad farewells and early deaths. Nina began to sing in her head; she'd been doing a lot of that recently. 'Slap 'em back, slap 'em back and walk towards the light' whirled words out of nowhere. She was interrupted by a bleary eyed and tousled haired Josie in the doorway.

'What are you doing down here, Mum?'

'Good morning, darling. I'm riding pink elephants around the kitchen cupboards! What about you?' Nina smiled, Josie didn't.

'You're weird, Mum! Can I have a drink?'

Nina creaked into an upright position, realizing that she'd been sat cradling her now lukewarm cup of tea for over an hour. She moved on automatic pilot despite the fact that Josie was more than old enough to get a drink for herself. Whatever had happened to the transition from mother of small child to mother of pre-teenager? She was, she suspected, hanging onto the former role for fear of the latter. So she got the drink, carried it to her daughter, and went back to make more tea. She carried two mugs upstairs, bidden by the soft remembered warmth of her bed. Malcolm grunted and turned his face to the wall as she put a mug down beside him. She crawled back into bed and sat sipping her tea and staring at the wall opposite. A dream from the waking hours of the night before began to gather in her consciousness.

In it, she was late for Josie's haircut and she was running out of time. The anxiety of the dream seemed to have spilled out into the day's reality; or was it, she wondered, the other way around? She needed to be there to organize Josie's haircuts, to rub her back at night if she got scared, to make her packed lunch, to fix her school bag, to help with homework when she could, to support her when her first period arrived, to sit on

145

the bathroom floor and listen to important snippets of the day's events, to say 'Good morning' at the beginning of the day and 'Goodnight' at the end. The thought that all this could be taken away was unbearable.

She glanced to her right and caught sight of a photo of her mother and father in a rare moment of togetherness at a cousin's wedding. They were grey-haired and smiling. She remembered all the times she had heard her mother rail against growing old and resolved there and then never to complain if ever she was allowed the privilege of old age. Old age, when she'd climb her Italian steps, up, up, into the sunshine and look out across the rooftops at the view. She thought back to the day before her operation, her day out with Lotty, when she'd bought the picture. It was still at the framers. She slipped out of bed and, with tea in hand, went to stand in the room at the end of the landing. She imagined where she'd hang it. She pictured her sculpture stand, her books and her tools. She sat on the sofa bed which was still piled high with outgrown clothes and wondered what to begin work on first.

She sighed in yet another effort to shift the clot of fear at the base of her throat. It was hard work. The banner of survival was heavy and unwieldy and she was tired of carrying it. Her family would be shocked. Phrases like 'fighting spirit' and 'resilient nature' echoed in her ears. Well, now she was tired. Tired of fitting the bill. Tired of doing battle.

For the first time, she realized that she couldn't fight alone. Gone were the illusions that she could manage by herself, the secret pride she took in not needing anyone else, the belief that she could do it all. In harbouring her pretence of strength, she'd slammed a lot of doors. No more. Now when Lotty rang to ask her how she was, she would tell her. Now when Mo came round to

146

drink coffee and offer to have Josie after school, she would accept. She would even ask for help. She would get Malcolm to go to Tesco's sometimes. Josie would make her own drinks. Little by little there would be change.

And no time like the present, she thought. It was half-term so she rang both Lotty and Mo and took them up on their offers to entertain Josie. She even insisted Malcolm take some time off. Before they knew it, the week was almost over and they were going to the dry-ski slope. A morning out in Berkshire in exchange for two weeks in Vermont. Ah well, such is life, thought Nina as she went to get dressed. Malcolm was eager to catch up on work so Mo had agreed to come with Abby and Beth. Josie was sitting on a chair chatting to her father as Nina began to dress. She was making slow progress, tucking her T-shirt into her jeans, when the stabbing in her solar plexus struck again; she caught her breath.

'What's the matter, Mum? What's happened? Are you alright?'

'Yes, I'm fine. I've just got this pain in my chest when I move sometimes. I think it's because the doctors had to remove some of my lymph nodes to see whether the cancer had spread.'

'What are lymph nodes?'

'They're little tiny things, I think, that help carry lymph around your body, stuff that helps you heal if you get an infection.'

There was a moment's silence while Josie took all this in. She sat quite still. Then suddenly in a totally uncharacteristic outburst of energy, she leapt up, threw herself on her parents' bed, clutched melodramatically at her chest and yelled 'Oh, me lymph nodes are killing me. Me lymph nodes are killing me!'

Nina laughed out loud. For the first time in months.

147

# Chapter Seventeen

The sports complex which housed the dry-ski slope was heaving when they arrived. The traffic had been bad leaving London and the children were tired of being in the car. As they walked into the crowded reception area, Nina looked at all the people around her and wondered if it showed that she'd been to hell and back while they'd been going to the office or doing the school run or enjoying the half-term holiday. Did it show in her face, in the way that she stood, in the way she held her right arm? She was sure it did. All she needed was the bell; unclean, unclean. Gone was the sanctuary of her hospital room where cancer was commonplace and good news was that it hadn't spread; here in the outside world the word 'cancer' struck terror in people's hearts and the good news was that everyone was free of it. Everyone, that was, except her.

Half an hour later she found herself standing in a freezing wind at the bottom of a slope made of giant toothbrush bristles watching other people hurtle from top to bottom. Insult to injury. I should be in the Green Mountains of Vermont without a care in the world, she thought, not trapped inside my own worst nightmare halfway between a hospital and an uncertain future. After a while she volunteered to go and get drinks and snacks. Not unusually for a British cafeteria in a building full of children at the end of half-term week, the highly inferior food was fast running out. There were very few staff to man the even fewer tills that were still working, and those there were could only be described as semi-delinquent teenagers of below average intelligence, all of whom seemed to be suffering from coordination problems. The queues were long and tempers were becoming frayed. Mothers argued with children, their faces set hard in anger. Indecisions mounted as more and more options were slashed from an ill-prepared menu and the staff lost whatever track they had had of what was still available. Nina felt at one remove from it all. She wanted to scream at each and every mother how lucky they were to assume that they would always be there for their children. How lucky not to be standing on the edge of her abyss. She swallowed silently. After what seemed like an age, she finally reached the front of the queue and took her tray in search of a free table. It wasn't long before the others appeared, Mo with Abby and Beth in tow and her arm round Josie who was ashen white.

'I'm so sorry, she's hurt her thumb I'm afraid.'

'It really hurts, Mum.'

Nina tried to stroke her forehead.

'She fell and caught it in the matting and bent it backwards I think. Abby, Beth, sit down for a minute.' Mo looked uncharacteristically frazzled.

They watched Josie's thumb swell up before their eyes. There was nothing for it but a trip back to hospital. It was a subdued group who made the journey home. Mo dropped them off and went to tell Malcolm the news.

The Accident and Emergency Department was no busier than usual. The little neon strip that ran above the heads of the ladies on reception cheerfully warned of a four-hour wait. Nina and Josie settled into two chairs in the corner of the waiting area from where they witnessed, in varying instalments, the day's casualties. There was the ghostly pale teenage girl in a blood-soaked sweatshirt who wandered around aimlessly, clearly still in shock. There were several elderly ladies who'd obviously fallen down whilst shopping, lined up in wheelchairs, bloodied hands clutching crumpled shopping bags piled high upon their laps. There was a young skinhead labourer who seemed unconcerned that he'd apparently removed most of the skin from one side of his face.

The minutes ticked into the hour and they waited. Josie was quiet and Nina didn't have the energy to engage her in conversation. Finally they were called through closed doors and asked to wait again in a small cubicle. Right outside the opened curtain, a frail white wisp of a woman was being treated in the corridor. She was bleeding profusely from her nose. The young doctor was obviously pushed for time.

'I need to stick a needle into your arm to take some blood.'

'What? Oh dear, more blood?' came the confused and weakened reply.

'We need to give you this. It tastes horrible, I'm afraid. Now I'm sorry to say that this will be a bit painful so bear with me.'

The little old lady's husband tried to shield her from the onslaught but events had already adopted their own momentum. As she watched, Nina marvelled at how small and insignificant people can so easily become in such situations. She dragged her mind back to Josie and tried to distract her by suggesting that they examine the posters depicting the insides of arms and legs. It seemed a marginally less gruesome occupation than watching the trauma in the corridor. When the doctor arrived, he sent them off to X-ray where they sat and waited yet

150

again, this time beside an anonymous patient on a trolley, tubes threaded in and out of his every orifice. Josie showed great clinical interest in this and Nina did her best to field her daughter's endless questions. Finally, three and a half hours after they had arrived, they emerged from the medical underworld of A & E cradling a bandaged thumb and the knowledge that it was fractured. Malcolm was waiting for them, full of remonstration.

'I knew dry-ski slopes were a bad idea.'

Nina had not the energy or the inclination to reply; she just wanted to go home.

Night-times were the worst. Tiredness set in and everything hurt much more than in daylight. Nina's resistance was especially low on this particular evening and the blackness of the night outside seemed to close around her, pervading her very spirit. She had let Josie stay up late to watch a video to take her mind off the pain. As it finished, Josie stood up, burst into tears and announced 'I don't feel very well.' Like mother, like daughter, Nina thought, as she gently helped Josie upstairs, fed her Calpol and listened to a long list of things which Josie suddenly deemed 'stupid'. Nina left her still quietly sobbing. Five minutes later, she heard her singing along to one of her CDs.

If only it was that easy. Nina sat in her bedroom next door, feebly trying to extract face cleanser from its bottle, suddenly defeated by even the smallest challenge. Tears welled up in her eyes and spilled down her cheeks, plopping again in rapid succession off the end of her nose and into her lap. She couldn't move. Malcolm put his head round the door and asked her what was wrong. She was unable to answer, she felt cold inside and out. He stood still, unsure whether to go or stay. Nina thought of her promise to herself not to bottle things

151

up and to speak out but even this task seemed overwhelmingly huge. Words were wholly inadequate in the face of the fear and the loneliness that held her in thrall but she did her best. 'I hurt all over and I don't want to die,' she managed to stammer between sobs. 'I don't want to die. I don't want to die. I don't want to die.' Again and again, as if by repetition she could lessen the force of the ties that bound her. Malcolm stood mesmerized, trapped in his own world of impotence and fear. It wasn't long before Nina's head began to pound. She decided to abandon the cleanser and get into bed. Malcolm turned the light off for her. She dozed into a fitful sleep and woke the next morning with a splitting headache.

It was Josie's first day back at school and two weeks since Nina's operation, the day she was due to see the consultant again. She struggled out of bed with a throbbing over her left eye and a bloated stomach. She was constipated again; the laxative syrup she'd been dosing herself with was clearly not up to the job. Apart from the ever-constant pain lodged at the base of her throat, she felt numb. Robot-like she went through the motions. With a good deal of moaning about how unfair life was, Josie left for school, brandishing her wounded thumb like a trophy.

The house was eerily quiet once she'd left. Nina wandered from one room to another without the energy to decide what to do next. When the noise of the phone ringing cut through the silence, she jumped.

'Oh hello, Nina, it's Jane's Mum here. I'm just ringing to find out how you are and what the latest results were. I'm at work so I can't talk long.'

Nina smiled to herself. 'Hello, Pauline. I'm absolutely fine, thank you. The results showed that the cancer hasn't spread, so that's good news.'

'Yes, but the trouble is these days knowing whether to believe in test results or not, isn't it?' She barely paused for breath. 'I mean you hear such awful stories about how they get things wrong all the time. My father-in-law was told that he was perfectly alright when in actual fact he had cancer of the pancreas. It's hard to know if you can trust them. I mean, you find out that they're not God after all.'

It took Nina several seconds to compose herself. When she did, she spoke in measured tones. 'Well, Pauline, whether that's true or not, I don't feel it's particularly helpful for me to go down that road at the moment. I need to live my life without that doubt.'

It was Pauline's turn to pause before replying. 'Of course. Yes. Anyway, what I really rang up to say was would Josie like to come back to tea with Jane today? I have to go out later, so I could drop her back to you.'

'I'm sure she'd like to. She may be feeling a bit fragile though, she fractured her thumb yesterday.'

'Oh no. Well, we won't do anything strenuous. They'll probably sit in front of the computer most of the time. I'll see you later then. Goodbye.'

Nina put the phone down and sat staring feebly at the carpet, amazed. Cancer did indeed cast a powerful spell.

Her appointment with the consultant was early afternoon. Malcolm had arranged to be back from work, reluctantly Nina felt. He'd said he'd meet her there in case of any last-minute hold-ups. She half expected him not to turn up as she took a seat in the crowded silent waiting room. Women, mostly much older than her, sat with their heads buried in the usual out-of-date magazines, vainly attempting to ward off the reality of their situations. Nina looked around at the faded grandeur that private medical insurance afforded. There were several light

153

bulbs missing from the chandelier which hung from the middle of the ceiling. The drapes around the windows had clearly been witness to far grander scenes and would have been more at home in a ballroom or a banqueting hall. The overall colour scheme was faded beige. Even the vase of fresh flowers had managed to adopt a brownish hue. The standard lamp in the corner leaned sadly to the left; several of its tassels were missing. There was an inevitability of defeat about it. The plant in the pot beside the disused fireplace seemed to have grown tired of waiting, its tendrils straining to escape across the floor towards the door.

The interminable waiting gave the room a leaden quality as the minutes ticked by on the tired face of the elderly clock on the mantelpiece. There was an air of dread, and a general desire to be any one of the healthy pedestrians passing to and fro in the streets outside the window. Every so often the consultant's head would appear round the corner of the door and another sheep would be ushered out for slaughter. Heads looked up briefly, only to bury themselves again as the door closed. Tensions rose. One woman stopped reading and rashly placed her magazine on the seat beside her. She sat staring at the space above the muted carpet in front of her, her fidgeting fingers picking at the skin around her nails. She's obviously forgotten about the risk of cuts leading to infections causing lymphoedema, thought Nina. The door squeaked open again and every head looked up. It was Malcolm this time, looking flustered and tired. There wasn't a seat free next to Nina so he settled on the end of a browbeaten sofa in the centre of the room. It was awkward to talk in the silence, so they didn't. The fingerpicking lady's name was called next, momentarily releasing her from her misery. Nina's leg began to shake as it had done at each instalment of her

154

nightmare. For want of something better to do, she decided to christen the consultant the 'Prophet of Doom' and was just toying with an insane desire to race around the room shouting at the top of her voice when the door creaked open again and he called her name. She and Malcolm followed meekly into the adjoining room.

'Hello. How are you? Take a seat.' He broke off half a chocolate digestive. 'Sorry! This is lunch – or is it breakfast?! Right, pop your things off and let's examine you. Hop up on here.'

Obediently, Nina stripped for the umpteenth time. She raised her arms when told to, she lay down when told to, she breathed when told to.

'Well, that all seems fine. You have some fluid which has gathered on your breast so I just need to drain that off for you. It is rather a large needle so it's probably best not to look.'

Nina needed no such invitation; she had not the least intention of watching while yet another instrument of torture was applied to her battered breast. Once the ordeal was over, she returned to her seat beside Malcolm to listen to the Prophet of Doom's interpretation of her notes. His 'team' had apparently met to discuss her case. The change of tone in his voice did not bode well. Nina found herself sitting with a thumping heart and fingers tightly crossed under the jersey on her lap, just as they had been when the whole nightmare began.

'Now as you know, you have a Grade Two cancer. We look at three aspects of the cancer and give each a score out of three, three being the worst and one the best. We then total the scores to give a grade. A score of 3–5 is Grade One, 6–7 is Grade Two and 8–9 is Grade Three. Your score is seven, the higher end of Grade Two but still Grade Two. Do you understand so far?'

155

Nina nodded weakly, wishing that she didn't have to hear any more. But his hands were already busy scribbling diagrams upside down so she and Malcolm could see.

'We look at whether the cancer cells are uniform in size and shape or whether they are irregular. You score a three there. We look at how similar they are in tubule formation to the healthy surrounding tissue. You score a three again. Finally, we look at how fast the cancer is growing, how quickly the cells divide. In your case we could see very little evidence of growth so you scored a one. Which makes a total of seven. Any questions?' Nina's head was reeling, trying to make out whether the news was good or bad. Malcolm was silent.

The Prophet of Doom continued. 'It's unusual to get a 3-3-1 score. We would expect the one to be higher which would of course push you up a grade but, there we are, it isn't.' He sounded almost disappointed. 'So there has been some disagreement over your future treatment. I would like you to think about having chemotherapy as well as radiotherapy.'

The mention of the word 'chemotherapy' struck instant unmitigated terror into Nina's already beleaguered heart. Why did the goalposts have to keep changing? Where would it all end? Each time she got her head around one thing and began to manage that, there was more horror round the corner. It was just not fair. Her panicked train of thought was cut short by his voice.

'You don't have to decide now. Go away and think about it. As I say, the team are divided over this. Some think it's overkill.'

Good choice of words, thought Nina as Malcolm found his voice. 'What would you advise if it was your wife in the same situation?'

The Prophet of Doom paused and smiled. 'I think if it was my wife, she would have a double mastectomy

156

and everything going! No, I think the thing you need to think about is whether the added protection chemotherapy will give you is worth the unpleasant side effects you may have to put up with. Could you face having a down day after each treatment? Would you mind getting more colds than usual? Could you cope with your hair falling out if it did? Could you manage being tired a lot of the time? Now I'm not saying that any of these things will happen to you. Everyone is different. What I would like is for you to have a discussion with Dr Barpin, the consultant radiologist, about it.'

And what I would like, thought Nina furiously, is not to have anything of the sort. But clearly the Prophet of Doom had mentally moved on to his next patient, and anyway there seemed little else to say. Nina stood up, sick with a new fear.

'I'd like to see you again in a week. Please make an appointment on your way out. Goodbye.'

# Chapter Eighteen

Nina woke with a start in a hot sweat. Bleary-eyed, she tried to focus on the clock beside the bed; it was 4 a.m. She struggled out of the reality of her dream in which she had been one of a team of air hostesses on board an experimental flight. But she'd got lost and the plane was only half-built and she'd spent most of the night striving to get where she was supposed to be. It seemed pointless trying to get back to sleep so she crept shakily out of bed and made her way silently downstairs. She pulled the curtains back and paced up and down the sitting room in the dark, searching for the vision of the future that had burned so brightly in the hours after she'd been given her results. But it was gone. In its place were the demons of the night echoing round the fear-filled valleys of her heart. They whispered of the horrible debilitating side effects of chemo, the return of cancer, of early death, of the great unknown. They fed the sickness and the pain inside her throat and took away her appetite. They made her think of Josie and imagine losing her. They showed her the sculptress she would never become, the work she would never produce. They turned her world in upon itself. They terrified her. She stopped pacing and curled up at one end of the sofa, unable to move. She was caught in a bottomless pit of fear and despair with no energy to begin the long crawl out. She felt as if the whole world was against her.

And as if that wasn't enough, she had a sore throat again.

At half past six, she made herself a cup of tea and sat, sullen and miserable, sipping it. She couldn't be bothered to face the world; she couldn't be bothered to smile and put on a brave face and say she was fine; she couldn't be bothered to make Malcolm feel better by pretending to cope; she couldn't even be bothered to jolly Josie along. The whole ordeal was running out of control; it was a great lumbering beast hurtling straight into darkness. Pains that had previously been perfectly manageable now became unbearable. Fears about the future assumed gargantuan proportions. Control was a dream and she began to fear the fear itself.

It was Josie who snapped her out of it. 'Can I have some breakfast, Mum?'

Nina knew that Josie was more than capable of making her own breakfast. However, on this morning, partly out of habit and partly to take her mind off darker things, Nina got up and walked into the kitchen. She moved through a haze, making toast, pouring juice, spreading jam and butter. She carried plate and cup into the sitting room and put them on the table beside Josie who was head deep in a book about computers. She grunted at her mother. Nina didn't have the energy to insist on a proper thank-you. Meanwhile, Malcolm emerged from the bathroom and called down the stairs.

'Have you seen my dark blue shirt?'

'Hanging up in the wardrobe, I think.'

'No, it isn't. I've looked. I need it for today.'

Wearily Nina trudged upstairs, opened the wardrobe in their bedroom, ran her fingers along the row of neatly ironed shirts and pulled out a dark blue one. She handed it to Malcolm who grunted.

'Sorry. Couldn't see it.'

She sat on the edge of the bed, gazing at his backview as he stood facing the mirror, tying his tie in a Windsor knot. He has absolutely no idea what I'm going through, she thought. Not an inkling. He has forgotten who I am, that is if he ever knew. He doesn't want to know. She knew it was pointless to try and speak. Instead she left the room, walked along the corridor and into her would-be studio; she leant against the closed door and shut her eyes. She felt like she was drowning.

'There has to be a me that is not wife or mother. There has to be an "I" that isn't dying.'

'Mum, are you in there? Who are you talking to? Mum, I need my PE stuff for school today? Mum? Mum?'

Nina breathed in deep and sighed out long and hard. 'I'm coming, darling.'

It was an hour later when she found herself alone again. She'd cleared up the debris of breakfast and the washing-up from the night before and was getting dressed in the bedroom. The early morning mist had cleared to reveal a bright blue springtime sky; sunshine poured in like honey through the window. She stood in its light, so bright and warm. Healing. It felt like a great yellow cloak of reassurance and protection, soft golden armour against the whims of the world outside. She thought about its source, an enormous ball of energy wielding the power of life and death in fiery hands. Perhaps that power could heal her. Perhaps. One of the hardest things, Nina found, was to trust. She had grown accustomed to control, and it was scary being catapulted into life without it. And fear was of itself, she knew, dis-ease. As surely as the cancer. Being forced to face her own mortality, it was the only weapon left. Faith. Trust in some higher power, trust in a collective positive energy. Perhaps if she could open up the doors, it would pour

160

in her the strength she needed. The strength to believe in a long and healthy future for herself. The strength to banish all those demons.

The ringing of the phone sounded from a muffled distance and it was a good few seconds before Nina moved to respond. She spoke quietly and uncertainly. 'Hello?'

'Hi, darling, it's Lotty. How's things?'

'Oh hello, Lotty. Not brilliant I'm afraid. I got told yesterday that I have to have chemotherapy as well as radiotherapy now. Every time I go to see a doctor, the news gets worse. I mean, where's it all going to end? When's it going to stop?'

'Oh God, I am sorry,' Lotty's voice was level. 'But listen, I know it's hard to see it now but there will be a time when it will all seem better, when it won't feel so threatening. Whether it takes six weeks or six months, there will be a time when all the treatment is over and you will only have to face the regular check-ups. You're going to live to a ripe old age, believe me. I need you, so that we can be eccentric old purple-trousered artists in our cottage on a cliff!'

Nina smiled, drinking in Lotty's faith.

'Are you still with me?'

'Yes, I'm here and you're right, I know you are. It's just getting from here to there that's the problem.'

'I know. I know. But you're going to get through this time and then you're going to seize whatever opportunities open up for you. I know you are. How's the studio coming on? You need to get working again and you can't do that without a space to work in. Have you cleared out the room yet?'

'Not yet. I'm reading the book you gave me though. And I'm working on the room. I was just standing in there this morning actually, thinking.'

'Well, if you're up to it, my advice is to get in there, girl. Life's too short for mucking about. It's not a rehearsal. Remember, none of us knows if we've got a tomorrow. All we have for certain is today, so make the most of it.'

'OK, OK, I hear you!'

'Right then. End of lecture. I'll ring you again in a couple of days. Bon courage and *carpe diem*. Bye.'

Nina could have hugged Lotty. In a few short minutes she had given her back a vision of the future where she'd go places and achieve things she would never have dreamed of were it not for the diagnosis which had ruined her daughter's tenth birthday.

She finished getting dressed, found some Bluetak, a pen and some coloured card and went into the spare room. She stuck the card to the wall and wrote on it in big letters a line from one of the get-well cards she'd received: *'You can't change the wind but you can adjust the sails'*. Fired with a sudden boldness of spirit and with the rekindled torch of positive thinking to light the way, she stepped back onto the road towards her future, flinging things into black dustbin bags as she went. The next two hours disappeared without trace. At 11 o'clock, she stopped to make herself a cup of coffee and had to fight her way past the accumulated line of bags on the landing to get downstairs. Just as she was attempting to stop the soya milk in her mug separating to form deeply unappetising clogs, the doorbell rang.

'Hi. It's only me and a bag of Danish pastries. Is the kettle on?' Mo spilled in through the front door all smiles and nurture.

'It's just this second boiled. You must be psychic! Come in.'

'God, is that your coffee? What on earth's happened to it?'

'It's this soya milk I'm trying. It's fine in tea but for some reason it separates in coffee. Looks disgusting doesn't it?'

'Is ordinary milk supposed to be bad for you then?'

'Well, I heard this programme on the radio about all the hormones that get pumped into cows through their feed to keep them producing milk. And there may be links between the hormones and cancer. Anyway, milk's not supposed to be particularly good for adults.'

'Blimey, shows how much I know! I thought milk was supposed to be healthy. A pint a day and all that?'

'Well, all I know is that they don't eat much dairy produce in the Far East and they don't get much breast cancer.'

'Oh, I hadn't thought of that.'

'Anyway, just at the moment, anything's worth a try. My body needs all the help it can get so I'm trying to eat as healthily as possible and put as few noxious substances into myself as I can.'

'Sounds all very sensible. So how are you feeling?'

'Well, the latest little gem is that I've now got to have chemotherapy as well as radiotherapy; which I could do without!'

'God, Nina, no. Why? That wasn't on the cards before was it?'

'Not as far as I knew, no. Apparently there's some disagreement as to whether to offer it to me or not. I think I'm sort of borderline. Probably five years ago or so, they wouldn't have offered it in a case like mine. I saw the "Prophet of Doom" yesterday. Possible "overkill" was the word he used, I think. Anyway I don't have to have it. It's up to me but I don't really see that I have a choice. What if I don't have it and the cancer comes back?'

'Have they said what the side-effects are likely to be? Do you have to go into hospital for it?'

163

'No, I don't think so, not overnight. I think it just takes a couple of hours. And they say it's not the hair falling out type of chemo and I shouldn't feel too sick but then everyone's different. So basically they don't really know.'

'I am sorry.'

Mo sat silent for a few seconds staring into her coffee, stirring it round and round with a spoon. Then she reached out to put her hand on Nina's arm.

'Look, I know you're going to get through this. Horrible as it is, I'm sure this is just one more step along the road to your recovery. Hang on in there, you can do it.'

Half-embarrassed at the urgency of her own words, Mo took a large bite out of her Danish pastry and changed the subject.

'So what have you been up to this morning?'

'Thanks, Mo,' Nina smiled at her friend. 'I've been clearing out the spare room actually. I'm going to make it into a studio for myself. I'm going to start working again.'

'Fantastic. Great idea! So what can I do to help? Can I see what you've done so far?'

'Sure. Come upstairs.'

The two women took their mugs and climbed the stairs, squeezed past the bags and into the room. It was bare now, save for the sofa bed and Nina's old desk in one corner. The walls looked dirty and the curtains hung limply to the side of the window at the end of the room.

'It needs a coat of paint and I'm going to buy a throw for the sofa bed when I finally unearth it! I want cushions in clashing colours. I'll have shelves and a working area here by the window. I'll get rid of the curtains...'

'What about a blind? That would give you maximum light.'

'Yeah, I thought of that. A really bright one.'

'Well, I'm the woman you need for cushions, the brighter the better, and I've got an empty car outside and I've got to go to Tesco's. Why don't I take these bags and dump them for you at the Children's Shop or the tip, whichever.'

'Oh, would you, Mo? That'd be brilliant. Thanks so much.'

'No problem, and if you want company to go shopping for material or anything else for the room, just let me know.'

'Thanks, Mo. You're a star!'

'I'll leave you to it then.'

Ten minutes later Mo was gone and so were the bags.

Nina spent the rest of the day making plans until it was time to pick up Josie from school. To do this she had to run the gauntlet of the inquiring faces in the school playground. There were those who said 'Hello, how are you?' with such smiles of pity in their faces that they clearly thought she already had one foot in the grave. She shuddered and moved on. The question was, did they really want to know or would they prefer the standard 'Oh, fine, thanks. I'm feeling really well.' Certainly the sarcastic option of 'Oh, absolutely marvellous, I'm really enjoying this whole experience' seemed a bit of a non-starter. The truth, of course, took longer and only served to increase the fear already rising in the inquirer's mind. She practised in her head responses such as 'It's like living through my worst nightmare and there's no waking up', or 'Well, since you ask, I'm absolutely terrified that I'm going to be dead this time next year', or 'I wake up every morning sick with fear and I'd give anything to be you, not me.' But they didn't really work. Instead Nina smiled, pretended to be jolly, and made the noises people wanted to hear until she could escape with Josie. They were just crossing the road when a voice called out, 'Hi, Nina, how are you?'

Not again, she thought and turned. 'Fine.'

'Are you really?'

'Yes, thanks. Really.'

'I hope you got all my messages. I didn't ring because I thought you might be resting.'

Nina smiled in as controlled a fashion as she could manage. She hadn't received any messages, indeed knew none had been left, and anyway resented the implication that she spent all her time in bed. She tried to walk on but the woman was like a terrier with a bone.

'Mo was telling me you now have to have chemotherapy as well?' Blast dear Mo and her openness, thought Nina.

'Yes,' she sighed as she prepared to say the words again. 'Apparently it's offered now in cases where it wouldn't have been before. So it remains to be seen whether it makes me feel ill or not.'

'Oh, it probably will though, won't it? I've heard it can be horrible. And so difficult for you feeling tired all the time with Josie to look after.'

OK. That's it! thought Nina as she grabbed Josie's hand and stomped off across the road. Her head was seething. No more Mrs Nice Guy, no more Mrs Manners, from now on you get it, both barrels, all you pitying women who look at me with scared eyes and sad smiles. How would you feel if I told you things were only going to get worse? What good would that do you? How exactly would that help?

'Mum, you're walking too fast. Slow down. What's the matter? And what does chemothingy mean?'

'Sorry, darling. I'm just a bit fed up. People say stupid things sometimes. Chemotherapy is just the name for some drugs that they inject you with to stop the cancer ever coming back, to make sure you stay well.'

'Is this chemowhatever going to make you feel ill, Mum?'

'I honestly don't know, darling. We'll just have to wait and see but there's no reason to suppose that it will.'

'My thumb hurts.'

'I'm sorry, darling.'

'Can Jane come round after school tomorrow?'

'Yes.'

Much later that night as Nina lay in bed waiting for sleep while her mortality stared her once again in the face, making her feel tiny and powerless, her mind wandered over the people of the day. In the weeks after her miscarriage she'd met them, the incompetent two-left-footed idiots outside school. She remembered the remarks. 'Never mind, dear. It was probably for the best.' 'The sooner you have another one, the better.' How desperate they had been to hear that she was doing well, how ready to deny the existence of her little half-formed baby boy. Then, as now, they seemed to fear that her trauma was contagious.

She could hear Malcolm's steady breathing beside her. Then, as now, he was out of his depth, his only thought to restore the status quo. She blinked hard in the dark, looking to the black to supply an answer. And it came. In the bedroom. At three in the morning. Elusive in its spirituality, it was there in the night none the less. Hope. The collective positive energy of the human spirit. After all, it had born witness to many miracles through many centuries. The trick was to tap into it, to stand in its light, and Nina had sensed it; somewhere on the wind or in the sunshine, she knew, it was there. She stopped looking, closed her eyelids, and let it wash over her.

# Chapter Nineteen

She woke the next morning to grey skies. A damp fine drizzle settled silently like mist on the garden. It was early March and the plants were on the starting line, bright little greens and brilliant yellows eager to be off. Nina stood at the bedroom window and felt, for no apparent reason, an overwhelming sense of being enfolded in a soft golden velvety future. She felt looked after. She had a powerful sensation that all would be well. It may have had something to do with her thoughts before sleep, a legacy of light at the end of the tunnel. Or perhaps it was the dream she'd had in which she'd developed stunning double-handed ground strokes and found herself in the Wimbledon quarter-finals! Her main concern had been that, when play resumed the following day, she didn't have a change of outfit. She had consequently spent the majority of the night worrying where to buy something suitable and what sort of knickers she should choose to accommodate the camera shots. Bearing in mind the miserable prognosis offered by the physiotherapist and the subsequent unlikelihood of her ever being able to play tennis again, she took the dream to be a positive message from her subconscious. The day could have continued as cheerfully as it had begun had she not decided to pay a visit to a local Christian cancer healing group.

A friend of a friend had told her about it. The

information had lodged in her brain and played there, resolutely refusing to go away. After all, she reasoned, what had she got to lose? Didn't she need all the help she could get? So, at 12 noon, feeling somewhat of a fraud, she turned up in great trepidation outside the doors of a very ordinary community hall tucked away in the back streets behind the shopping centre. She ventured nervously inside to be greeted by an extremely cheery 60-something-year-old who stood behind a small table on which were spread blank name labels in neat rows. Beside the labels lay a red felt tip pen and a blue one. Their significance was soon to become apparent. All 'patients', as the group was pleased to call those who had been touched by the dread hand of cancer, were given labels written in blue ink, while their healthy friends and relatives were given ones written in red. Nina searched her experience over the past weeks to find any justification for the title of 'patient' but she could find none. She had never felt ill; and the only pain had been that caused by the medical profession. How then was she a 'patient'?

Her train of thought was interrupted by a general movement towards a group of tables on which were laid pots of coffee and tea. As people nibbled nervously on the corners of biscuits, Nina took stock. The average age around the room seemed to be about 70. Any head of hair that wasn't grey belonged to a relative or friend. She deduced this from the colour of the name labels. How she longed to swap her blue one for a red one! It was several seconds before she realized that she was being asked a question.

'Do you live near, my dear?' A rather overweight 'jolly hockey sticks' type of septuagenarian had plonked herself heavily in the chair next to Nina's.

'Er, yes, quite close. Just down towards the river.'

169

'Ah ah, a veritable local then. Of course I remember what this town was like during the war. You'd hardly recognize it now of course. Everything's changed of course and it's not for the better, if you ask me.'

Nina hadn't, but this was not going to deter her companion from delivering a 10-minute lecture on life during the war. When she next drew breath, it was to ask, 'So what's happened to you then, my dear?'

'I was diagnosed with breast cancer a few weeks ago and operated on three weeks ago today.' Nina listened to her words; they still stuck in her throat as she said them. Half of her continued to believe she was talking about someone else.

'You're very young, my dear, aren't you?' A fact which Nina hardly needed reminding of as she scanned the room for any sign of a kindred spirit. 'So what happens to you now?'

I don't want to think about it, thought Nina, as she summoned the energy for a reluctant reply.

'Well, I'm waiting now to begin radiotherapy and also mild chemotherapy.'

'Oh, I see. Of course it will be difficult being tired from all that. Do you have any children?'

'Yes, one,' Nina replied miserably as she made a desperate attempt to escape by engaging in the conversation on her other side. She was briefly introduced to a smiling woman with immaculately cut grey hair, smart trousers and a jacket. It turned out that the hair was not her own and she had been given six months to live about nine months earlier. Nina was just thinking of making her excuses and a run for it when everyone began shuffling chairs, discarding tables and arranging themselves in a large circle around the room. Reluctantly she joined them.

It was the turn of an elderly vicar to hold court. While he waxed lyrical about the healing power of

God's love, Nina felt more and more of a hypocrite by the minute. She envied churchgoers their faith and their ritual, their means of managing mortality. But she had never felt a part of their exclusive club. Whilst she was sure that there was a power at work in the world that was infinitely greater than any individual human being, she was not at all sure she would call that power 'God'. Which meant that, on this grey afternoon in March, sitting where she was sitting, she felt like a fish out of water, a hat without a coat.

Dragging herself back to the present, she realised with horror that a very nasty little hand-held microphone and power unit were being passed around the circle in her general direction. People were 'sharing' information about their current medical state. Her heart began to pound. Finally it was her turn.

'I ... er ... think my blood pressure's just shot through the roof at the sight of this microphone approaching!' Nina said, attempting to lighten the atmosphere. There were some sympathetic smiles. She took a deep breath and continued. 'My name is Nina, as you can probably all see from my name badge,' she hesitated wondering whether to say more on the subject of badges but decided against it. 'I was diagnosed with breast cancer on my daughter's tenth birthday. I've since had a lumpectomy and I'm facing the unknown again waiting to find out what sort of chemo and radiotherapy they think I should have.'

She wondered whether to continue by confessing her agnosticism but decided there were too many evangelical hopes at stake.

'I have to say I'm feeling a bit isolated here. I may be flattering myself but I feel much younger than anyone else with a blue label. I have a young child and I believe that makes a difference.'

171

'My dear young lady!' said a very dapper gentleman in highly polished shoes. 'What do you mean "*younger*"?'

A few more sympathetic smiles were followed by silence.

The microphone wended its weary way round the rest of the circle until it was handed to a very elderly man who appeared to have been asleep throughout most of the proceedings so far. He spoke slowly and hesitantly, clearly struggling with the weight of his emotions.

'What ... er ... I ... er ... would like you ... er ... all to pray ... er ... for ... er ... is ... er ... my wife.'

He went on to explain how his wife was dying, consumed with bitter resentment at everyone around her including God. The old man, who Nina learnt had been blind for 60 years and was himself dying of cancer, could not bear his wife to end her life in such a way. Nina sat immobilized by the poignancy of their situation but she was soon shaken from her reverie by the noise of chairs being pushed back as everyone stood up to hold hands. Nina took the hand of the woman with the wig on one side and an incredibly overweight woman on the other who was unable to rise from her wheelchair. Her drugs, Nina learned, had been halved because they were doing nasty things to her nerve endings. Nina smiled at her and wondered at the horror of cancer.

At last it was over and she was breathing the fresh damp air as she strode out for home, wondering if it had been worth it. They clearly all believed in the power of their collective healing energy and it seemed no bad thing to tap into it in whatever lopsided way she could. On the other hand, the image of the lonely old man, the immaculate lady in the wig and the overweight woman in the wheelchair took their toll. Nina was not sure it would be helpful to return.

The following morning she woke with the now familiar

lump of anxiety in her throat and a shaking in her soul. What horrors were due out of the medical hat today? What vestige of control would be whipped from under her feet? This was the day she went again to see the Prophet of Doom and then his partner in crime, the consultant radiologist. On balance, there didn't seem to be a lot of point in getting out of bed. She turned to face the wall and sighed heavily in an effort to shift the sickness at the base of her throat. It didn't work. In fact it was still there four hours later when she found herself, together with an ever-silent Malcolm, sitting in the now equally familiar waiting room of faded glory, watching the obligatory 'head in magazine' routine. After what appeared to be the statutory delay, the door opened and the Prophet of Doom beckoned them in.

'How are you?'

'Physically I'm absolutely fine.'

'Physically?'

'Well, I can cope with the present. I've made up my mind about the chemo and I can manage that. What still terrifies me is the future and whether I have one.'

'I would say your chances are very good. Take your things off and let's have a look at you.'

For yet another time, Nina stripped bare to her waist, moved her arms when bidden, sat while her scars were prodded, lay down while her breast was pommelled.

'You've got quite a band that's formed under your arm. This often happens with thinner people.'

Good, thought Nina, at least the diet's still working!

'I can do something about it but it will be painful. Will you allow me to do it?'

He was standing close to her right side, holding her arm tightly by the wrist, high above her head. Nina felt even sicker than before. She glanced at Malcolm, who looked down at the floor.

'I don't suppose I have much choice, do I?' she asked.

Almost before the words were out of her mouth, he yanked her arm straight upwards with incredible force. There was a horrible scrunching sound from deep within her armpit and a razor-sharp stab of pain shot through her shoulder. Involuntarily she kicked the small steps which were tucked under the couch she was sitting on.

'I'm sorry. I know it hurts.' It was the nearest the Prophet of Doom had ever got to showing compassion. Without pausing to draw breath, he produced a large syringe and proceeded to puncture her battered breast a second time to draw off fluid. After the pain of a few moments ago, this last ordeal was a breeze. The day's torture over, Nina was permitted to get dressed and sit down. Almost, she felt, as if she were a normal human being!

'Well, I'm happy with your progress and I'm ready to hand you on. I'll see you in six months. Goodbye.'

Oh whoopee, thought Nina, out of the frying pan into the fire. An hour later and they were once again sitting waiting, this time in a corridor between two closed doors next to a busy hospital X-ray department. Malcolm was just considering his second cup of coffee from the machine when one of the doors opened and they were ushered inside. Nina instantly remembered the kindly round face of Dr Barpin from the sentinel node mapping on the day before her operation.

He was a Humpty Dumpty sort of man, gentler and less intimidating than the Prophet of Doom. He seemed in no particular hurry and began to regale them with stories. There was the one about the conversation that never happened between himself and his hearing aid and an elderly lady patient and her hearing aid to the background accompaniment of workmen drilling holes in the consulting room walls. Then there was the one about the long-term patient who got so used to her appointments that she would start undressing as soon as she saw him, which worked fine until the day they met at a cocktail party. Along the way he took some notes, gave detailed explanations of what to expect from radiotherapy and closely scrutinized the papers on his desk. He was clearly about to draw the meeting to a close when Nina could bear it no longer.

'I'm sorry, but I thought the purpose of this meeting was to have a discussion about chemotherapy.'

'Ah ... oh ... I see.' Humpty Dumpty was clearly taken aback. 'Yes. I was thinking you would get your radiotherapy over and done with and then we would discuss any further treatment.'

'I understood that the chemo, if I was to have it, would start first and then the radiotherapy would fit in to the middle of it.'

'Well, we can play it several different ways. I can certainly feed in your chemotherapy once the radiotherapy is under way if that's what you'd like.'

What I'd like is never to have been diagnosed with cancer. What I'd like is to be one of those other women out there who've never had to go through half of what I've been through. What I'd like... Nina sat silent.

'Perhaps if I explain what is involved? You would be given a combination of three different chemotherapy drugs. Two are given intravenously and one as pills, in a monthly cycle over six months. You would need to come into hospital for a couple of hours on day one and then again on day eight each month.' He was drawing little line diagrams as he spoke. 'You would be taking pills from day one for two weeks, then nothing would happen for two weeks and the cycle would start again. Does that make sense?'

Nina nodded.

'You see, there is a risk of the side-effects of the radiotherapy being enhanced by the chemotherapy, so I would rather have the radiotherapy well under way before introducing the chemotherapy.'

'And if I have the chemotherapy and the worst happens and the cancer returns in the future, will it lessen my chances of being treated because I've had chemo this time?'

'No, not at all. There are hundreds of different chemotherapy drugs we can prescribe and hundreds of different combinations of them so it would make no difference to future treatment.'

'And how bad are the side-effects likely to be?'

'That's a tricky one to answer because everyone is different. I can tell you that we are not proposing an aggressive regime of chemotherapy in your case so it's unlikely that you would lose your hair. And there is no reason to suppose that you would feel particularly sick, we are much better at controlling that now. You might feel a bit more tired than usual and want to take it a bit easy, especially the day after the drugs have been administered. On the other hand, you may be relatively unaffected. It's similar to the radiotherapy, some people retire to bed, others carry on in full-time jobs.'

He paused, leant back in his chair and smiled. 'First things first. We need to get you started on the radiotherapy, so I'll arrange a session for you on the simulator, that's the machine we use to measure you up before beginning the radiotherapy. Is there anything else you'd like to ask me at this stage?'

It was Malcolm who spoke first. 'What are the long-term effects of either treatment? In what ways will Nina be different?'

'As far as the chemotherapy is concerned, any side-effect symptoms will cease shortly after treatment has finished. With radiotherapy, there may be permanent loss of underarm hair and you'll be the proud possessor of four tiny permanent tattoos. Nothing too awful. You'll be as right as rain!'

He smiled again at Nina as he began to gather up the piles of paper in front of him. For her part, Nina couldn't begin to think about how she would be after the treatment, she was too busy channelling all her energies into coping with the here and now.

'I'll wait to hear from you then. Thank you. Goodbye.'

She and Malcolm drove to the station in silence. Malcolm was catching the train back to work where he was going to stay till late into the evening. Nina hadn't the energy to challenge him. She dropped him off and drove to collect Josie from Jane's house. On the way, she devised all sorts of strategies to protect her from having to confront Pauline, but in the event, none of them worked. No sooner had she pulled up outside the house than Pauline was on the doorstep inviting her in for a cup of tea. She declined the tea but failed to avoid stepping inside the front door.

'How are you?' came the inevitably over-solicitous enquiry.

'I'm fine. Yeah, I feel very fit and healthy, thanks.'

'You look very drawn, not surprisingly of course.'

Well, that's wiped the smile off my face, thought Nina. Silly me, my mistake, there was I thinking that I looked quite good considering all I've been through! Obviously I got it wrong. Oh well, you can't win them all and thanks a lot for pointing out my error, it's made me feel a whole lot better. She wasn't sure what expression had settled on her features during this inner rant and decided that a swift retreat was probably the best policy. She thanked Pauline for having Josie and made a run for it with a disgruntled daughter in tow. Josie had wanted to stay longer and was not pleased to be going home with her mother.

'Will Daddy be at home when we get there?'

'No, I'm afraid not darling. He had to go back to work to make up the time he missed when he came to the doctor's with me today.'

'It's not fair, he's never at home. When will you stop having to go to the doctors all the time?'

'Soon I hope, darling, soon. How was your day at school?'

'Fine. Except my thumb still hurts. Can I go on the Internet when we get in?'

'Yes. I suppose so.'

Moments later, they walked into a cold dark house. It felt momentarily unlived in, even Charlie seemed to have vanished. He was getting very old now, more set in his ways and less tolerant of the human race in general. Josie rushed upstairs and Nina went to put the kettle on. As she did so, the thought crossed her mind that it would be good to have a dog to welcome her home. Malcolm was not an animal person, however. It was as much as he could manage to tolerate the cat. Nina shrugged as she poured boiling water onto a herbal tea bag. It had been another tough day.

# Chapter Twenty

The next morning she picked the post up from the floor. *'The following appointment has been made for you ... please report to the Simulator on Level A. We enclose a pre-registration form which should be completed and returned by post unless your appointment is within the next three days, in which case please bring it with you...'*

Within the next three days? It was within the next three hours! Luckily, Nina had nothing planned. So a little later, for the second time in as many months, she stepped through the automatic entrance doors of the spanking new Cancer Centre and walked down corridor after corridor of polished floors and clean walls decorated at militarily regular intervals with brightly coloured prints of various sizes, mostly depicting flowers. She followed the signs to 'The Simulator' and turned a final corner half-expecting to be confronted with Dr Who's Tardis or at least an encounter of the third kind. Instead she was met by a frail old lady propped up on cushions on a trolley in the middle of the corridor, attended by two concerned nurses.

'We're going to get the doctor to come down and see you, Mrs Avery.'

'What dear?'

'We're going to get the doctor to give you something for the pain.'

Despite the fact that people three corridors away could easily have heard this last sentence, the old lady seemed not to have registered. She sat surrounded by tubes and scrunched up pieces of paper towelling, hunched over in her trauma. Nina found a chair a little further down the corridor under a sign which read that the simulator had been sponsored by a large local insurance company. Specializing in life insurance policies, no doubt, thought Nina. She wondered idly what her chances really were as she waited and half-listened to the nurses' now muted conversation about the old lady, who had taken to moaning quietly.

Trolley loads of strange objects began to emerge through the closed doors of the simulator room, to be wheeled off in different directions. First there was a pile of what looked like giant colourless yoghurt pots with four small bolts on the top of each one. Next came a load of clear plastic breast-shaped moulds. With a pang in her heart, Nina wondered how many single-breasted women with shattered lives the nonchalant pile of plastic represented. Before she had time to speculate further, the door of the simulator room swung wide open and a young lad marched out closely followed by and handcuffed to a policeman. Right behind them came a second officer. Nina was just debating whether the policeman would have been simulated along with his prisoner when her name was called out from down the corridor. She was ushered into a large room full of massive machines with a little office-like area screened off in one corner.

'Good morning,' came a disembodied voice from behind the screen, 'And welcome to the torture chamber.'

'Isn't he awful?' giggled one of the nurses.

'He certainly knows how to inspire confidence,' replied Nina, smiling a little wearily as she began to remove her shirt and bra for what seemed like the thousandth time. Humpty Dumpty had appeared from behind the screen and was standing over her, smiling a warm smile.

'We're just going to do a lot of measuring and lining up today, that's all. It's a bit tedious I'm afraid but nothing too bad.'

As it turned out, he was right. It wasn't too bad as long as you didn't mind lying in a relatively uncomfortable position for half an hour while several monoliths of modern technology whirred and hissed and made menacing turns around your prostrate body. Lots of X-rays, countless biro marks and four permanent pinhead tattoos later, Nina was free to leave.

She drove home and sat in the sunshine at the back of the house, listening to the birdsong, drinking in the yellow of the daffodils and trying to re-establish some connections with the outside world. She had a week before she was due back to begin the real thing.

For want of something better to do, she volunteered to spend a day at Josie's school helping the children make chocolate muffins for Red Nose Day. She didn't much enjoy cooking, and spending time with other people's children was not usually her idea of fun, but she would have done anything to try and take her mind off the lion's den which awaited her. It was the waiting which was the worst. She wanted it over and done with. She wanted to start so she could finish. She wanted a chance to live the life she'd put on hold for too long. But it all took time. Bloody time. So she found herself elbow deep in melting butter, muffin cases and red-nosed glace cherries. Group after group of excited children arrived in a steady stream throughout the morning. Would Year Three's teacher have to shave his head by the end of the day? Would the Head get a bucket of cold porridge poured over him and would Miss Pring really eat the roses? The sickly-sweet smell of chocolate muffins began to pervade the air in the windowless resource area and the temperature rose each time the oven doors were opened. Two hours flashed by and Nina's shoulder began to ache. She contemplated sitting down, but the production line had taken on a menacing momentum of its own. And so it continued; the children kept coming, the butter kept melting, the mixture kept baking, the muffins kept cooling.

Lunch hour provided a welcome break. Or it would have done had it not been for the member of staff who, having enquired how Nina was, proceeded to regale her with the details of her own scare at discovering a lump which had turned out to be nothing at all to worry about. Nina returned to the fiery hell of the muffin area burning with a sense of injustice. Nearly 2,000 muffins were sold by the end of the day and over £300 raised. Nina collected Josie and returned home almost too tired to be scared. Sadly it didn't last.

It seemed as if she hadn't set eyes on Malcolm for days. He had taken to leaving even earlier in the morning than usual and returning late into the evening. She had tried on a couple of occasions to talk to him, but he was totally unable to address what was happening. She could almost see him squirm with a need for everything to be alright, for life to carry on as normal. And that, of course, was impossible. But he was not ready to acknowledge that and she lacked the emotional energy to help him. So they sank silently into a mire of individual isolation. He never spoke of work and she never asked. She gave up trying to explain how she felt and he seemed relieved not to have to listen. In her heart she longed for the warmth of a supportive hug or a daily dose of positive words but neither came. They began to lead more and more separate lives as Nina rallied all her energies to face her next ordeal. The week was up.

She had been told to arrive 20 minutes early in order to see the nurse. Mo had offered to accompany her but

Nina opted to go it alone, promising to accept next time if the experience proved too awful. There were never any parking places; a small fact which made any visit to the hospital or the Cancer Centre just that bit more trying. As luck would have it, though, the nearest supermarket was only a ten-minute walk away and the attendants who cleared the trolleys didn't seem to be too vigilant. Nina parked, put up her umbrella against the early morning drizzle and walked briskly towards the new building. Once more she braved the shiny automatic doors which slid apart slowly on her approach. The woman on the desk pointed down the nearest corridor and told her to wait at the end. She sat down in the corner of a square of chairs, many of them already occupied by grey-haired men and women. No sooner had she taken off her coat than a business-like nurse appeared and called her name. She got up and followed her into a small windowless room, housing a table and two chairs.

'Now, Mrs Salis. I just need to run through a few details with you concerning your treatment.'

Oh well, one up on Mrs Hayes, thought Nina, nodding meekly and fearing the worst.

'Is this the first time you've had radiotherapy?'

Too bloody right it is and it better be the last, she thought, as she said 'Yes.'

'Well, everyone responds differently. Some of our ladies find their skin gets very sore as the treatment progresses, but not all. We recommend aloe vera gel, you can get it at any good health food shop. We used to advise no washing at all of the affected area but we now say a shower is fine, but we recommend that you don't lie in a hot bath.'

Bang goes my major means of relaxation, thought Nina, as she nodded attentively.

'We recommend you don't wet shave the armpit or use a normal deodorant. You may lose your underarm hair and this may be permanent.'

No great loss on that score then.

'It's most important that you don't sunbathe and you may want to wear loose clothing and no bra. Have you any questions?'

Nina tried desperately to hang on to some sort of positive thought in the midst of all this negativity. She had taken herself off swimming on a few occasions since her operation to try to improve the flexibility of her arm.

'Can I still go swimming?' she asked.

'No I'm afraid that wouldn't be a very good idea, not while the treatment is going on; the chlorine might affect the skin. I'm sorry.'

So am I. Ah well. 'What about jogging?'

Nina asked this last question more for something to say than because she seriously intended to jog every day. But then again it would provide a means of getting fit and the fitter her body was, the better she would be able to manage the continuing onslaughts.

'I don't see that that should be a problem as long as the breast is well supported. Probably very good for you to get the whole system going.'

The nurse was already on her feet; the interview was obviously over. Nina returned to the square of chairs and joined the queue. She looked around. There were bright yellow and black signs everywhere: 'Radiation. Controlled Area. No Unauthorized Entry.' It was like something off the set of a disaster movie. Was she seriously going to allow lethal doses of radiation to be aimed at her mangled breast? Was she mad? Writhing snakes fought for position in the pit of her stomach while her old friends, sickness and anxiety, bubbled at the base of her throat. The old lady opposite her was called in. As she struggled to stand, she turned towards Nina.

'You have to put your card in the little box, dear, there ... by the door.'

'Oh thank you,' Nina replied, realising the woman could barely walk and offering her an arm to lean on. It was gratefully received. The nurse moved across the waiting area to take over and Nina went to put her appointment card in the small plastic box beside the entrance. She went back to her seat. Fifteen minutes later the old lady was wheeled out in tears. She was dabbing at her eyes with a scrunched up tissue. There followed a few moments of frenzied activity while the nurses tried to locate a doctor for her to speak to. Nina was ushered in through the doors and could only wonder what was to become of her elderly companion.

The room she entered was similar to the one which had housed the simulator. The nurse pointed to a chair and Nina stripped. She lay down and raised both arms above her head. The 'surrender position' she had once heard it called, and never did the name seem more apt. The bed moved; the machines moved; pencil-thin beams of light aligned with pinpoint accuracy. Finally the nurses scurried like frightened rabbits for the safety of another room while, for 47 seconds, Nina lay alone and still, listening to the deceptively cosy hum of the gamma rays as they punctured her body. When it was safe, the nurses returned to realign the machine and the whole process was repeated. Then it was time to go. Nina took her card and ran for the daylight and the world outside.

Every other day, bar a couple of public holidays, for the next six weeks, Nina made the same pilgrimage to the grim doors of the Cancer Centre. She longed to make the journey in the privacy of her car but, not surprisingly, the supermarket staff had noted her hasty retreat in the opposite direction and she had been politely advised that this constituted incorrect use of company premises. She had tried shouting 'I've got cancer! Leave me alone!' but to no avail. She was therefore forced to use public transport and would watch the faces around her aching with envy, longing to be any one of them making any one of their journeys instead of her own. But there was no escape.

Each visit afforded a new snippet of human suffering. There was the man who emerged from his radiotherapy one day balancing a bright white gauze bandage on the back of his hand which he held out in front of him. Seemingly transfixed by it, he moved slowly and methodically as if engaged in some obscure, long-forgotten dance, and then wandered off unseeing down the corridor. There was the smartly dressed business-woman who kept looking at her watch, clasping her jewelled hands together while uncrossing and recrossing her stockinged legs. Clearly her diagnosis of cancer had seriously disrupted her schedule. The conversations were invariably entertaining.

'One learns so much from one's dogs.'

'And do you attend dog training classes?'

'My dear, I wouldn't miss one for the world. Betsy so enjoys them.'

'I learnt such a good trick for "Heel" the other day.'

'Oh, do tell.'

'Frightfully simple. Once they start pulling on the lead, just turn abruptly and walk in the opposite direction, giving a good tug and shouting "Heel". After a few steps, set off in the direction you want to go again.'

Images of demented dog owners spending hours

walking backwards floated across Nina's mind. Then there were always the snowy-haired ladies, sitting with their husbands, staring into space as if in an effort to remove themselves from the world in which so much horror was being inflicted on their frail and vulnerable bodies. Occasionally an attentive husband would make a remark which would drag them back to the reality of their situation for a second or two. One such couple seemed more animated than the rest. Nina had exchanged smiles with them and on one occasion, while his wife was being zapped, the old man broke the silence.

'She's so brave, my Reenie. She's my second wife, you know. My first wife died of cancer. Died on Reenie's birthday as it happens. Strange old world, isn't it?'

He smiled and paused for breath. 'I blame our children! My son, he married Reenie's daughter you see. Funny how things happen. One Christmas they invited me to stay and asked if I would bring the mother-in-law. That was Reenie, you see. And things just went from there.' He paused, momentarily lost in thought. 'Nine years we've been married now and goodness knows how many grandchildren. One of them's six foot tall and sends his grandma all sorts of inappropriate cards! Sent one last week that brought tears to her eyes, he did!'

Before Nina could respond, Reenie reappeared and the two of them walked off hand in hand, leaving Nina to wish that she too was at the comfortable end of her life. But then maybe it would have been a wasted life. Maybe cancer was the kick up the backside she needed. On good days when she felt strong, she could grasp the future in both hands. On bad days when the waiting areas were empty and it was very quiet, the shadowy spectres would return to fly around the silent walls and whisper tales of death. Then nothing but the barest attempt at survival seemed possible. Then she longed to wake up and lie in the blissful morning realization that it had all been a very long bad dream. But the waking never came.

# Chapter Twenty-One

The days turned into months. Nina stopped swimming and began jogging. The trauma of the radiotherapy turned into the trauma of the chemotherapy. For a wild and heady two-week period, she was having both at the same time. It was then that the skin on her breast began to peel in sheets. She remembered Humpty Dumpty's words of warning about the chemo drugs enhancing the effect of the radiotherapy and, in dismay, went out and bought an even larger tube of aloe vera gel. Her daily jog along by the river became a test of endurance as her drying skin bounced and stretched and pulled at every step. It was like running with no bra and strips of sellotape attached to half your chest. Each and every movement was painful. All part and parcel of the treatment, she supposed, until on one of her final visits to the echelons of the Cancer Centre, she bumped into Humpty Dumpty as she walked through the car park. She told him what was happening to her skin and he said he would come and see her when she was having her treatment. Thirty-five minutes later she was stripping off and explaining the situation to the nurses who were less than sympathetic.

'Yuk, that does look revolting.'
'Are you sure you've been washing regularly?'
'It's not a pretty sight, is it?'
Under any other circumstances Nina would have been

able to cope with these remarks. As it was, she felt gutted. Tears of defeat began to prick behind her eyes; she fought them back. A few minutes later, she and Humpty Dumpty were in their by now familiar relative positions; she lying on her back bare to the waist and he smiling down at her. He began to pick at her breast with his fingernail.

'Now, let's see what you've been up to here.'

'Ouch, that hurts.' Nina flinched, fearing the worst.

'Do you know what I think we have here? A bad case of over-gelousness! Get it? Over-gelous, that's not bad for me. You, my dear, have been a bit heavy-handed with the aloe vera. What you need to do is go home and have a good long soak. I think you'll find that your skin underneath is in excellent condition.'

The nurses had a good laugh while a tidal wave of relief flooded over Nina as she stood up to get dressed. Not one of the people around her had the tiniest inkling of the horrors she had been imagining. For days she had lived with visions of a red, raw and bleeding breast and of months making a lengthy recovery. Had they not told her to avoid soaking in the bath? Had she not followed their instructions implicitly? She went home, walked into the house, up the stairs, into the bathroom and turned on the taps. Within minutes she was soaking, peeling the softened layers of aloe vera gel off in sticky layers. She felt like a new woman and jumped up and down on the spot while she was drying just to prove to herself that the pain was gone.

In celebration she took herself off in search of a sturdy table on which to work. The spare room had now begun to look like a studio. Mo had made her a bright yellow blind, a cover for the sofa bed and several vibrant-coloured cushions. The walls and the floorboards of the room were now so white that the Dulux dog would have been impressed. She herself was quietly pleased with how things were going and secretly excited at the prospect of sculpting once again. She wished she could share what she was feeling with Malcolm and with Josie; she longed to take them with her down this new road upon which she'd set her first few tentative steps. But they were reluctant travellers. Malcolm had put his head round the door one evening and grunted.

'Bit white, isn't it?'

'I wanted it white. It's my blank canvas, my future.'

'What do you mean, your future?'

'Well, going back to work again is a means of proving to myself that I have a future. That I'm not going to die. That the cancer is not going to come back.'

'That's ridiculous. Of course you have a future. Of course it isn't coming back. Everything is OK now, or it will be once you've finished the chemotherapy.'

'How do you know, Malcolm? How can you possibly know that?' Nina felt instantly irritated.

Malcolm shrugged and shifted from one foot to the other; he leant against the door frame, disgruntled. 'I don't know why you want to sculpt again anyway. It's not as if you ever made much money out of it.'

Nina sighed. 'I'm not doing it for the money. I'm lucky enough not to have to. At the moment at least.'

'I've got work to do anyway,' Malcolm cut in, and the conversation ended as most of their conversations had taken to ending, abruptly, with Malcolm retreating under the pretext of work.

Enthusiasm was no easier to illicit from Josie. She half-listened as her mother outlined her plans and then asked if she could go and watch television. She showed no further interest in the ongoing work on the room and Nina stopped trying to share it with her.

So it was that she stood very much on her own in the

191

darkened storeroom of a small junk shop in the back streets of town.

'You take yer time, luv. Have a good look around. Lord knows what's stashed away back 'ere. Bloomin' black hole of Calcutta it is! I'll leave yer to it then.'

'Thanks very much.' Nina smiled and blinked into the shadows.

There was a long narrow corridor that seemed to go back and back forever, becoming progressively darker as it did so. The odd bare light bulb swung silently from the ceiling, illuminating blankets of dust and lacelike cobwebs. The walls on either side were stacked high with abandoned possessions perched precariously one on top of the other. The flotsam and jetsam of the furniture world. As she peered into the gathering gloom, Nina doubted that she'd ever find anything amongst the jumble of wood and plastic. But something told her not to turn back. Against her better judgement, she stumbled on while the light from the little shop front far behind her faded into the distance. She felt like Aladdin in search of the lamp.

And then it happened. The pocket of her jacket caught on the corner of something and she was jerked abruptly backwards so forcefully that for a moment she thought some invisible hand had grabbed her from behind. She was about to shout out when she realised there was no one there. She turned to dislodge her jacket from the handle on which it had ripped and noticed the table. It appeared to be large and made of solid oak, like everything else it had a mound of debris piled on top of it. She could see a single large shallow drawer with an old brass handle. She ran her hand along what little surface was showing; a trail of warm brown wood appeared through the dust beneath her fingers. She made her way immediately back to the front of the shop. It was empty.

'Er ... hello? ... Hello ... Are you there?'

There was a clatter of footsteps on some stairs. 'I'm 'ere, luv. Just makin' meself a quick cuppa. Parky in 'ere it is.'

'Um ... I've found a table right in the back. I wonder if I could have a better look at it. There's loads of stuff on top of it, I'm afraid.'

'No bovver, luv. Let's see now, shall we.'

After several minutes of laboured panting and puffing, the amicable overweight proprietor dragged the table into the meagre light.

'It's comin' back to me now. This table's right old. Left 'ere it was, by the old geezer I bought the place off. Forty-odd year ago now it was. Funny old bloke. Had this shop all his life and his old Mum and Dad before 'im. Used this table they did, the family. Solid old bit of wood, it is.'

Nina didn't hesitate. She agreed a price and arranged a day for it to be delivered.

'No problem luv. That'll go in me van, no bovver. The best of the day to yer.'

She almost skipped out of the shop and along the pavement, realising that for the first time in months the search for the table had afforded her a whole 45 minutes free of the throat-gripping clod of fear which had become her constant companion.

The day on which the table was to be delivered was also the day of her second visit to the hospital for chemotherapy. The first visit had been nerve-wracking but uneventful and, apart from the debacle of losing her 'skin', she had survived the first week symptom-free. She had waited to feel sick, which she hadn't. She had waited to feel tired, which she hadn't. She had waited for the constipation which never came. She scoured the basin for any telltale signs each time she washed her hair, but

193

nothing seemed to be falling out. Despite all this, it was with only slightly less trepidation that she headed back for a second dose seven days later. Part of her couldn't believe that she was willingly allowing herself to be injected with syringe-fulls of poisonous substances; part of her wanted to run a mile and never come back. But the other part of her knew that if the cancer returned and she hadn't had the chemo, she would regret not doing all she could. Anyway it was not going to come back, she told herself, as she had taken to telling herself at regular intervals throughout each day. She told herself as she walked through the hospital doors. She told herself as she sat waiting for the blood test which she had to have every time she came. A slightly nervy middle-aged woman ushered her into a small room across the corridor.

'Right then. What are we doing today?' Nina hoped this was a rhetorical question. 'Ah, yes, we only need a little. Now let's see if we can find a vein. It's this arm is it?'

'Yes, it has to be that one because the other one has had lymph nodes removed.'

'That's a shame, because the veins are so much better on that side.'

Nice of you to point that out, thought Nina who was not fond of needles or blood tests at the best of times, let alone when they served only as painful precursors of worse to come. The woman seemed increasingly edgy as she fixed a tourniquet round Nina's arm and handed her a blue plastic ball to squeeze. She tapped the inside of Nina's elbow with her finger.

'Oh dear, it's so hard to find a vein. Right. Let's try here.'

Nina turned her head away, closed her eyes and gritted her teeth. The nails of her other hand dug deep into her palms. There was a sharp stab and silence.

'Oh dear, I am sorry. I just can't seem to get any blood. Could you press on that for me while I go and find my colleague. I think he'd better have a try.'

Once again Nina fought back tears as she was left alone in the tiny room balanced uncertainly between one trauma and the next. After about five minutes, the door opened and a younger dark-haired man in a white coat swept in. He had the air about him of someone in a hurry, as if his mind was several hours ahead of his body.

'Let's see if we can't sort out these problematic veins, then.'

The whole process was swiftly repeated. The stab was harder the second time. And then it was over. For the time being.

'You know where to go next, don't you?'

He was out of the door before Nina had time to roll down her sleeve. Her arm throbbed insistently as she walked along the corridor and down the stairs to the day ward where she sat to wait again. It began to bleed and she had to go in search of a nurse and ask for another plaster before returning to her seat. There were about six chairs grouped around a coffee machine and a water dispenser.

Opposite her were a father and son. She presumed the man must have had a hole in his throat because he had a flap of plaster attached to his neck which blew outwards each time he spoke. His voice was gravelly and barely audible. His son was clutching a packet of Polos and a can of Dr Pepper. He was wearing wellies. They seemed to be sharing a silent joke about whether the boy was going to allow his father a sweet. His dad grinned broadly while the child's eyes twinkled as he giggled. Next he tried to open his can but gave up and handed it to his father who succeeded in spraying his son's whole face with sticky fizzy liquid. They both laughed again and then settled down to read.

Nina looked down at her arm and wondered at the unspeakable horrors the man must already have been through, the trauma his family must be suffering and why it was that his young son was sitting with him in the hospital. She wondered if Josie would want to come and see what chemotherapy was all about; somehow she doubted it, but resolved to offer her the opportunity anyway.

The wonders of private medical insurance meant that, on this occasion at least, the chemotherapy was administered by the consultant himself. Humpty Dumpty was unfailingly kind. He inserted the cannula quickly and confidently into the back of her hand whilst regaling her with the shortfalls of the NHS system, the long waiting lists and how he had enough forms to fill out per patient to wallpaper a lighthouse. She learnt about his bad knee, his garden, his grandchildren, and his wife's recent accident with the carving knife.

'Right, all done. That wasn't so bad was it? You'd better just stay put for 10 minutes or so, just in case you stand up and keel over in the corridor. It's never happened before, but you can never be sure. I'll see you in two weeks' time. Goodbye.'

Nina in fact made it into the outside world without mishap. She supposed she blended quite quickly into the mass of people on the pavement; only the small round plaster visible on the back of her hand gave her away. She had an hour before the table was being delivered and then she had to collect Josie from Mo's house. They'd gone swimming. She decided to treat herself to a cup of coffee. As she sat at a small table in the window watching the world go by, she realised she was shaking. She stirred the froth and chocolate powder into her cappuccino and put the spoon down on the napkin beside her cup. A dark stain spread out from the teaspoon and formed an irregular circle. Nina stared at it idly and, without thinking, reached into her bag for a pen. She drew a line around the stain, around and around, until there was a thick band of blue encircling the brown. Then she drew arrows pointing in from the outside of the circle, more and more of them, until she had filled the square of the napkin. She sipped her coffee and looked at what she'd drawn. That'll keep it at bay, she thought, as she began the long walk home.

Her new-found friend from the junk shop rang the doorbell at 5.30, just as arranged. He'd brought his nephew with him to help unload. Nina had explained that she wasn't supposed to lift anything too heavy. He was a gangly spotty youth who wore a baseball cap back to front and trousers so baggy that there seemed no logical reason for them to stay up. It took them a while and a lot of arguing and juggling of position, but they finally managed to get the table up the stairs and into the room.

'Bit of a job that, luv. Hope we 'aven't scratched yer paintwork too bad. There's a load of papers and stuff in the drawer which I didn't bovver to chuck out. See ya then.'

Nina looked at her watch. She wanted to go and admire her table; she wanted to root through its drawer for hidden secrets but the phone rang and she was forced to answer it instead.

'Hi, Nina. It's Beckie. Lotty told me the news and I've been thinking about you such a lot. It's so dreadful. I just thought I'd ring and find out how you are. Sorry I haven't rung before. I guess the radiotherapy's making you feel pretty tired.'

Beckie was a friend from art school days. They spoke at irregular intervals and exchanged Christmas cards.

'No actually, I'm feeling fine thanks, Beckie.'

'No, really, are you? Well I suppose that's good. Perhaps it won't hit you till you've started the chemo. A friend at work had breast cancer a year ago and she had to have chemo – made her really sick and I think her hair fell out too. She's still not back to working full-time.'

Nina could feel her blood pressure rising.

'Yes, well, everyone's different. I have actually started the chemo and so far haven't had any side-effects so I'll just have to hope that lasts.'

'Oh, I didn't realize you'd started it already. That's quick.'

'Well, I think I'm lucky in that I live in an area where the team treating me seem to be very up with the latest research. Something to be grateful for!'

'Grateful! I shouldn't think grateful is a word which figures very largely in your vocabulary at the moment! I should think anger is more what you feel. I mean, you must feel angry at what's happened, don't you?'

'Not really, no,' Nina could answer truthfully. By this stage she was eager to get off the phone. She was becoming increasingly irritated and had no wish to be regaled with the gruesome details of someone else's experience of chemotherapy.

'I have to go now, Beckie. I've got to pick up Josie.'

'Oh, OK. How is poor Josie?'

'She's absolutely fine.'

'Oh, right. Well, I'll ring you again in a week or so. Hope you feel better soon. Bye.'

Nina put the phone down, screamed at the dining-room table that she wasn't feeling ill and grabbed the car keys, slamming the front door behind her as she left.

She was still cross when she arrived on Mo's doorstep.

'Hiya. How's things? How did it go today?' Mo hugged her friend warmly.

'Oh Mum, do we have to go already? We've just started something on the computer. Can't you have a cup of tea?' Josie's voice ricochetted down from upstairs, accompanied by the singsong chorus of Abby and Beth's 'Have lots of cups of tea'.

'It's fine by me,' Mo smiled.

'Hi, darling, nice to see you too. Hi, Abby. Hi, Beth. Half an hour then and we'll have to get home,' Nina shouted up the stairs.

Mo put the kettle on and the two women sat at the kitchen table.

'Beckie rang just as I was leaving. Regaled me with the horror stories of someone she knows who's had cancer. She just wouldn't believe that I was feeling OK. It really pisses me off.'

'I guess it's just people's fear. Like if you're feeling alright and you've had cancer and they're feeling alright, then they might have cancer. Or something like that.'

'You're probably right. I've been thinking about how some people look at me as if I've already got one foot in the grave and I've come to the conclusion it's all because we don't have public executions anymore.'

'What on earth do you mean?' Mo grinned, passing her a mug of tea.

'If you think about it, when people die these days, they do it in hospitals or somewhere removed from everyday life and anyway they don't die as often as they used to. How many children do you know who've died?'

'None, I don't think.'

'Exactly. Most of them live to grow up, they don't die in childhood right, left and centre like they used to.'

'So?'

'So I reckon we've been left with a gap in our culture

somewhere. It's led us to become preoccupied with anything traumatic, gory or life-threatening.'

'Hence all the programmes on the telly.'

'Exactly, we lap it up. Whether it's paramedics scraping people off the roads, child sex abuse, or real-life hospital dramas. Not only do we get coverage of all the latest atrocities around the world but we get in-depth follow-up reports of all the repercussions in terms of human suffering. I mean, when did you last read a newspaper report about all the thousands of women who've survived breast cancer? I rest my case!'

'I'm still not sure I see the connection with the Beckies of this world.'

'It's the same thing. The same cultural preoccupation that leads people to refuse to allow me to be well. I have to be feeling "very drawn" or "just beginning to get my strength back" or about to be made ill from further treatment! Forgive me if I'm being naive, but what possible good can it do me? Where's people's sense of altruism, that's what I want to know.'

'Overridden by their fear?'

'Yeah, you've hit the nail on the head. It's the same old fear that makes people cross to the other side of the road, so frightened of saying the wrong thing that they say nothing at all, so frightened that the trauma is contagious that they have to keep their distance.'

'Listen, you're doing really well, Nina. You carry on refusing to feel ill. They're the ones with the problem, not you. Don't let the bastards get you down!'

Nina smiled; her anger had abated. 'Thanks for listening to me ranting and raving. I can't talk to Malcolm these days.'

'You haven't told me how the chemo went.'

'Oh, it was fine except that they couldn't get any blood. One woman tried and failed. Then she left me sitting there while she went to get someone else to have a go. So that was a bit painful.'

'What was painful, Mum?' asked Josie, who had appeared from upstairs.

'Bat ears!' smiled Nina. 'Just the blood test I had to have today.'

'Abby says can we have some sweets please?' Josie turned to Mo with her politest smile.

'Of course you can, darling. They're in the tin.'

'And then we must go, Josie. It's getting late.'

# Chapter Twenty-Two

Several hours later, after Josie was in bed, Nina remembered the table and its drawer. Malcolm was still out; these days he rarely seemed to come home before she was asleep. She made herself a cup of tea and went upstairs to her studio. The congenial shop owner had dusted the table down for her; apart from a few small scratches on the surface, it was in remarkably good condition. It suited its position against the white wall; out of the murk and dust, returned to a rightful place in life.

Nina pulled out the drawer, put it on the floor and sat down beside it, her back against the sofa bed. It was large and shallow and would, she realized, provide an excellent home for her sketches. There were several old invoices scattered about, handwritten in spidery swoops of ink. It appeared that the Windward family had run a milliner's shop, and quite a successful one at that. They also, it seemed, undertook minor alterations as there were several entries for 'hemming', tucking' and the 'insertion of plackets'.

A couple of small spiders scuttled over some jumbled old newspaper cuttings and escaped over the side of the drawer at one corner. The newsprint was faded brown and the yellowing paper brittle with age. Gingerly Nina unfolded a page; it crackled to reveal a date – 1 March 1932. There was a faint line of pen around one of the paragraphs. She read: *'Owner Wanted for 4000 Hats. Police are seeking an owner for 4000 hats, most of which were found under a railway arch in Manor Place, Hackney.'* According to the article, the owner of the arch had the rest of the hats stashed away in his front room at home awaiting collection by the rightful owners. The Windwards perhaps. There was another small scrap of paper, barely a sentence or two, encircled in jagged edges where the paper had been ripped. *'Hospital Delays – London Doctors Protest'* the headline read. *'The Committee is deeply concerned by the reports which reach it of many patients who have died but whose lives might have been saved had energetic action been taken to secure medical and nursing attention for them at the time when practitioners endeavoured to obtain their admission to hospital.'* That was all.

Then something caught her eye at the very back of the drawer; it was a small wooden box with an engraving of two butterflies on the top. She lifted it out and took it to the light. Carefully, slowly, and with a sense of invading unknown privacies, she opened up the lid. Inside were some old photographs and two small rolled-up scrolls of paper, one tied with a thin pink ribbon, the other with a blue. Minute particles of dust floated in the air around them hanging in the light like dancing snow as Nina held them in her hand. She pulled at the pink ribbon and slowly unrolled the paper. It was in fact two pieces of paper, a birth certificate and a death certificate. The other scroll was the same; she laid them side by side, held them flat, and read. *'Certificate of Birth ... Agnes Mary Windward ... 7th March 1923.' 'Certificate of Birth ... Edward John Windward ... 7th March 1923.'* Twins, thought Nina, as her eyes scanned the other two pieces of paper. *'Certificate of Death ... Agnes Mary Windward ... 3rd March 1927.' 'Certificate of Death ... Edward John Windward ... 3rd March 1927.'* It was hard to decipher the rest of the writing; she couldn't make out the cause of death but assumed that the children must have fallen victim of the hospital delays reported in the newspaper article.

She wasn't sure how long she sat staring at the four stark scraps of paper; they rolled up on themselves immediately she let go as if to guard their sad secret. Her tea, long forgotten, grew cold as her mind rang at the loss of two small children on the same day. She thought of her own two miscarried babies and could only imagine what it must have been like for the Windwards.

Suddenly she remembered the photographs; she took them and spread them out gently on the surface of the table. And there they were. Right before her eyes. Curly-haired, chubby limbed and big-eyed. Sitting angelically on their parents' laps. Laughing mischievously. Crouching intently over a bucket in a small back yard. Flying a kite. Agnes and Edward Windward staring back at her through the brown mist of time-faded images. After a while she carefully replaced the certificates and the photographs in their wooden box and put the drawer back in the table. The pictures though continued to dance in her head and she felt an overwhelming urge to bring Agnes and Edward back to life. Indeed, she would have started to do so if she'd had any clay. As it was, she had to satisfy herself with some rough sketches. She was still engrossed in her drawing when she heard the sound of Malcolm's key in the front door and his footsteps on the stairs. His hand appeared around the door, reaching for the light switch.

'Hello.'

'God, you gave me a fright,' he said, 'I thought you'd left the light on by mistake. What on earth are you doing up at this time? It's past 2 o'clock.'

'I didn't feel like sleeping. Anyway, I could ask you the same question.'

Malcolm looked slightly sheepish.

'Oh, you know. Work. Trying to beat the backlog. I'm whacked. I'm going to have a shower and get to bed. Goodnight.'

'Goodnight.'

Nina placed her sketches on her table, went downstairs, got herself a glass of water and swallowed her chemotherapy pill, climbed into bed and turned out the light. Something told her not to tell Malcolm about Agnes and Edward, and something told her not to ask where he had really been.

She half-woke on a couple of occasions through the night, aware that she was soaked in sweat. Half-asleep, she felt her way to the bathroom. She was having to drink copious quantities of water to counterbalance the effects of the chemotherapy drugs, so she was growing accustomed to these nightly forays.

In the morning she awoke determined to put the finishing touches to her studio so that she could begin work. She now had two subjects for her first piece and they were not going to let her rest. As soon as she returned from walking Josie to school, she phoned the electrician; she needed brighter lighting. After that she began carrying in the reclaimed bricks which had stood in the garden for years waiting for a chance to be useful. With them she built six small walls about 18 inches apart and 12 inches high at right-angles to the wall against which her table stood. On top of these she laid a long length of shelving and then built bricks again until she had a long, low bookcase with a wide top to house her work in progress. Next she unearthed the shelving and brackets she had bought several weeks earlier on one of her shopping jaunts with Lotty. Armed with a Black and Decker drill, a screwdriver, rawlplugs, a bag of screws, and a new sense of urgency, she set to work. Four hours later she realized she was hungry. She stepped back to admire her handiwork. Three rows of shelves adorned the wall above her table. Beside these along the same wall above her homemade bookcase, two shelves slightly further apart stood ready to display her work. The sofa bed with its sky-blue cover and her desk stood against the opposite wall; things were really beginning to take shape.

She made herself a sandwich piled thick with organic salad vegetables, took it and two pieces of fruit upstairs, and began unpacking her art books. Trying to eat at least five pieces of fruit a day was proving quite a challenge. So was giving up cheese. After reading several articles on the links between dairy products and certain cancers, she had decided to give it a go. But cutting out all dairy products was easier said than done. It certainly made sandwiches a lot less interesting. Organic products, too, added pounds to the weekly shopping bill, but she decided that Malcolm could afford it, luckily, and anyway, she reasoned, how do you put a price on life?

She rooted in the loft and found the small easel she used for displaying any photographs she needed to work from; she also found her sculpture stand. Having not been able to afford the best at the time, she took one look at her old friend and remembered its several annoying eccentricities. Still, it was better than nothing. She set the two up beside her table near the window. She was just about to leave the house to collect Josie from school when the phone rang. It was Lotty.

'Hi, sweetie. Just a quick call. Wondered what you were doing for lunch tomorrow.'

'Er ... nothing I don't think. Working on my studio probably.'

'Good. Then you can spare me an hour. I'll be with you about twelve. We can go out.'

'Or I can make us some bread and soup or something.'

'OK. Great. See you then. Gotta go. Bye.'

The rest of that day and the evening passed uneventfully. Unusually Malcolm arrived home before 8 o'clock and was able to help Josie with her maths homework. Nina cooked and they ate in silence. She tried to inquire about work but he seemed reluctant to talk. He also seemed reluctant to know how she was feeling, as he didn't ask. She decided to broach a new subject.

'I don't think Charlie's very well. He's not been eating and he seems to sleep nearly all the time. He also looks really stiff when he moves.'

'Probably just old age. We'll all end up the same,' Malcolm chuckled. It was the nearest he came to cracking a joke.

I wish, thought Nina, the ever-present knot of fear stirring in her throat.

'Do you think I ought to take him to the vet?'

'Not unless you think he's in pain,' Malcolm paused, obviously searching for the right thing to say. 'But take him if it'll make you feel better.'

'It'll take more than that to make me feel better.'

'You know what I mean,' replied Malcolm with a hint of impatience.

He got up from the table and began clearing the plates. Nina went to check on Charlie. She found him in his usual place, curled up on the uncharacteristically uncluttered sofa bed. He half-opened one eye at her approach and closed it again. She could barely see him breathing. Quietly she got her camera from her desk and took several close-up pictures of him. He hardly stirred. She stroked him, wished him goodnight and left him.

The next morning, after Malcolm and Josie had left

the house, she found him in exactly the same place. She looked at him long and hard, not wanting to believe what she saw. She looked again. There was no sign of movement. Lying in virtually the same position as the night before, he seemed peaceful. She reached out a tentative hand and touched his back; he was cold and stiff. Instantaneous tears welled up, spilled over and splashed onto his fur in little silver circles. He had been a loyal companion over the years and, apart from feeding him, she had paid him little enough attention over the past few months. She wished she could make it up to him now. But it was too late.

She found an old sheet and wrapped it round his lifeless body. She was going to bury him in the garden but then decided to wait in case Josie wanted to see him. She found a box, gently laid him in it and left him by the back door. The sense of loss which then flooded over her was totally disproportionate to the place Charlie had occupied in her life. She cried for her failing marriage; she cried for the child she couldn't relate to; she cried for her family's inability to support or understand her; she cried for her buried creativity; and she cried because she had cancer. When Lotty knocked on the door two hours later, she was a complete mess.

'Good God, what's happened? You look awful!'

'Oh, it's nothing really. Charlie died this morning, that's all. It's silly of me, I know, but I can't seem to stop crying.'

'Well, it just so happens that I've got something which might cheer you up a bit. Wait there.'

Lotty disappeared in the direction of her car. What reappeared looked like a large headless package on legs. 'Never let it be said that I don't treat you,' said the label on the package.

'Happy Unbirthday!' said Lotty, beaming. 'Happy Rest of Your Life! Whatever! Just as long as you use it.' Lotty dumped her enormous parcel at Nina's feet just inside the front door.

'What on earth is it?'

'Well I can think of one way to find out!'

And then it dawned on Nina. 'Oh Lotty, you haven't!' She started ripping off large strips of wrapping paper. 'Oh brilliant! I don't believe it! You have!'

She put her arms round her friend and hugged her tightly. Beside them, leaning against the wall, was a brand spanking new, state-of-the-art, easily adjustable, lightweight, collapsible sculpture stand.

'You must be telepathic. When you rang yesterday, I'd just got my old one out of the attic and I was just remembering all the things that were wrong with it. But this one is fantastic, it must have cost a bomb. Thanks so much. I can't wait to get started. Come and see what I've done with the room.'

'Love to, sweetie, but first things first. The old caffeine levels are pitifully low. Any chance of a quick top-up before we go any further?'

'Of course, sorry. I've got some real coffee all ready.'

Lotty was impressed with the new studio. Over bread and soup, Nina told her all about the Woodwards and their table, about Agnes and Edward and how they were going to be her first subjects.

'Sounds to me like you're finally on the road again, girl. Well done!'

'But what if I can't do it, Lotty? What if I'm rubbish?'

'What if you are? What's the worst that can happen? Anyway it's the doing it that matters. Remember the book? What does it say? *It's far harder and more painful to be a blocked artist than it is to do the work.'* Or something like that. So go for it!'

'I know. You're right. I will. I am. That's one more good thing about cancer; it certainly alters your definition of scary!'

'Yes, I imagine it does.'

When Lotty left to return to work, Nina carried her new stand upstairs and set it up in the window. The top cranked up and down easily, it could be spun round or held firmly in position, and the legs folded for carrying. She packed away her old stand and carried it to the bottom of the stairs. Then she rang a firm she knew and ordered some clay. Now there was no turning back. That done, it was time to collect Josie from school. They were about half way home when Nina decided to break the bad news.

'I'm afraid I've got something sad to tell you.'

'Has the cancer come back?' Josie blurted without pause for breath. 'We're not going to have to cancel another holiday are we?'

'No, darling, it's nothing like that. I'm afraid Charlie died today. I found him this morning and he wasn't breathing.'

Josie's face showed no emotion. 'Where is he now?'

'I've wrapped him up and put him in a box in case you wanted to see him before we bury him.'

Josie walked a few steps in silence. 'Could I cut him open and see what he looks like inside? You know, dissect him?'

For a moment, Nina was horrified and lost for words. This strange child of hers never ceased to amaze her.

'Well, I hadn't really thought of doing that, darling. I mean it wouldn't really be very nice for poor Charlie would it?'

'But he's dead isn't he? He won't know anything about it. Oh please, Mum, it'd be cool.'

Nina had visions of Charlie's peace being shattered

for eternity. She saw him lying in small pieces on the kitchen table, reeking of decay. She couldn't bear it.

'No, darling, I'm sorry. I think we'll just bury him in the garden. You can help me do that if you like.'

'Do what you want, I don't care. You're such a spoilsport, Mum.' Josie's face set in sullen defiance as it often did these days. She stomped off a few paces ahead of her mother. When they got indoors she stormed upstairs, flinging her school bag down behind her as she went. Nina heard a door slam and loud music. She went into the kitchen and made herself a cup of tea wondering if after all she should allow her faithful cat to be cut into small pieces. But she felt unequal to the experience and decided to leave things as they were.

A little later she went out into the garden on her own and dug a large hole under the lilac. A solitary thrush was bursting its lungs with song. The ground was hard with weeks of winter and it took her a long time. She wondered whether her arm would swell up in retribution but decided that Charlie was worth the risk. It was getting quite dark by the time the hole was big enough. She called Josie to ask if she would like to come and take part but was met with a perfunctory 'No'. So, still alone, she carried the rigid body and laid it under the lilac tree and shovelled earth on top of it.

When she had finished she was panting slightly and unsure whether to say anything out loud or whether just to go indoors. It was cold and she could see her breath in the light from the rooms inside. Feeling slightly foolish, she half-whispered 'Thank you, Charlie, for being such a good friend for such a long time.' And then she went in. Josie managed to sulk for the rest of the evening. Even Malcolm's early arrival home for the second day in succession did little to alleviate the gloom.

211

He responded to the news of Charlie's demise by muttering that it was probably for the best. Nina knew it would take a few days for the dust to settle.

# Chapter Twenty-Three

Before she knew it, it was time for another dose of chemotherapy. Each visit followed a horribly similar pattern; waiting, surviving a blood test, a lot more waiting, having a cannula inserted in the back of her hand, and finally being injected with the chemotherapy drugs themselves. The three of them, she discovered, cyclophosphamide, methotrexate and fluorouracil, were called 'CMF' by those in the know. Two of these were injected. One, she wasn't sure which, produced a peculiar and almost instantaneous tingling sensation around the vagina which lasted for several seconds, not wholly unpleasureable it had to be said, a fact which the depressing Bacup leaflet failed to relay.

In fact, the cancer charity Bacup's information sheets were all unremittingly gloomy. They listed every possible side-effect of chemotherapy ranging from sickness and diarrhoea to mouth ulcers and blurred vision, from infertility and hair loss to reduction in bone marrow and liver failure. Whilst reassuring their anxious readers that each person's reaction was unique and some people had very few side-effects, this catalogue of potential disasters did little to reassure.

Nina had determined early on not to feel ill. She decided instead to take it as it came and, as far as she could, to expect nothing bad. Miraculously it worked. Apart from the odd cold sweat, a few days of constipation and the monthly trauma of the blood test (surely if that was all they did all day, they should be better at it), it was fine. Not a barrel of laughs but not nearly as bad as the endless well-meaning individuals like Beckie had predicted.

Her old friend, fear, however, the frog in her throat, did manage to gorge himself shamelessly each fortnight on the visits to the hospital, causing her chest to tighten, her vision to blacken and her legs to start shaking. When this happened, her best weapon of defence, she found, was work. And it was going well. She would race back from the hospital and head straight for her studio where Edward and Agnes would be waiting.

It was ten days since the clay had been delivered and Nina had spent every spare moment bringing the children to life. It was not easy. The photographs were old and faded. Even a magnifying glass could only produce the haziest of features; soon her easel was covered in blown-up snapshots. As she worked, the days passed and the bond between her and the children grew. She finished a maquette in a few days. She decided to model two figures in terracotta a little under life size, crouched down either side of a bucket, deeply intent on whatever lay within. The piece would be sculpted in three separate parts so that she could play with the relative positions when it was finished. She had worked a lot with life forms in the past but never, she realized, with children. The affinity with them which swept over her in the days and weeks that followed amazed her. It was the first time she had sculpted since becoming a mother, and a new-found compassion seemed to seep from her finger tips.

While she worked, there was a sort of peace. Some days she would play music, some days she would work in silence. Some days she would look at the sofa bed and think of Charlie. Some days she would wonder what Malcolm did till late into every night, and whether she really wanted to know. Some days she would remember Josie when she was Agnes and Edward's age. She remembered Lyme Regis and red wellies and spilt milk. Some days she would walk by the river and feed the ducks and watch the children, storing up new images for the future.

Much to her surprise and sooner than she'd expected, Lotty's words came true and she found herself, bolstered by Edward and Agnes, setting off to hospital for the last time. When she emerged three hours later, she wasn't sure what to do. Should she run, jump, scream, get drunk, go on holiday, indulge in retail therapy or have a slap-up meal? As it was, it was time to pick Josie up from school so she had to put all of these possibilities on hold.

It was that evening that Malcolm suddenly asked, 'Do you think we could get a babysitter for Thursday night?'

Nina smiled at the 'royal we'.

'Maybe. I could try. Why?'

'I've booked a table at Gimigiano's. I tried for Friday or Saturday but they were full. I thought we could go out.'

Nina was gobsmacked. She couldn't remember the last time Malcolm had made such a suggestion.

'What's the special occasion? Did I miss someone's birthday?'

'No occasion. I just thought we'd go out but if you'd rather not...'

'No, no,' Nina interrupted, 'I think it's a novel idea. Great. Let's do it! We could even celebrate the end of my chemo.'

'Oh, of course. Today was the last day? How was it?'

'Oh marvellous, marvellous,' Nina smiled back at him with more than a hint of sarcasm.

'Well at least it's over. You don't have to think about it any more.'

Nina sighed. If only. What Malcolm meant was that he didn't have to think about it anymore.

There were two days in which to find a babysitter. She was a little out of practice. However, the teenage daughter of a neighbour further down the street was always in need of extra pocket money and only too happy to oblige. Nina didn't see Malcolm on either of the two intervening evenings. He seemed more edgy than usual on the brief occasions that their paths crossed during the early morning routine. With hindsight it was not hard to see why. Thursday night arrived and they got changed without conversation. Malcolm seemed to be paying even greater attention than usual to the minutiae of his appearance. He had arranged for a taxi to pick them up so that they could both drink with impunity, despite the fact that Nina hadn't touched a drop of alcohol since day one of the nightmare. On this particular night, though, she didn't argue; something told her that she might need a drink before it was all over. Malcolm seemed agitated, like a swimmer treading water and fearing for the worst. They sat in the back of the taxi in silence.

The restaurant was small but always busy. Malcolm ordered a large whisky and soda for himself and a glass of mineral water for Nina; they found a table by the bar, sipped their drinks and studied the menu. After they had ordered, Nina became absorbed in the faces and half-heard conversations around her. It was several seconds before she realized that Malcolm was trying to say something. He was shifting from one side of his chair to the other, continually adjusting the knot of his tie and trying to clear his throat.

'Nina, we need to talk,' he finally blurted out as the colour rose in his neck.

'OK.' Nina spoke quietly and calmly. It was as if she knew what he was going to say before he said it.

'I ... er... I ... I ... well, that is ... I mean ... I have something to tell you,' Malcolm struggled on. 'The fact is that ... there isn't an easy way to say this ... the fact is that I've been having an affair for nearly nine months now.'

The words finally out, he slumped back in his chair.

'I know,' said Nina quietly.

There were a few seconds' silence.

'I don't understand.' Malcolm looked astonished. 'What do you mean, you know?'

'I mean that I know and that I have known for quite a long time. What I don't know is what you intend to do about it.'

Nina felt remarkably calm. As she spoke, the realization dawned on her that she had indeed known for a long time but hadn't admitted it to herself. Now it was out in the open, she felt a great sense of relief. Malcolm, on the other hand, seemed more agitated than ever. He'd recovered from his initial shock at her response and now looked as if he were flailing about in increasingly mountainous seas.

'I ... er ... I don't really know ... I mean I think perhaps we ... I mean, I'll break it all off if that's what you'd like me to do.'

At this point the waiter arrived to tell them that their table was ready. Nina picked up her handbag, her glass and the remains of her marriage and followed him into the body of the restaurant. She was pleased to see that they had been given a table in the corner at the far end. The bottle of wine that Malcolm had ordered was waiting. When the waiter offered to fill Nina's glass, she didn't refuse.

'Who is she? Do I know her?'

217

Their starters arrived. Nina tucked into hers without waiting for an answer. To her surprise she found she was ravenously hungry. Malcolm was obviously not. He chased small amounts of food around his plate with his fork, staring miserably into the centre of the table.

'Er ... no, you don't. She joined the company about 18 months ago. She's my PA.'

'Amongst other things,' smiled Nina with no hint of malice. 'What's her name?'

'Is that really relevant? I mean, do you really need to know?'

'Well, if you're going to spend the rest of your life with her, then I think it would be helpful if I knew what to call her.'

'Her name's Patricia,' said Malcolm gloomily.

Nina said nothing while she finished her mango and avocado salad. It was Malcolm who spoke next.

'I hadn't actually got as far as thinking about spending the rest of my life with her.'

'What exactly had you got as far as thinking then, Malcolm?'

'I'm not quite sure. I mean I didn't expect you to react like this.'

'How did you expect me to react?'

At this point a bevy of waiters arrived with their main courses and vegetables. Nina sat back and sipped her wine. She was enjoying the treat and felt as if she were watching the scene being played out on a stage. The plot was hardly original. Malcolm was speaking again.

'I mean I don't want to hurt you, more than I have done already, that is. I know you've been through a lot this last year.'

'So have you by the sound of it!'

Malcolm was silent. Nina decided not to waste the

food. As she ate, she glanced across the room and caught sight of a couple she guessed were in their mid-fifties. They were not speaking and neither one looked particularly happy. At least, it seemed, she and Malcolm would be saved that.

'For God's sake, Nina, say something,' Malcolm burst out suddenly. 'Shout at me. Tell me I've been a bastard. Something. How can you be so calm?'

Nina looked him directly in the eyes. 'Have you thought about Josie?' He avoided her gaze.

'Yes ... I mean, no ... I mean, I don't want to hurt her.'

'Don't you think it's a little late for that?' Nina heard the edge in her voice harden. She felt guilty that she had somehow failed her daughter by not holding her marriage together more successfully.

'In fact, I think it's a little late for a lot of things that might have happened differently. But they haven't. So we have to decide where we go from here and what we do about Josie.'

Malcolm, who hated waste of any kind, gave up the unequal struggle to do any sort of justice to his food. He put his knife and fork together and pushed his plate away from him.

'What do you want me to do?'

'No, Malcolm. No. This time that's not good enough.' The old irritations Nina had felt for so many years B.C. came rolling back. The tide was turning.

'This time it's up to you. You have to take responsibility for the future. The time for trying to please is past. This is life and it's not a rehearsal. No more running away.'

A solitary waiter arrived and asked if they'd like to see the dessert menu. They declined but ordered coffee.

'I need the gents. I won't be long.'

219

The wine was beginning to go to Nina's head and she felt faintly dizzy. Slowly it was dawning on her that she was standing on the edge of yet another precipice. She cast her mind back a few months to the cliff she'd stood on in her hospital room while she waited for the Prophet of Doom. She was tired. How much more was there to come? But then she remembered Agnes and Edward. She was proud of them. They would be fired by now and she would be able to collect them soon. With a supreme effort of will she focused on what she knew she had to do. Malcolm sat down again opposite her. The coffee had arrived.

'You tell me what you want me to do and I'll do it.' What might have felt magnanimous to him sounded simply limp to Nina but it gave her the courage to continue.

'Alright. If I must. I think we should get a divorce. I presume you would move out and do whatever it is you're going to do with Patricia. Or is it Pat for short? I'll stay in the house, unless we can't afford it, in which case I'll have to move too. I guess Josie would stay with me because it's near to school and she could see you at the weekends. We'll have to talk to her together. Perhaps we should ask her what she wants to do.'

'God, you sound as if you've had all this planned for months.'

'The strange thing is, Malcolm, that I think I probably have.'

They were both exhausted by the time they walked through the front door. Nina paid the babysitter, who was engrossed in some romantic comedy on the television and obviously reluctant to leave. Malcolm poured himself a large whisky and collapsed into an armchair. Nina poured herself a large glass of water, took her chemotherapy pill and went upstairs to run a bath. As she closed the bathroom door, she heard Malcolm's hushed tones on his mobile phone. She awarded herself no prizes for guessing who he was talking to.

# Chapter Twenty-Four

It seemed strange to carry on as normal the following morning when the whole world had shifted for the second time in the same year. Malcolm disappeared off to work without a word.

Nina, meanwhile, took Josie to school and then went for a long walk by the river. She tried to piece together the new jigsaw and make a picture of the future. Had she not lived through the previous ten months, she would have been terrified. As it was, there seemed little room for any more fear. She looked deep into the quietly flowing water and thought about her marriage. All she'd ever really been to Malcolm was someone to stand at his side at corporate functions and be a housekeeper and mother at home. She tried to fathom out her feelings. Was she sad, relieved, excited, tired? Shocked was the one thing she knew she was not. But she was worried, though. Worried about Josie and how she would react; worried about the practicalities of divorce and how she would manage; worried about her capacity to be a single parent; worried about living on her own again after so many years. But if she was honest, the prospect also fizzed with possibilities. Malcolm would no longer cast a shadow over her creativity; she would no longer need to live the lie of her marriage; her weekends would be free; she could even get a dog!

On her return home, she felt brave enough to test the

water. So she rang Lotty. 'Hi. It's me. Is this a good time or are you very busy?'

'Hi sweetie. No, it's fine. I've just got myself a cup of coffee and I'm sitting here contemplating me navel. How are you doing now the chemo's finished?'

'Fine. Actually that's not the only thing that's finished, which is partly why I'm ringing. Malcolm told me last night that he's been having an affair for the last nine months.'

'Bloody hell! Not Malcolm! I don't believe it! God, after all you've been through, too. His timing leaves a lot to be desired, I'll say that for him.'

'I think his timing speaks volumes, actually. He just hasn't been able to face what's been happening. The strange thing is that I knew about it all the time. It wasn't hard to see. His horror of the whole cancer thing and his need to escape, the endless late nights, his trips away for work. You didn't need to be a genius.'

'You sound horribly calm. Why aren't you ranting and raving? I know I would be.'

'I don't know really. Don't think I can summon up the necessary energy.'

'Have you told Josie yet?'

'No, he only told me last night and then disappeared off to work first thing this morning. I think we need to talk to her both together so that will be a little treat in store for the weekend! No prizes for perfect parenting here!'

'Now don't start that. That's one cudgel you definitely do not need to beat yourself about the head with. You've given up body and soul for that child for nearly eleven years with very little thanks, if you don't mind me saying so. And I could say the same for what you've done for Malcolm. Have you ever wondered why it's taken you this long to get your sculpture stand out of the attic?'

Nina was silent.

'Hello, are you still there?'

'Yes, I'm here.'

'Do you want me to come over? Or do you want to meet somewhere to drown your sorrows?'

'Yeah, that'd be good. I could meet you somewhere halfway. I don't think I'm going to get a lot of work done today. I just need some time to absorb what's going on, and to work out how to speak to Malcolm this evening – if he comes home this evening, of course. If he can drag himself away from Patricia!'

'Is that her name? Who is she?'

'Oh some bimbo at work. I don't know her. Probably in her twenties with long blonde hair and legs up to her armpits. I only hope he's got the stamina!'

'Ah, good, I detect a hint of anger.'

'No you don't! Well, yes, actually, you probably do.'

'Well, you have every right to be angry. Bloody men, waste of space!'

There was the sound of a voice in the background.

'Listen, someone's just come in. We'll talk more over lunch. I'll meet you at that wine bar, you know, where we met once before. Gino's or Dino's or whatever it's called. About 12.30?'

'OK. See you then. Bye.'

Nina achieved very little during what was left of the morning. She took a cup of what purported to be a coffee substitute, although it bore no resemblance whatever to coffee, up to her studio and sat on the sofa bed staring into space. Her mind wandered back over the past months and she looked for Malcolm in all that she'd been through. It wasn't hard to picture what had happened. The new PA working late to impress her boss. She was young. Malcolm was flattered. He'd taken her out for a meal. There'd been an office party. It had been too late to get home. Nina didn't know whether to smile or cry. Her hiking boots got heavier as each new mountain rose before her. But the miracle of miracles, she realized, was that she was still climbing.

Lunch was a bonus. The two women laughed a lot and drank a bottle of champagne at Lotty's insistence, 'To celebrate your future!' They planned holidays while Nina tried to get her head around the notion that Josie wouldn't always be living with her.

'My God, my mother! I've only just thought of her! God knows what she'll say! She'll be horrified. A divorce in the family. Unheard of. I'll be persona non grata for the next ten years or more! She'll kill me!'

'Nina,' Lotty's tone was sotto voce, 'I really don't think that your mother is the most important consideration at this moment in time.'

'I know, but how am I going to tell her?'

'What about "Hi Mum, just rang to let you know that Malcolm and I are getting divorced"?'

'I'll have to break it to her more gently than that or she'll have a heart attack!'

'Look, Nina, my friend, this is your life and the only way you're going to live it to the full is to take responsibility for doing what you know is right for you. You haven't even mentioned trying to make it work. Have you thought about that? Are you sure you want a divorce?'

'Yes, I am. I think I've known for a long time that it wasn't working out, but I just wasn't brave enough to admit it to myself or to do anything about it. That was B.C. – A.D., it's taken all my energy just to keep going.'

'I'm sorry ... B.C? A.D?'

'Before cancer and after diagnosis. Also I didn't want to hurt Josie.'

'I 'spose you've considered that you might be hurting

her more by struggling on in an unhappy relationship? I bet she knows other children with divorced parents.'

'Oh, she does. Several of them. In fact she once told me she felt the odd one out because we weren't divorced!'

'Well, there you are then.'

'I know. It's just that it all feels so hard. I'm not sure I've got the energy to go through all this as well as everything else.'

'You have. I know you have. You've got this far and you're doing great. You've already started on the road, this is just an extra hill to climb. But climbing it is going to be a hell of a lot easier than going back, I'm sure of it.'

'Oh, Lotty I wish I had your faith in my future.'

'It's easy. What was it someone said? "Undoubtedly we become what we envisage" or something like that. So get envisaging, girl, and you'll get there!'

Nina approached the school gates that afternoon with an unexpected spring in her step. For a few heady hours, she felt like she could take on the world. Wasn't she the woman who had just lived through her worst nightmare? Everything else was chickenfeed. It didn't last, of course. By the time she had been at home with Josie for a couple of hours, she wasn't sure of anything. How she felt, how to speak to Malcolm, how to tell Josie, how to get from one day to the next. As Josie was safely tucked away upstairs behind a closed door, she decided to risk breaking the news to Mo.

'Hi. Sorry we can't get to the phone right now. Leave a message and we'll get back to you.'

So cosy, Nina thought as she left a brief message, the collective 'we'. Happy families. Where did hers go? She went to make herself another cup of tea and was reminded of another occasion when all she had been able to do was make herself tea. If life carried on in a similar vein, she decided, an option in tea shares might be well worth considering. She was not looking forward to the evening.

Malcolm's key turned in the lock more tentatively than usual, shortly after 7 o'clock. Clearly he had decided to face the music as it was quite early in the evening.

'Hello. How are you?'

'Oh marvellous, marvellous,' Nina retorted. 'Exactly how do you expect me to be after last night's little revelation?'

'I don't know,' Malcolm replied gloomily. 'Look, Nina, I've been thinking. I don't want to hurt you. I think we should give it another go. I'll tell Pattie it's all over and we'll carry on as before. There's no need for divorces and moving houses.'

'Ah, but the trouble is, I think there is, Malcolm. Even if we could carry on "as before" as you put it, which I don't think is possible anyway, I've decided that I don't want to. I want more from life and I can't afford to wait around before trying to find it. We none of us have the luxury of a guaranteed tomorrow. If this last year's taught me anything, it's taught me that. So we have to live for today and that's what I'm going to try and do.'

'But we could live for today together. If we split up, it will make things very hard for Josie.'

'Well, you should have thought of that a whole lot earlier, don't you think?'

Malcolm slumped onto a kitchen chair. It was the first time in months that he had not poured himself a drink and gone straight upstairs to change. Clearly events were taking on a momentum he had not planned for.

'I don't blame you Malcolm,' said Nina more gently. 'I know this last year has been really hard for you too. I can see how much of a threat the whole cancer thing has been. We haven't talked about it, but I'm sure it's brought back all sorts of memories about your mother. I know that you've desperately needed to escape. Even the computer screen wasn't big enough, was it? So I'm not surprised that you looked elsewhere.'

She paused, waiting for a response. Malcolm said nothing so she continued. 'I'm sorry, but I think it's time to move on. And we'll just have to cope with the harm it does to Josie as we go along.'

She was also sorry, although she didn't say it, that Malcolm was unable, even now on the brink to which he'd brought himself, to face up to all that the last year had meant. Before either of them could speak again, there was the rumble of feet on the stairs.

'Hi, Dad. You're home early. What's the matter?'

'Nothing, darling, just thought I'd come home and see you.' Malcolm smiled weakly.

'Now's as good a time as any,' cut in Nina, seeing that Malcolm was about to run away. 'Josie, darling,' she continued, 'Daddy and I have something to tell you.'

'Oh Mum, there's always something! Don't tell me, you've got to go into hospital again.'

'No, no, it's nothing like that.'

'Daddy's got to go into hospital, then.'

'No, no one's going into hospital.'

'What is it, then?'

Nina glanced at Malcolm to see if he was prepared to take up the reins but his legs were crossed, his arms were folded and he was staring resolutely at the floor in front of him. Nina took a deep breath and continued.

'Give me a chance, darling, and I'll tell you.'

Josie plonked herself in a chair next to her father, folded her arms like him and pouted.

'It's not easy to explain. You know Daddy and I both love you very much.'

228

Josie was staring at the table. She didn't move.

'Well, it's just that we've decided not to live in the same house any more.'

There was a silence while Josie hugged her folded arms tighter into her body.

'What do you mean?' she asked looking at last from one parent to the other.

'I mean that we've decided to separate.'

'But why?'

'Well, for all sorts of reasons really,' Nina glanced at Malcolm, who continued to stare at the floor.

Before she had the chance to say any more, Josie exploded. 'It's all your fault, Mum! Why do you have to keep spoiling things? You're always leaving us!'

Nina was taken completely off guard by the ferocity of her daughter's outburst. Malcolm found his voice and intervened, 'Josie, darling, that's not exactly fair.'

'Yes it is,' Josie's eyes were wild with anger and her voice was becoming more and more high-pitched. 'It was Mummy's fault she got cancer. It was her fault we had to cancel our holiday. She left us to manage on our own and now she's making you get divorced!'

'No, she is not,' said Malcolm firmly. 'Mummy is not making us do anything. If you want to blame someone, blame me,' he added miserably.

'I don't want to blame you. You haven't done anything!'

Malcolm seemed at a loss for words.

'Josie, darling,' said Nina in a voice wavering with emotion, 'this isn't anybody's fault. It's just...'

'Yes it is! It's yours! It's your fault! And I hate you!'

This was too much for Nina, who sunk backwards into a chair, tears welling up as she absorbed the brunt of Josie's pent-up passion. Josie herself stormed out of the kitchen, thundered up the stairs and slammed her bedroom door shut behind her.

229

'Do you think I should go after her?' Malcolm asked.

'No, leave her. Give her a chance to calm down a bit. Then we'll try to talk to her again. I don't think I can take much more right now.'

'Do you want a drink?'

'No thanks. Just an end to all this pain.'

Malcolm looked as if he was about to say something but stopped himself. He poured himself a whisky and soda and crept upstairs to change. Nina was left, head on hands, tears dropping slowly, rhythmically, onto the kitchen table. The phone rang and made her jump. She blew her nose and answered. It was Mo.

'Hi! I got your message. Is this a good time or not?'

'Oh Mo. It's a long story. I'm not brilliant just at the moment, I'm afraid.'

'Why? What's happened?' Mo's voice was suddenly edged in panic.

'Nothing too ghastly,' said Nina quickly. 'We're all alright, well, sort of. Malcolm told me last night that he's been having an affair for months and we've just talked to Josie about how we're going to live apart for a bit and she's just gone off in a terrible state having yelled how much she hates me and it's all my fault!'

'Oh Nina, I don't believe it! Oh how awful! How unfair! I'm sure she didn't mean it, she's just very upset. Did you tell her that Malcolm's been seeing someone else?'

'No, how could I? I couldn't load all that on to her as well as everything else.'

'No, I suppose not. Oh Nina, I don't know what to say. It's just not fair that all this should be happening to you now after all you've been through over the past few months.'

'Life's a bugger, isn't it? But, you know, it's not all bad. At least I know what I want to do. I mean, it's not as if this has come as any surprise. What I hadn't bargained for was Josie's reaction, I just don't know how to cope with it.'

'Give her time. I'm sure she'll see reason. I'm sure she doesn't really believe that it's all your fault and remember, love and hate are always two sides of the same coin.'

'Thanks, Mo. Look I can't go on talking now. I need to sort out what's happening upstairs. Could we meet on Monday? Have a proper chat then.'

'Yes, of course. Why don't you come here for a coffee? When you've dropped Josie off at school?'

'OK. Thanks.'

'See you then. I'll be thinking of you over the weekend. Bye.'

'Bye.'

Nina put the phone down and went to stand at the bottom of the stairs. She could hear voices and knew Malcolm and Josie were talking. She crept up the stairs and sat on the top step outside Josie's bedroom not knowing whether to go in or not. She felt very alone.

'But what's going to happen to me?' Josie's voice was pregnant with the sobs she was trying to suppress. 'Where will I live? I don't want to move, what about my things? Where's my bedroom going to be?'

'Darling,' Malcolm's voice was soft and measured as if in this way he could contain the emotional fall-out. 'Nothing is going to happen in a hurry. We'll discuss all those things with you and we won't make you do anything or go anywhere you don't want to go.'

'But why can't you just stay together?'

There was a silence while her father struggled to find an answer. 'We just can't, darling. It's not that we don't love each other and it's certainly not that we don't love you. It's just that it would be better for all of us if we didn't live in the same house anymore.'

'It wouldn't be better for me,' Josie snapped. Malcolm was silent. Nina took the opportunity to venture to the door.

'We'll do our absolute best to make things as easy as possible for you, darling,' she said. 'You never know, it might be fun to have two homes and two bedrooms!'

'Oh great! So I get to be a suitcase kid like in the book! No thanks!'

'Only if that's what you want.'

'So who's going to live here? And who's going to move out?'

'We haven't discussed all the details yet, sweetheart. There's plenty of time for that. We need to think everything through very carefully.'

Nina listened to him, unsure whether it was himself or Josie he was trying to convince. Josie looked from one to the other of her parents.

'Is that it, then? Because I was in the middle of something on the computer.'

'Yes, that's it,' said Nina, 'We'll talk about it more later. I'm going to cook us some supper. We can all eat together. Would you like that?'

Josie shrugged as she got off her bed and moved towards her desk. Her parents left the room as the weight of the world settled quietly around her young shoulders.

# Chapter Twenty-Five

The weekend was not easy. Malcolm and Nina walked on eggshells both in respect of each other and of Josie. Josie spent much of her time pretending that nothing had happened while Malcolm tried to come to terms with the idea of divorce. Nina suspected that he'd hoped she would beg him to return to the family fold. When she didn't, he seemed quite lost. In fact, of the three, Nina was the only one to feel a sense of purpose in the trauma. Bleeding as she was from her daughter's onslaught, she knew in her heart that she was doing the right thing.

Ironically, they passed quite a pleasant family weekend; they went on family walks, ate family meals and even managed a game of Rummikub. It was almost as if the value of what they were losing had crystallized to be celebrated in a final swansong. Sunday evening came before they knew it, and Nina was about to have a bath and go to bed. She resolved to take the opportunity of a few moments' peace with Malcolm.

'Have you talked to Patricia or Pattie or whatever it is you call her since Friday?'

'Only briefly. Why do you ask?'

'Well, I wondered what you and she were planning for the future.'

'To be honest, Nina, we haven't planned anything. Things are moving so fast, I'm not sure where I stand.'

'What exactly did you expect, Malcolm?'

'I don't know really. But I certainly didn't expect you to be so amenable about it all.'

'I don't see that there's much point in my being anything else. Are we going to tell Josie?'

'About Pattie do you mean?'

'Yes.'

'Do you think we should?'

'Well, that rather depends on what you intend doing, doesn't it? I mean, if "Pattie" is going to be a permanent fixture in your life, then it would be a trifle tricky not to mention her to Josie, wouldn't it?'

'I suppose so.'

'Don't be ridiculous, Malcolm, of course it would!'

Malcolm hesitated. 'Do you think we could not say anything just for the moment. Until I've sorted out what's going to happen, I mean.'

'Well, OK. but don't leave it too long. I don't think I'm prepared to lie to Josie forever. It seems I'm already sufficiently in her bad books without adding insult to injury.'

'Oh she'll come round. She didn't mean what she said.'

'Maybe she didn't, but that doesn't alter the fact that she said it, and it doesn't take away the hurt.'

'I know, and I'm sorry.'

'Anyway, I'm going to have a bath. Goodnight.'

'Goodnight ... and Nina, I'm sorry for everything.'

'I know you are,' she said.

The following morning dawned bright and blue. In fact the whole of the south of England was enjoying an Indian summer and the early autumn warmth fell like a welcome blanket on the troubled waters of the Hayes household. Malcolm left for work as usual and Nina delivered Josie to school. Josie's attitude towards her mother had softened over the weekend; nothing more had been said on the subject of the future. Nina sat in the sun on Mo's front doorstep, waiting for her to return from the school run. She closed her eyes and lifted her head to absorb the energy-ridden light. It wasn't long before a car drew up and a rather flustered Mo staggered up the path under the weight of several assorted carrier bags.

'Hi! Sorry I'm late. The traffic was awful and then I had to get some milk and some bread. Have you been here ages?'

'No, not long. And anyway it's lovely sitting in the sunshine.'

'Give us a hug!' said Mo coming to a halt in a sea of plastic bags and opening her arms wide. 'I can't believe what's happening to you. Don't you ever ask where it's all going to end?'

'Not if I can help it! Someone might tell me!'

Mo laughed. 'Come in and I'll put the kettle on.'

The two women walked into the kitchen. Nina leaned against the work surface and watched Mo as she began to clear away the aftermath of breakfast.

'So tell me exactly what he said. Where were you when he told you?'

'We were out. Gimigiano's. Malcolm's suggestion.'

'Blimey, I bet you smelt a rat when he suggested going out. When was the last time he did that?'

'Can't remember. Somewhat naively I thought we might be celebrating the end of my chemo. More fool me!'

'Oh, Nina. It's just not fair!'

'Don't worry, it's not that bad. In some ways it's a relief if I'm honest. It's taken the pressure off me to do something about it. My marriage I mean.'

'I knew things hadn't been too brilliant but I didn't know they were that bad.'

'Well, there didn't seem much point in talking about

it if I wasn't prepared to take any action. Anyway, I've always felt too guilty about Josie.'

'How is she? You said she yelled at you the other night.'

'Oh yes, something along the lines of "It's all your fault and I hate you Mummy!"'

'You know she didn't mean it, don't you? She's probably just very upset and angry about everything and you're the safest person to direct it all at.'

'Yes, I know that objectively. She's been so subdued over the whole cancer thing. Hasn't ever said anything, never asked any questions after the initial ones. Bit like Malcolm, now I come to think of it. So I guess all that pent-up emotion had to erupt at some stage. It's still pretty hard to hear though.'

'Of course it is. You must feel so hurt. Especially as none of it is your fault.'

'Ah, but it takes two to tango.'

'Yes, but ... where was Malcolm? What did he have to say while all this was going on?'

'Oh, you know Malcolm, hardly forthcoming at the best of times. I think he really is not waving but drowning at the moment. Maybe that's why I'm not angry at him; I almost feel sorry for him.'

'Well, you're a better person than me. I'd be bloody furious.'

'I don't think you would, not if you'd been through what I've been through the last few months. Being so full of fear all the time tends to drain you of emotional energy. I haven't got enough left to be angry. Also, I need to hang on to what I want. For me. Not me as dishwasher, ironer, mother and wife. Not me who loses sight of the person I am. I have to try and stick to my dream and I need to save all my energy for that.'

'So there's no chance you'd consider having another go, trying to make it work, I mean?'

'I think we've both gone too far past the point of no return. Malcolm's just not capable of understanding that I need to work, and sadly I don't think he ever was. What he's always wanted is a secure home and a happy wifey in the background. I've played the game for nearly eleven years, I've tried to be fulfilled by it but it just hasn't worked. And the time has come for me to face up to it and do something about it.'

'I'll take that as a "no" then! Shall we go and sit in the garden?'

Mo led the way over the obstacle course of abandoned toys and swept the children's accumulated debris off the garden bench onto the ground. They sat side by side facing the sun, bits of Barbie doll and Lego scattered at their feet.

'So what happens now?'

'I'm not entirely sure. I've not done this before. What I need is a step-by-step guide to divorce; there must be one out there!'

'Does Malcolm move out? Is he going to live with whoever he's been having the affair with? Will you have to sell the house?'

'I suppose so, I haven't a clue, and I don't think so! I don't think Malcolm knows what he's going to do. He and "Pattie" will have to work that out between them. Good luck to her, that's all I can say!'

'Oh, "Pattie" is it? Do we know her?'

'No, she's relatively new to the office. His PA or something.'

'Do you think it'll last?'

'I honestly don't know and, apart from how it will affect Josie, I honestly don't care. Just for once in my life, no twice actually, I'm going to put myself first. I did it when I went to art school and I can do it again now – at least I think I can!'

237

'Well, good for you, that's all I can say. Go for it! Life's too short not to, as you know only too well. And you know if there's anything I can do to help, anything at all, all you have to do is ask.'

'Thanks Mo. You've been really great. I wouldn't have been able to get through all this nearly as well as I have if it wasn't for people like you and Lotty being there for me.'

'Well, we ain't going to go away, you can count on that.' Mo smiled awkwardly and shifted in her seat. 'More coffee?'

'No thanks. I'm going to pick up my first two figures. They've been fired and I can't wait to see them. They're my stepping stones back on the road. Agnes and Edward. I'll introduce you to them if you want to come over and see them.'

'Great. Yes, I'd love to. I'll give you a ring.'

Nina walked home along the river in the sun and watched the million diamonds sparkle on the surface of the water. She felt, not for the first time, enveloped in a golden blanket of warmth and well-being. The world was on her side. She was going to be alright.

She collected Agnes and Edward, wrapped them and their bucket painstakingly in several blankets, and drove them carefully home in the back of the car. She set them on the floor in her studio and spent a good two hours playing around with their relative positions. She liked the warm red hue of the terracotta. It had a softness she'd not used before. An earthy feeling that enhanced the sculpture. She could barely contain her excitement; her body tingled with a sense of achievement. This work was good, she knew it beyond a shadow of a doubt. She also knew that she could never have produced anything like it in the years after she left art school. This was something different; this transcended the superficial, the competent, the pleasant, and the bland. She looked at them and knew she had captured the spirit of their childhood. Oblivious, crouched intently over their bucket, they played on across the years.

It was time to collect Josie from school. Mother and daughter walked home in silence. Ten yards from the front door, Josie spoke. 'It's not fair, Mum. I don't see why you have to make everything change.'

Nina paused to consider her response. 'Sometimes in life, sweetheart, you have to leap even if you're not sure where you're going to land. You have to be brave enough to change things for the better.'

'But I liked things the way they were.'

'I know you did, darling, but I'm afraid you're not the only person in the jigsaw puzzle.'

'What do you mean, jigsaw puzzle?' Josie spat back at her mother.

'I only mean our family and how we all fit together.'

'Well, we all fitted together very well until you got cancer.'

'Josie, you have to understand that it was no one's fault that I got cancer. And it's gone now. I don't have it any more and we have to move forwards from where we are. Much as we might like to, we can't turn the clock back.'

'But I'll never see Daddy if he moves out.'

'Oh, of course you will, darling. As often as you want to. I'm sure he won't move far away. You never know, you might even get to see him more than you do at the moment. I mean, he's hardly ever home before you're in bed and he's often working at the weekends. Perhaps all that will change.'

They had reached the front door. Nina turned the key and opened it. Awkwardly, Josie clasped her hands fleetingly around her mother's waist, then threw her school bag down and ran upstairs. Nina stood in the hallway, savouring the moment and drinking in the possibility of a better future relationship with her daughter.

The next weeks slunk by rather uneventfully. Malcolm and Nina co-existed in their resignedly separate lives. If anything, Malcolm spent more time at home than he had done for many months, as if grasping at the straws of his old life while it slipped relentlessly through his fingers. They agreed between them for Josie's sake to stay together for one more Christmas and for her birthday. Malcolm began to look for a flat to rent somewhere close by. He didn't say, and Nina decided not to ask, whether he would be moving in alone.

Then something unexpected happened. She bought a puppy. She didn't mean to, it was an accident. She had only gone into the local vet's because she was passing and to see if they had any lists of puppies for sale. In case, she told herself, she should ever need the information in the future. She had hardly got in through the door when she was accosted by a small bundle of black and white fur which bounced around her ankles in instant adoration. The receptionist was already out from behind her desk and attempting to retrieve the animated mass.

'I'm so sorry. This wee chap has just been left in a box on our doorstep this morning. Apparently the family can't afford to keep him. We're just trying to sort out his future but he seems rather reluctant to wait!'

'Don't worry,' smiled Nina, bending down and putting her hand out to the small creature who immediately rested his chin in her palm and looked up at her with big brown eyes. 'I'll have him.'

She heard the words come out of her mouth and couldn't believe that she'd said them. It occurred to her, in spite of the pun, that she'd gone completely barking mad.

'Oh well, er, I'm not sure...' The receptionist seemed equally taken aback. 'I would have to check if that's possible. Are you in a position to look after a puppy?'

'Yes,' said Nina, marginally more confidently. 'In fact, I was just coming in to see if you had any lists of puppies for sale. I work from home and I have a garden and I walk every day as it is.' She wasn't sure which one of them she was trying to convince.

'I see. Well, if you'd like to take a seat, I'll go and see what the position is.' She scooped up the mass of fur and disappeared through a door towards the back of the building. A few minutes later she was back without the puppy.

'If you'd like to leave me your telephone number, apparently we need to try and contact the family who left him here and, if they are agreeable, there seems to be no reason why you shouldn't have the puppy as long as you're in a position to be able to afford the necessary injections and such like.'

'That won't be a problem and I think you've got my number. My cat, Charlie, was registered with you. The name is Salis, Nina Salis.'

'OK then, Mrs Salis. I'll give you a ring later on today or possibly tomorrow morning.'

Nina walked out onto the street in a sort of haze. Had she really just done that? She didn't even know what size it was going to end up; it could be a Rottweiler! But then no, that didn't seem likely. Its paws were small as far as she could remember. It was a mongrel, definitely. 'Jumble', 'Checkers', 'Cookie', 'Scruff'. The names played in her head as she walked home. She wondered what on earth Malcolm would say, until she remembered that she didn't have to worry about that any more. She wondered

241

if Josie would approve. What the hell! What she had done was take a leap of faith. Somehow they would muddle through. 'Muddle', she thought, now there's a possibility for a name.

# Chapter Twenty-Six

Muddle's arrival the following morning was chaotic. It all happened too quickly for there to be any semblance of order about it. Nina ended up having to pile boxes and chairs across the opening into the kitchen in an effort to corral the bundle of boundless energy somewhere where she could wipe the floor. She rescued one of the boxes, lined it with an old towel and put it in a corner to serve as a bed. Then she spread newspapers over the floor. She found an old bowl, filled it with water and put that down in another corner. Lunch consisted of a handful of all-in-one puppy food hastily bought at the vet's and liberally soaked in chicken stock; it was gone almost before the bowl had hit the ground. A small black nose and eager brown eyes looked up for more.

'More? You ask for more!' Nina laughed out loud and the puppy bounced about her ankles in reply. She sat down on the kitchen floor and Muddle bounded over to her, and, limpet-like, curled up on her lap, tucking his nose neatly under his tail. He closed his eyes in perfect trust. Nina sat stroking him, reluctant to disturb his peace by moving. The house felt suddenly less empty.

When Josie returned from school, Nina was unsure what to expect. Her daughter had never warmed to Charlie and she had had no time to prepare her for Muddle's arrival. She decided it would have to be a complete surprise. Josie stepped into the hall to be confronted by the makeshift Fort Knox in the kitchen doorway.

'Mum, what's going on?' She turned to look quizzically at her mother.

'Someone to meet you, darling.'

Josie turned back to be greeted by a small ball of fur being mercilessly wagged by its own tail.

'Oh Mum, it's so cute! Hello sweetie. Who's is it, Mum? What's it doing in our kitchen?'

'It's ours. His name is Muddle and he arrived this morning,' replied Nina rather tentatively.

Josie had already burst through the line of defence and was on the floor, getting acquainted. For the first time in months, she hadn't disappeared straight up to her room. She and Muddle played and played and played. Nina was amazed. Far from being indifferent, Josie seemed to latch onto this small creature, showering it with love and attention. The weeks that followed were no exception; there was a new spring in her step as she raced home from school to see him. Despite Nina's suggestions, she seemed unwilling to share him with any of her school friends, preferring instead to keep him all to herself. Nina wondered at what allowed her child to lavish so much affection on a dog when she found it so difficult to do the same thing with people. In any event, she was pleased that Josie'd found something to counterbalance her sense of lost stability.

Malcolm, on the other hand, kept his distance. He was not fond of animals, and Muddle was no exception. He had found a flat and was concentrating on moving out. Slowly. He seemed reluctant to move too many of his possessions at once. Nina let it go. She focused on her work and on Muddle. The season of school fairs and plays was soon upon them. Before they knew it, even Christmas had been and gone.

Almost exactly a year had passed since the original diagnosis; time for Nina to face a mammogram and an annual check-up. Through the weeks the fear had never left her. Sometimes it would lurk quietly just under the surface, still and silent, generating the barest hint of a ripple. At other times like the days leading up to this first check-up, it would burst into the light, stamping and screaming for attention, throwing her into a world where death was only a footstep away. It was a burgeoning monster devouring everything in its path, thriving on a diet of mammograms and blood tests. On these occasions, and Nina knew there would be more of them, the only weapon she had was life. She would reinvest every ounce of her emotional energy into living.

It was then that she was at her most creative. She worked with a fire she doubted she'd ever possessed before. Children out of the ether swam before her eyes, jostling for position. She sketched till late into the night, anxious not to lose a face, a gesture, a backward glance. The puppy seemed to sense these unseen presences; he would curl up at Nina's feet, reverential, motionless, nose tucked under paw, fearful of disturbing the energy at work. In the days that followed, individual maquettes would take on life forms around the studio. Nina would name them, alter them, play with the shape of them, and Muddle would go without his daily exercise. Slowly the little community in her studio was growing. Agnes and Edward had company. Soon she felt she would be in a position to mount an exhibition, and she began searching for a venue.

Malcolm had all but left. Josie seemed to have settled to her new life with Muddle for company; even her computer had taken a back seat for a couple of months. Nina survived her return visit to the hospital and her mammogram, although it wasn't pleasant; the memories it triggered were huge. The Prophet of Doom was as thorough as ever; he prodded and pummelled and left it to the end of the visit to tell her that her mammogram showed no cause for concern. She walked out into the crisp morning air, free for a further six months. Malcolm, to his credit, had offered to accompany her. She'd decided to try going it alone. He rang in the evening to ask how it went.

Slowly, a pattern was emerging. Josie would spend one night a week and most weekends with her father. They ate out a lot, apparently. Nina waited for any reported sightings of 'Pattie' but none came. Either she was being the model of discretion, or things were not going according to plan for Malcolm. Nina was only glad that Josie never asked, and there was therefore no need for her to lie. The Easter holidays were fast approaching when Nina received a phone call from Malcolm. 'I was thinking of taking Josie to a hotel by the beach for a week.'

Nina was somewhat taken aback. 'But you hate the sand and sea, Malcolm!'

'No I don't. Well, not that much, anyway. I thought Josie might enjoy it. It's a hotel that caters especially for children. But if you think it's a bad idea...' his voice trailed off miserably. He sounded put out.

'No, no, I'm not saying it's a bad idea. I'm just surprised, that's all. Where is the hotel?'

'Studland Bay in Dorset. Some chap at work has been there with his children. Apparently they had a great time. Special meals for the kids and stuff to play on and the beach within walking distance.' Malcolm was clearly very pleased with himself.

'It sounds great, Malcolm, for a five-year-old. Don't you think you're a few years too late?'

'What do you mean?'

'I'm sorry to pour cold water but Josie is eleven. She'd really much rather have dinner with you in the evenings and probably go somewhere with more to do than build sandcastles.'

'What about if she could bring the dog?'

It was the last thing Nina expected him to say. 'Surely you can't take the dog to a hotel?'

'Oh, yes. Not only child-friendly but dog-friendly too.'

'Sounds just the place for you!'

'I'm not going for me,' came the faintly irritated reply. 'I'm going for Josie.'

'And you really want to take the dog as well? You hate dogs.'

'I'm sure I can manage with it for a week.'

'Well, if that's what you want. She certainly does seem to have grown very attached to him.'

'That's putting it mildly. She never stops talking about it, seems hard-pushed to live without it, it seems. Hence my idea.'

'Shall I ask her then or do you want to?'

'No, you ask her and see what she says.'

It was all arranged for the first week of the Easter holidays. Josie was beside herself with excitement and spent long hours into the evening explaining the details of the planned trip to Muddle who sat dutifully listening, head cocked, ears pricked and tail wagging. When he got tired of listening, he would lie on his back, all four paws in the air while Josie rubbed his tummy and continued to outline her plans.

At some point before the end of term, it struck Nina that she would have a whole week's freedom. It begged the question what to do with herself. She could stay at home, safe, and work. Or she could take a leap into the unknown. She ran through her mind a list of places she'd always wanted to visit, she weighed up whether

247

she was brave enough; she counted the cost. She ran the idea past Lotty and Mo one evening when, Josie-free, she'd invited them both for a meal.

'I'm thinking of possibly going abroad for a long weekend. What do you think?'

'Great, go for it, girl!' enthused Lotty without so much as a moment's hesitation.

She was filling up their wine glasses; they were on to their second bottle.

'What about Josie and the dog?' asked Mo. 'Do you want me to have them?'

'No need, thanks, Mo, it's really kind of you but Malcolm has arranged to take them both to the seaside.'

'I'm sorry, could you repeat that?' grinned Lotty. 'We are talking about Malcolm here.'

'Yes I know, both of them. Can you believe it?'

'Both of them? But I thought he hated dogs and sand!' said Mo.

'He does. But this apparently is an exception.'

'Guilt, no doubt,' muttered Lotty helping herself to more salad.

'Whatever,' grinned Nina. 'I'm free for a week.'

'Well, I think you're very brave to even consider going abroad. I'm sure if I was you I'd just stay at home.'

'Not if I could help it, you wouldn't,' Lotty cut in vehemently. 'Whatever happened to the feisty female we all knew and loved?'

'She grew up and became a mother, I suppose,' said Mo rather ruefully.

'Rubbish,' Lotty continued. 'You're only as safe as you feel.'

'Ah yes, safety,' Nina smiled. 'I vaguely remember such a thing. It fell out of the window a year and three months ago, along with a lot of other presumptions.'

'Nothing ventured, nothing gained,' said Lotty, raising

her glass. 'Or is it "no pain, no gain"? Anyway, whatever, I'll drink to it! Or if you're not careful, you'll end up spending the rest of your life cooking great meals for me and Mo. We'll get horribly fat and you'll get horribly bored!'

# Chapter Twenty-Seven

When the day dawned, it was a scary sort of beginning. Nina felt other-worldly as she stepped out of the front door and turned the key to double lock it. It was a bright crisp morning and the air washed her face as she walked a brisk ten minutes to the tube station. A mantra formed in her head in time with her steps – passport, money, tickets, passport, money, tickets, pmt, pmt, pmt. Not something she had to worry about any longer as the Tamoxifen, or was it the chemo, had plummeted her into an early menopause many months ago. She smiled as she showed her pass and stepped onto the escalator. Just over an hour later, she emerged among the bright lights and the bustle of Heathrow airport. She followed the signs, 'Check in for Hand Baggage Only'. Then she went in search of, what she considered to be, a well-earned cappuccino. So far so good. It felt strange, very strange, to be sitting alone, on such a brink. But then she'd been there before. This was no big deal.

The plane took off an hour late. She watched from her window seat at 35,000 feet the patchwork quilt of greens, yellows, purple-blues and chocolate browns. She watched them turn to licheny greens and muted mauves as the cloud cover thickened enough to form a muslin haze. Unannounced, some 30 minutes later, the great snow-capped crags of the Alps broke the surface. Wrapped around with pure swathes of virgin snow, their rocky peaks fell away into gentle rolling pastures which lapped at the Heidiesque shores of the Alpine villages nestling in their midst. Unseen air currents rose to buffet the plane, a reminder of the power beneath. The safety belt sign bing-bonged on above Nina's head. She noted with interest her lack of fear; two years earlier and she would have been bombarded with images of crash landings, fireballs and carnage. As it was, she relaxed into the mild turbulence and watched the mountains fade into the distance. It wasn't long before the captain was announcing their imminent arrival under cloudless skies. She looked down and caught her first glimpse. Domes and towers and spires sprung up out of a sea of terracotta roofs. Tiny boats zipped from left to right. Small brown patches of land dotted the surface of the water. Venice.

Her heart beat fast with anticipation as she walked out into the arrivals lounge. A smiling woman with an American accent was holding a card with her name on it. She said she would phone for a water taxi and suggested that Nina buy herself a three-day ticket for the waterbuses while she waited. Twenty minutes later and the Venetian wind was whipping around Nina's head as she sped across the lagoon towards the city. The way was mapped by clusters of chunky timber posts sunk into the water, grouped in threes or fours, all leaning in towards each other like so many army veterans rubbing shoulders at a reunion. Workmen were busy sinking new timbers into walls to stem the relentless tide. There was a couple in the taxi with her; they sat huddled undercover, oblivious to the view. Even when the boat turned in to the first canal and the shuttered walls of the houses rose up on either side, they seemed not to notice. For her part, Nina could not move her head quickly enough to take everything in. Her whole being was consumed with the first sights and sounds of the city she had dreamed so long of seeing. The silent couple got out at the entrance of a very smart five-star hotel.

'You're not staying here?' the woman asked or rather stated as she stood up.

'No,' Nina smiled.

The boat chugged on, more slowly now, with its solitary passenger. It rounded a corner and Nina caught her breath as she realized where she was. The Grand Canal. There were boats everywhere. Larger ones with flat tops packed with people; these were the waterbuses. Smaller ones stacked high with boxes of fruit or filled with freezer units advertising milk or yoghurt. Sleek, highly polished wooden water taxis buzzed this way and that like angry bees intent on reaching their different destinations. And then there were the gondolas, those that crossed back and forth across the waterway and those that cradled packs of solemn-faced Japanese tourists or mildly embarrassed couples being serenaded by accordian-playing Latin tenors. Before Nina had time to take it all in, her boat turned into a narrow waterway under a small arched bridge and came to rest beside some wet stone steps.

'Hotel Biorgi!' shouted the smiling taxi boatman, gesticulating wildly in the direction of a tall church on the far side of a little square. Nina grabbed her bag and stepped out of the boat, and he was gone. The first thing she noticed was a sign which read 'Dog Shop'. She wondered fleetingly how Josie and Malcolm were managing with Muddle. She crossed the little piazza to the side of the church and saw the hotel straight in front of her. She walked into a wood-panelled foyer, fresco-walled and warm. The staff were friendly and spoke very good English; her room was on the first floor. It was small but had everything she needed.

Taking barely enough time to pause for breath, Nina repacked her rucksack with maps, money and a water bottle and set out to explore. Within minutes she was immersed in the magic of Venice. The lump of fear which had remained stubbornly lodged at the base of her throat for months was temporarily forgotten. The weight of anxiety which usually nestled behind her breastbone dissolved. As she followed the little signposts high on the walls towards St Mark's Square, every corner produced a new cameo, an eye's-blinked glimpse of another narrow street, another intricate little bridge, another waterway. In and out she wove her way until finally she stepped out into the late afternoon sunshine which splashed down onto the corner of St Mark's Square. People and pigeons danced around each other to the sound of the music from the cafés lining the sides of the square. She walked as if in a dream around the edges of the scene past the exquisitely decorated little rooms of Florian's, crystallized in a time when Dickens sat drinking coffee there, past the commercial contrast of the expensive shops and on towards the gilded splendour of the Basilica di San Marco. She stood at the entrance, her neck craned back to see the glittering mosaics which lined every wall. She knew she ought to be impressed, and she was, but the golden extravagance of it all was almost too much. An hour later she emerged dazed with the excess of it and in need of fresh air.

She treated herself to a large pistachio ice cream and wandered along the waterfront where giant ferries and rusty tankers edged their way up and down the channel of water, bizarrely incongruous reminders of the twenty-first century. She looked back and saw the Campanile, the bell tower, of St Mark's rising up towards the sinking sun. She resolved to see the view from the top the following day.

She made her way slowly and attentively back towards

her hotel, pausing every so often to take a picture. When she got back to her room, she ran a deep bath and lay in it, summoning up the courage to go out to supper on her own. The worst that could happen, she reasoned, could hardly be more difficult than what she had been through in the past year. She took a book for company and set out. The early evening air was still warm. She felt remarkably safe as she zig-zagged her way through narrow streets and over little bridges in search of a little restaurant frequented by the gondoliers which she had read about in one of the guide books. Finally she came upon it more by luck than judgement. There was a long noisy queue outside. She was about to abandon the idea when a plump red-faced waiter appeared at the narrow doorway holding one finger in the air.

'Solo? Just one?' he shouted.

Nina stepped forward and was whisked into the colourful red and white-checkered interior. The waiter plonked her into a chair at a tiny table between the bar and the wall; it was a good vantage point. The noise, if anything, was louder inside than out. Above the diners' conversations, the waiters yelled instructions to unseen chefs in the kitchen at the back. They moved with alarming speed in such confined a space. Her book languished untouched as she ate the delicious food and absorbed the spirit of the place. She noticed that every so often a group of loudly gesticulating Italians would be ushered in past the waiting queue and mysteriously tables would be found for them at the back; gondoliers, she presumed. By the time she returned to her hotel, she was exhausted. She slept well, a fear-free sleep, full of excitement for the future.

Bright and early the next morning, she was back at the Campanile before the queues of the previous day had a chance to form. Within five minutes she was in the lift. Within ten she was stepping out high above the city. The sight that met her eyes was one she would never forget. A comfortable jumble of terracotta tiles wrestled for space. Tables, chairs and plants in pots perched precariously on wooden platforms clinging to the roofs in impossible positions. Amongst the quiet chaos nestled domes of enormous proportions, like giant mushrooms dwarfing their neighbours. Towers sprang up out of nowhere and rose skyward at odd angles. It was hard to imagine that the whole scene was floating on a watery foundation. Several groups of tourists came and went as Nina walked round and round the tower, taking in every detail of the view from every side. She thought about the families who lived under the countless roofs, she wondered what traumas they had suffered and whether they were happy. She wondered how many children they had and how many, like her, they had lost. She was curious to know what fears they lived with.

Her train of thought was interrupted by the arrival of an Italian family; a mother, father and children ranging in age, Nina guessed, from about two up to thirteen. There were four of them, two boys and two girls. She watched as they took in the view and raced around the tower. The eldest girl linked arms with her mother and seemed to be pointing things out to her. Every so often she would reach up and kiss her mother on the cheek. The two boys soon got tired of looking at the view and began to wrestle on the floor. The youngest, a girl, ran for the sanctuary of her father's arms and snuggled in to his shoulder, twiddling the hair at the back of his head in her little fingers. He responded by burying his head into her chest and making her roar with laughter as his rough skin tickled her. Nina envied them their physicality, their closeness and their sense of fun, but most of all she envied the mother her relationship with her daughter. She tried to remember if she and Josie had ever stood like that. She knew they hadn't. She turned away and returned to ground level.

On her final day, she took a boat to the birthplace of Venice, a small and largely deserted little island called Torcello. The sky was clear and blue and the sun beat down on her back as she walked the stony path beside the canal leading inland from the boat. Tiny blue flowers like spark-eyed daisies lined the way and birds sang in the hedgerows. There were fields and the odd garden.

On the far side of the little canal stood a big house just visible in the distance, set in its own grounds. The path wound on past two small restaurants and then led into a grassy square. Two ancient churches flanked the square, both predating anything built in Venice itself. There was a warm air of quiet mystery about the place. After the splendid decadence of St Marco, the muted golds and softened shades of the ancient mosaics of the Basilica di Santa Maria Assunta struck a chord somewhere deep inside her.

She crept into the hushed interior of Santa Fosca, the smaller of the two churches, and sat down. The cupped hands of the rounded walls enfolded her within their centuries-old embrace. She felt at peace in a way that she had not felt for a long time. She sat down and, in the stillness, felt the wisdom of the stones soak into her being. She thought about the struggle to make her marriage with Malcolm work, the eleven-year effort she had put into creating a home for them in which to play happy families, the sadness of her miscarried babies, the disappointment of lost years with Josie. She thought about the terror of the cancer, the nightmare of the treatment, and the endless encounters with the medical profession. And she thought about her work. She knew she was on the right track with her children. Agnes and

Edward had been a gift from the unknown; proof, if any were needed, that there was a great creative force at work in the universe, there for the taking. She emerged into the sunshine of Torcello quite sure that she had a future.

Late that night she said her goodbyes to the Grand Canal on the way back to her hotel. She sat at the front of the water bus and watched as it chugged past the faded facades, past the intricately carved cherubs adorning pillars and castellations and doorways, the house where Byron lived, the rooms where European royalty gambled opulent nights away. Cut-glass chandeliers lit high-up windows and whispered of ages gone by when literati met and royalty dined. Under ornate ceilings, their light spilled out onto huge portraits hung along the walls.

And underneath it all, the dark green seaweedy waters of the Grand Canal licked hungrily at the hearts of the palaces, biding their time, waiting their chance. For Nina, they mirrored the fear that had licked at her heart since the day of the diagnosis. But, she reasoned, her heart was strong and she would survive, just as the palazzi on either side of her had survived. Tides of black water had swept under the bridge in the days since Josie's tenth birthday. It had been a long hard road. She had no idea where her journey would end. But much more importantly, she finally knew for certain that, at last, it had begun.